Catherine Tinley has loved reading and writing since childhood, and has a particular fondness for love, romance and happy endings. She lives in Ireland with her husband, children, dog and kitten, and can be reached at catherinetinley.com, as well as through Facebook and @CatherineTinley on Twitter.

Also by Catherine Tinley

**The Chadcombe Marriages
miniseries**

Waltzing with the Earl
The Captain's Disgraced Lady
The Makings of a Lady

Discover more at millsandboon.co.uk.

THE EARL'S
RUNAWAY
GOVERNESS

Catherine Tinley

MILLS & BOON

First published in Great Britain 2019
by Mills & Boon, an imprint of HarperCollins*Publishers*
1 London Bridge Street, London, SE1 9GF

Large Print edition 2019

© 2019 Catherine Tinley

ISBN: 978-0-263-08171-8

MIX
Paper from
responsible sources
FSC
www.fsc.org FSC® C007454

This book is produced from independently certified FSC™ paper to ensure responsible forest management. For more information visit www.harpercollins.co.uk/green.

Printed and bound in Great Britain
by CPI Group (UK) Ltd, Croydon, CR0 4YY

To all my women friends—colleagues and school friends, college and GAA pals. And to the activists, campaigners and supporters in my life.

You are my sister writers, maternity co-campaigners, repealers and WHO Code supporters.

I feel your support in Women Aloud, the Unlaced Harpies, branch and regional volunteers, conference organisers and maternal mental health champions.

I salute you all.

Chapter One

Cambridgeshire, England, January 1810

Marianne tiptoed along the landing towards the servants' staircase as quietly as she could manage. How different everything looked at night! A sliver of silver moonlight from the only window pierced the curtains, pointing at her. *Look!* it seemed to say. *She is trying to escape!*

Her skirts whispered as she moved through the darkness and her cloak billowed behind her like a black cloud. The creak of a floorboard under her feet sounded unnaturally loud, and she had to be careful not to allow her bandboxes to crash against the walls or the furniture. Shadows, unfamiliar and darkly threatening, loomed all around her, growing and shrinking ominously as she passed, her small candle gripped tightly in her right hand.

Downstairs a window rattled in a sudden gust of wind, and in the distance a vixen called mournfully. The candle flickered briefly as she reached the end of the landing, sending shadows scuttling and then reforming all around her.

She paused, listening for any sound, any indication that someone might have heard her.

Nothing.

Her heart was pounding—so much so that it was hard to hear anything above the din of her own blood rushing rhythmically through her body. Her mouth was dry and her palms sticky with fear. But she must not tarry! The longer she delayed, the greater the chance of being discovered.

Raising her candle, she carefully lifted the latch on the door to the back staircase. It gave way with a complaining click and Marianne bit her lip. She moved inside in a swish of silk and closed the door behind her.

She released her breath. Her first task was accomplished safely. Now for the next part.

She stepped down the stone stairs, her stout walking boots making a clatter that sounded thunderous to her ears. But with a closed door behind her hopefully it would not be loud enough to awaken anyone.

Reaching the bottom, she scuttled along the narrow passageway until she reached the chamber that the housekeeper shared with her daughter. The door was ajar, as arranged, and as she reached it Mrs Bailey opened it wide and bustled her inside, closing it securely behind her.

'Oh, Miss Marianne! I never thought to see this day!' Jane, the housekeeper's daughter—Marianne's personal maid—was sniffling into a handkerchief.

'Hush now, Jane!' Mrs Bailey admonished her daughter, though she herself also looked distressed.

Marianne set the candle down and touched the girl's hand to soften her mother's words. 'We talked about this. You know it is for the best, Jane.'

They spoke in whispers, conscious that the housemaids were asleep in the chambers on either side. 'But surely I should at least come with you?' Jane protested.

Moved, Marianne enveloped her in a brief hug. 'I love it that you would be willing to do so, but we all know there is no sense in it. Your place is here with your mother.'

Mrs Bailey, despite her stoicism, wiped away a tear. 'Your own poor mother would break her heart if she knew you were running away from home, miss!'

Marianne felt the familiar pain stab through her. Mama and Papa had died over six months ago, yet she felt their absence still. Every waking moment.

'Mama would want me to be safe, and I am no longer safe here.' Even talking about it caused a wave of fear to flood through her.

'I know, Miss Grant. It is best that you go.' Mrs Bailey shook her head grimly. 'Now, what have you packed?'

Marianne indicated the bandboxes in her left hand. 'I fitted in as much as I could. My other black dress, two clean shifts, slippers, my reticule and my jean boots. A book. And Mama's jewels.' She lifted her chin. 'I refuse to leave them here for *him*!'

'They belong to *you*, miss. That was clear from the will, so they say. And when your parents made Master Henry your guardian they believed it was for the best.'

'I know.'

Mama and Papa had refused to accept the truth—that Henry had no kindness in him, no sense of right and wrong. They would never knowingly have placed her in danger.

'He is your brother, after all.'

'My *step*brother.' That had never seemed so important. 'You know my real father died when I was a baby.'

Mrs Bailey acknowledged this with a nod.

'The master and mistress were good for each other. Both widowed, both with a child to rear. It seemed a good marriage.' She hesitated for a moment. 'I have often wondered,' she confessed, 'if losing his own mother so young changed Master Henry.'

Marianne had no time to consider this. 'He is who he is. I only know that I must escape before he...harms me.'

'Of course you must.'

Unspoken between them was the fact that Mrs Bailey had rescued Marianne when Henry had cornered her a few hours earlier, in her chamber. He had been drunk, of course, but his unnatural interest in his stepsister was of long standing.

Marianne had been keenly aware of how the servants had kept her safe these past months, ensuring that Henry had no opportunity to be alone with her. Until today nothing had ever been said, but the butler had instructed the second footman to fit a new lock to Marianne's chamber door just last week. Behind the locked door she had been able to relax a little.

Until tonight, when he had lain in wait for her within her own chamber.

Believing Henry to be still drinking with his raucous friends, in what had been her mother's favourite drawing room, Marianne had hurried upstairs to seek the sanctuary of her room. Sighing with relief, she had closed her door and turned the key, only to hear him murmur silkily, 'Good evening, my dear Marianne.'

She had whirled round to see him lying on her bed, his cravat loosened and a predatory look in his eye. Her mind had frozen for a second, and then wordlessly she had turned back to the door and unlocked it.

Before she had been able to open it properly he had been upon her, grabbing her from behind and muttering unspeakable things in her ear. Her shriek had not been loud enough to be heard in other parts of the house, but luckily Mrs Bailey had been nearby and had bravely intervened.

'Oh, sir!' she had said, bustling into the room. Pretending not to notice Marianne's distress, or the position of Henry's hands, she had gone on, with mock distress, 'One of your friends has been violently sick and they are all requesting your presence.'

'Damn and blast it!'

Henry had released her and stomped off, but not without a last look at Marianne. *I shall win*, it had promised. *You cannot escape me for ever.*

Mrs Bailey had stayed to soothe and calm Marianne. 'Oh, my poor dear girl! That he would *do* such a thing!'

'Please go—do not draw his anger,' Marianne had urged, though her whole body had been shaking. 'If the mess is not cleaned up quickly who knows what he will do!'

'The footmen are already cleaning it,' the housekeeper had reassured her. 'My maids will not serve them in the evenings.'

They both knew why. The maids had also experienced the licentious behaviour of Henry and his drunken friends.

During the day their behaviour was rowdy, but they were usually reasonably restrained. In the evenings, however, fuelled by port and brandy, they became increasingly vulgar, ribald and uninhibited. And the entire household suffered as a result.

Marianne, pleading the conventions of mourning, had always avoided the ordeal of eating with them, choosing instead to consume a simple dinner each evening in the smaller dining room. She barely knew who was here this time—apart from his two closest friends, Henry's guests were different for each house party.

Oh, their hairstyles and clothes were more or less the same—they were all 'men of fashion,' who spent their wealth on coats by Weston or Stultz, boots by Hoby and waistcoats by whichever master tailor was in fashion at that precise moment. Their behaviour, too, was more or less the same—arrogance born of entitlement and the belief that they could do whatever they wished, particularly to defenceless women. Including, it seemed, Marianne herself.

Knowing he would be criticised by society if he continued his customary carousing in public too soon after the tragic deaths of his father and stepmother, Henry had told Marianne that he had hit on the 'genius notion' of inviting all his friends for a series of house parties. Every few weeks, her home had been invaded by large groups of young men. They stayed for five or six nights each time and were up for every kind of lark.

The housemaids had learned to be wary of them, and Mrs Bailey had hired three older women to serve them, keeping Jane and the other young housemaids as safe as she could. Some of the servants—maids and footmen—had left already, to take up positions elsewhere. Very few long-serving staff remained—chief among them Mrs Bailey and Jane. Mrs Bailey had expressed the hope that once their year of mourning was completed, in March, Henry would return to his preference of living in the capital, and they would again have peace.

His attempt to assault Marianne herself this evening had changed everything.

While the behaviour of Henry and his friends had been gradually worsening, last night's incident had been different. It had not been simply a lewd comment or a clumsy attempt to embrace a chambermaid. Henry had dark intentions, and Marianne now knew for sure that she was in danger. Running away was her only option. Mrs Bailey agreed.

'Here is the direction for the registry I told you about.' The housekeeper pressed a note into Marianne's hand. 'I have heard that they will place people who come without references. Lord knows we may need it ourselves before long.'

'Thank you.' Marianne secreted the note in her pocket, where her meagre purse also rested.

Although she had never wanted for food, new clothes or trinkets, and had a generous allowance, nevertheless she did not normally need access to much cash. This was an unusual and urgent situation, so she would have to make do with the pin money she'd had in her room. She drew her cloak around her and picked up her bandboxes again, this time hefting one in each hand.

'Mr Harris will meet you at the gates.' The housekeeper named one of the tenant farmers. 'He will take you in his cart as far as the Hawk and Hound, where you can catch the stage at five in the morning. It comes through Cambridge from Ely and you will be in London by night-fall. I've also written down the names of two respectable inns. Hopefully one of them will have a room free. Stay there until you find a situation as a governess.' She gripped Marianne's hand. 'I am so sorry that you have to leave your home, miss. Please take care of yourself.'

'I will.'

Marianne nodded confidently, as if she knew what she was doing. But as she walked up the drive in darkness, away from the only home she had ever known, her heart sank.

How on earth am I to manage? she wondered. *For I have never before had to take care of myself!*

Grimly, she considered her situation. She had been gently reared, and could play the harp and sing, sketch reasonably well and set a neat stitch. She had been bookish and adept at her lessons when she was younger.

But she had no idea how to buy a ticket for the stagecoach, or wash clothes, or manage money.

She had also never been in a public place unaccompanied before. Mama had always been with her, or her governess, or occasionally a personal maid. But those days were gone. She must learn to dress by herself now, and mend her own clothing, and dress her own hair. And somehow she must keep herself safe in the hell that was London.

London! She knew little of the capital—had never visited the place. But in her mind it was associated with all kinds of vice. London was where Henry lived. London was where his arrogant, lecherous friends lived. London, she had come to understand, was a place overrun with wicked young men, drinking and vomiting and carousing their way through the streets, gambling dens and gin salons.

Mama and Papa had hated to visit the place, and had always exclaimed with relief when they'd returned home to country air and plain cooking. They had never taken her with them, leaving her safely in the care of her nurse or governess, and Marianne had never objected. Even as a child she had understood that London was a Bad Place, and she had been puzzled by Henry's excitement at going there.

When he had become old enough he had insisted on having lodgings of his own in the city, and with reluctance Papa had given in to his son's demands. Henry had moved to London, rarely coming home to visit, and everyone at home had breathed a little easier.

And now here she was, leaving home in the middle of a cold January night, with little money, no chaperone, and no notion of how she was going to manage. And she was choosing to go to London, of all places.

She stifled a hysterical giggle. Strangely, the absurdity of it all had cheered her up. That she could laugh at such a moment!

She lifted her chin, squared her shoulders, and trudged on.

Netherton, Bedfordshire

William Ashington, known to his friends as Ash, rubbed his hands together to keep away the cold. The vicar's words washed over him. 'For as much as it hath pleased Almighty God in his great mercy to take unto himself the soul of our dear brother here departed: we therefore commit his body to the ground—earth to earth, ashes to ashes, dust to dust...'

Ash threw a handful of earth onto John's coffin, feeling again the loss of the man who had been much more to him than a cousin. In truth John had been like a brother to him—at least until that summer when they had both turned eighteen. In recent years they had recovered something of an awkward friendship, but it had never been the same.

How could it?

He turned away as the service ended, accepting a few handshakes and murmuring appropriate responses to the expressions of sorrow being offered.

'My Lord?' It was the vicar. Ash started, realising the man was addressing him. Strange to think that because of John's death he was now not simply Mr Ashington but the Earl of Kingswood.

'Yes?'

The vicar shook his hand and thanked him for attending the service. 'A funeral is always a sad occasion, but laying to rest such a young man is doubly sorrowful. Why, he was not much more than two and thirty!'

I know, thought Ash. *For John and I are— were—almost the same age.*

'And to think of his widow and daughter, now left alone in the world…' The vicar sighed, then looked at Ash intently. 'Lord Kingswood—er… the *previous* Lord Kingswood spoke about them often to me in his final weeks.'

'Indeed.' The last person Ash wished to think about was John's widow. Thank goodness women did not attend funerals.

'He also spoke about you.' The vicar's warm brown eyes bored into Ash's. 'I think he regretted the distance between you.'

Ash was feeling extremely uncomfortable. He was unaccustomed to discussing his personal affairs with someone he had just met. In truth, he was unaccustomed to discussing his personal affairs with anyone. He preferred it that way.

Adopting his usual defence in such moments, he maintained an even expression and said nothing.

The vicar made a few more general comments and Ash listened politely. He thanked the man and turned away to where his coachman, Tully, waited with the carriage. If he left now he could be back in London by tonight.

'Er...'

The vicar. Again.

'Yes?' Ash's patience was beginning to wear thin, but he forced himself to maintain a courteous expression.

'I was asked to pass this to you.' He offered Ash a sealed note.

Ash frowned but took the paper. Opening it, he ran his eyes over the contents.

'Confound it!' he snapped, causing the vicar to raise an eyebrow. 'I am requested to go to the house after the funeral. By the family lawyer.'

The vicar looked bewildered at his reaction to what must seem a perfectly reasonable request. They were literally standing together at the Fourth Earl of Kingswood's funeral, and Ash was now the Fifth Earl.

But he had never expected to accede to the title.

Why, John had been only thirty-two, with plenty of time to sire a son with Fanny. Everyone—including Ash—had assumed that John would eventually have sons, and that he—Ash— would never have to worry about the responsibilities John had carried for so long.

Ash debated it in his mind. Could he ignore the note and leave immediately for London, as planned? He could ask the lawyer to see him there. *No.* It would look churlish and impolite. *Damn.* He would have to comply as a courtesy. Which meant possibly seeing *her* again.

Fanny. John's wife—John's *widow*, he corrected himself. After all these years of successfully avoiding her.

Placing his hat firmly on his head, he bade farewell to the vicar and made for his carriage. If he must face this ordeal, better to get it over with.

Chapter Two

Marianne reminded herself to breathe. Her shoulders were tense and she could feel fear prick her spine. She had paid the fee and entered her name into the registry book at the office recommended by Mrs Bailey, and now she waited.

Well, she acknowledged, not her *actual* name. Her made-up name.

She had decided during the long journey to London that she must not go by her usual name, for fear Henry might look for her. She would use her father's surname—her *real* father—as it would give her comfort, and she was confident Henry would not remember or recognise it.

After being known as Marianne Grant for most of her twenty years, she would now go back to the surname she had been given at birth—Bolton. Charles Bolton had given her her dark brown eyes, her dark hair and, according to Mama, her placid nature. The Grants were altogether more fiery.

She was seated in an austere room with a dozen other would-be servants, all patiently awaiting their turn to be called. Among the would-be grooms, scullery maids and footmen she had espied two other young ladies, respectably dressed, who might also be seeking employment as governesses. She had exchanged polite smiles with both of them, but no one had initiated conversation.

It was greatly worrying that on a random Tuesday there were three young ladies of similar social standing all seeking positions at the same time.

The door to the inner office opened and everyone looked up. The young man who had been called a few moments earlier now emerged. His demeanour gave no sign as to whether he had been offered a position or not, but he kept his head down as he left.

I wonder, thought Marianne, *if he is a footman?*

'Miss Bolton? Miss Anne Bolton?'

With a start, Marianne realised that it was her turn. The lady in charge—the one who had been calling people in for the past hour—was standing in the doorway. Anne Bolton was, of course, the false name Marianne had written in the registry book, and her ears had not responded when the name had been called.

Blushing, she stood. 'I am Miss Bolton.'

My first lie. Or is it?

The lady eyed her assessingly. 'Come with me.'

Trying to maintain a dignified expression, and hoping that her shaking hands were not obvious, Marianne followed her into the inner chamber and closed the door.

'Please sit, Miss Bolton.'

Marianne complied, watching as the registry lady took her own seat behind an imposing rosewood desk. So much depended on the next few moments and this woman's decision!

'I am Mrs Gray.'

She was a stern-looking lady in her later years, with iron-grey hair, dark skin, piercing dark eyes and deep lines etched into her face. She wore a plain, high-necked gown in sombre grey and no jewellery. Despite this, it was clear that she was a person of authority. It was something about the way she carried herself, how still she was, the way those dark eyes seem to pierce right through Marianne's flimsy defences.

'I see that you are seeking a position as a governess,' she stated, 'but you have come with no recommendation. Tell me about your situation and why you are here.'

Mrs Gray's tone was flat, expressionless. Marianne could feel her heart thumping in her chest.

Haltingly, then with increasing fluency, Marianne told the tale she had concocted. Mrs Gray listened impassively, giving no indication whether she believed any of it. Doubt flooded through Marianne. Perhaps she should not have pretended that her father was a lawyer and that he had left her with little money and no connections. What if Mrs Gray asked for some proof? Her heart fluttered as anxiety rose within her.

'When did your father die?'

'Six months ago.' Marianne's throat tightened as it always did when she thought about Papa.

Mrs Gray's eyes narrowed. 'And your mother?'

'Also dead.' Marianne swallowed. Her hands clenched into fists as she fought the wave of grief that threatened to overwhelm her.

Mrs Gray's gaze flicked briefly to Marianne's hands, then she leaned back slightly in her chair. 'Tell me about your education, Miss Bolton. What are your talents?' Mrs Gray spoke bluntly, giving no clue as to whether she would favour Marianne.

Hesitantly, Marianne spoke of drawing and painting, of her musical skills, her ability to sew and to converse in French and Italian—

'And what do you know of Mathematics, Logic and Latin?'

Marianne blinked. Mrs Gray had asked the question in perfect Italian! 'I have studied the main disciplines of Mathematics,' she replied, also in Italian.

Mrs Gray quizzed her on these, then switched to French, followed by Latin, to discuss the finer details of Marianne's knowledge of Logic, improving texts and the Classics.

Thankfully Marianne's expensive education had equipped her well. She had been an apt student and had enjoyed her studies. Was that, she wondered, a glimmer of approval in Mrs Gray's eye?

The woman paused.

Marianne forced herself to sit still. *Please*, she was thinking, *please*. If she could not gain a position as a governess she had no idea what she would do. Returning home was not an option. That door was closed in her mind. She had no home. So everything depended on Mrs Gray.

This house is freezing, thought Ash, stepping towards the fireplace in John's study. Hopefully he could be on his way quickly—the last thing he needed was a prolonged encounter with the grieving widow.

He paused, holding out his hands to the pathetic fire, but there was little heat to be had. The door opened and closed, sending smoke billowing into the room. Ash coughed and stepped away from the fire.

Have the dashed chimneys ever been cleaned?

He had not been in Ledbury House for many years, but he could not remember it looking so dilapidated.

'Lord Kingswood, thank you for coming.' The lawyer, a bespectacled gentleman in his middle years, bowed formally. 'My name is Richardson.'

Ash nodded his head. 'I received your note asking me to come to the house after the funeral. I understand you wish to read the will immediately.'

He kept his tone polite, despite his impatience with the entire situation. Every moment he spent here meant a later arrival in London.

'I am required to outline the extent of your inheritance, plus a number of other matters added by the Fourth Earl to his will.' The lawyer pushed his spectacles up his nose, where they balanced precariously. He went behind John's desk and began taking papers out of a small case.

Ash stood there, wishing for nothing more than to leave and never return. Every part of him was fighting the notion that he was now Earl of Kingswood. The last thing he needed was *'other matters'* complicating his life further.

'What other matters? And why did John—my cousin—see fit to *add* to the responsibilities of the Earldom?'

Mr Richardson sniffed. 'That is not for me to say. My role is simply to see that the requirements of the will are carried out.' He arranged the papers methodically on John's desk.

'I see.'

But he didn't. Not at all. Why had John added to his burdens, knowing how much he would hate it? Particularly when they had not been intimate friends for fourteen years?

John had settled into life as a country earl, staying in this rundown mausoleum of a house with his wife and daughter and rarely visiting the capital. Ash, on the other hand, barely left London, unless it was to attend a house party. Life in the country was intolerably tedious.

Perhaps, Ash mused, *John has left me a memento—something from our childhood or youth.*

Still, if he was forced to stay for the reading of the will it meant that he would not be able to avoid running into—

'Mr Richardson! Thank you so much for being here in our time of need.'

Ash turned to see Fanny glide into the room, followed by a girl who must be her daughter.

Fanny had always known how to make an entrance. Her black gown was of the finest silk, with self-covered buttons and black lace detail at the sleeves. Her blonde hair was artlessly arranged in an elegant style, and her matron's cap did nothing to dim the beauty of her glorious features. The cornflower-blue eyes, cupid's bow lips and the angelic dimples that had driven him mad with desire all those years ago were all still there. If anyone could make mourning garb look attractive it was Fanny.

Despite himself he felt a wave of recognition and remembered longing which almost floored him. For a moment he felt eighteen again.

She stopped, as if noticing him for the first time. 'Why, Ash! I did not know you were here already.'

She was lying. The servants would have told her of his arrival—and the fact that he and the lawyer were in the library for the reading of the will.

He bowed. 'Hello, Fanny.' He made no attempt to take her hand. Or kiss it.

'This is most unexpected,' she murmured. It was unclear whether she was referring to the immediate reading of the will or to his coming into the title.

'For me, too.' Pointedly, he eyed her daughter. 'And this is—?'

'My daughter, Cecily.' The girl, as pretty as her mother—though with John's hazel eyes—curtseyed politely, then looked quizzically at him.

'I am an old friend of your father. And I am also his cousin.'

'We were *all* friends, Ash.' Fanny seated herself on a faded sofa and smoothed her skirts, indicating with a gesture that Cecily should sit with her. 'May I offer you some refreshments? Tea, perhaps?'

'A brandy would be preferable.' He would need something stronger than tea if he was to endure the next half-hour.

She pressed her lips together and reached for the bell.

Ash sighed inwardly. Fanny had not changed one iota.

Mrs Gray had been making notes throughout her quizzing of Marianne, but now she lifted her head to fix Marianne with a steely stare. 'It is difficult to find a situation for a governess who comes with no reference, no recommendation.'

'I understand.' With some difficulty Marianne kept her expression neutral. It would not do to show desperation. 'But I assure you I will make a good governess. When I lived with my parents

I taught our maid to read and to write. I found it enjoyable, and I believe I have an aptitude for it.'

That is mostly true, she thought. *I did teach Jane—though the implication that she was our only maid is misleading. Oh, dear—how hard it is to be a liar!*

Mrs Gray tapped her finger on the table, considering. 'There is one possibility. A young girl in need of a governess. Her father died recently, too—indeed, my understanding is that he was to be buried today.'

Marianne felt a pang of sympathy for the unknown girl. She knew exactly how it felt to lose a beloved parent.

Mrs Gray was watching closely, and now she nodded in satisfaction. 'She lives quietly with her mother in the country.' She eyed Marianne sharply. 'You do not mind leaving London and living in some quiet, out-of-the-way place? Will you miss the excitements of the capital?'

Marianne shuddered at the very thought of the 'excitements' of London. Since arriving in London last night she had been almost overwhelmed by the noise and the smells and the feeling of danger all around her. It had reinforced her notions of the city, gleaned from second-hand tales of Henry's activities and from the behaviour of the London bucks he had brought to her home.

'I have no desire to live in London. I am myself country-bred and will be perfectly content in the country.'

It would also make it harder for Henry to find her. If he even bothered searching for her.

'I have one further question.' Mrs Gray eyed her piercingly. 'Those who come to me for a situation know that I sometimes place those whom other registries will not touch. But I insist on my people being of good character.'

Marianne's chin went up. No one had ever dared question her character before! 'I can assure you, Mrs Gray, that my character is blameless.'

'No need to get hoity-toity with me, Miss—' she glanced down '—Miss *Bolton.*'

Marianne blushed. Mrs Gray was making her scepticism about the name obvious.

The woman's dark eyes fixed on Marianne, bored into her. 'Are you with child?'

Marianne gasped. 'Of course not! I've never— I mean I wouldn't dream of ever— I mean, *no.*' She kept looking at Mrs Gray. 'It's impossible.'

'Very well.'

As if she had not just asked Marianne a perfectly outrageous question, Mrs Gray took a fresh sheet of paper, and began writing.

'You will receive board and lodging and will

be paid a yearly wage and a tea allowance. You will be entitled to two days off per month. Take the Reading stage from the Angel on Thursday and get out at Netherton. I will arrange for someone to meet you there and take you to Ledbury House.'

She looked up.

'Remember, Lady Kingswood and her daughter, Lady Cecily, are in mourning, so they will live very quietly. I have placed servants and staff there before, who have left because the situation is too remote. I believe it is why Lady Cecily's last governess left. The child needs someone who is willing to stay for a long time. After losing her father—'

'I understand.'

Living quietly sounded perfect! Marianne had loved her quiet, easy life with Mama and Papa, visiting neighbours and friends and never aching for the so-called delights of the city.

'Lady Kingswood had been focused, naturally, on nursing her husband through his last illness, which is why she has entrusted the appointment of a new governess to me.' Mrs Gray handed her the paper. 'Do not let me down!'

Marianne assured her that she was to be relied upon, then looked at the document. It gave the address as Ledbury House, Netherton, Berkshire. It also included a summary of Marianne's terms of employment.

Her hand shook a little as she accepted it. Amid the relief which was coursing through her there was also a sense of unreality. Strange to think that from now on she would no longer be Miss Marianne Grant, a young lady of wealth and status, but instead plain Miss Anne Bolton, governess, orphan, and near-pauper.

She swallowed. The alternative was absolute poverty or—God forbid—returning to Henry. Fear flooded through her at the very thought. She would have to make this work, be careful and, crucially, be effective as a governess. She would also have to learn to respond to the unfamiliar name.

She looked at the page again. The wage she was to be given was shockingly little. It was much less than her allowance—the pin money that she had so carelessly spent each quarter on trinkets, stockings and sweetmeats. She had no idea how to make economies. Now she was expected to make this meagre amount cover all her needs, including her clothes.

She lifted her chin. *I can do this!* she told herself. *I must!*

* * *

'And now to the family bequests.'

Mr Richardson, Ash thought, would have made an excellent torturer. Not content with bringing him into this godforsaken house and forcing him to endure Fanny's company, he was now reading—very slowly—the entire Last Will and Testament of John Ashington, Fourth Earl Kingswood. Ash had sat impassive as the lawyer had detailed the property that was now his—the main element being this house, with its unswept chimneys. Thankfully, the lawyer was now on to the family section.

Ash took another mouthful of brandy. He would be out of here soon.

Fanny sat up straighter, a decided gleam in her eye. Only the house and gardens were entailed, therefore the rest of the estate would likely be placed in trust for Cecily, perhaps with a sizeable portion for Fanny herself.

He wondered, not for the first time, if Fanny had chosen John because of his title. Had *he* been the Earl when he and John had both fallen in love with the same girl, would she have chosen him?

Ash forced himself away from cynical thoughts and tried to pay attention to the lawyer.

Mr Richardson read on—and what he said next

made Fanny exclaim in surprise. Cecily was to receive only a respectable dowry and John's mother's jewellery. So Fanny was to inherit everything?

Ash stole a glance at her. She was quivering in anticipation. Ash averted his eyes.

'To my dear wife,' Mr Richardson droned, 'I leave the Dower House for as long as she shall live there unmarried...' He went on to specify a financial settlement that was again respectable, though not spectacular.

'What? *What?*' Fanny was not impressed. 'If he has not left everything to Cecily, or to me, then to whom...?'

She turned accusatory eyes on Ash. *'You!'*

The same realisation was dawning on Ash.

'The remainder of my estate I leave to my cousin, the Fifth Earl Kingswood, Mr William Albert James Ashington...'

Without missing a beat the lawyer detailed the unentailed lands and property that Ash was to inherit. But there was more.

'I commend my daughter, Lady Cecily Frances Kingswood, to the guardianship of the Fifth Earl—'

'What? *No!*' Fanny almost shrieked. 'Mr Richardson, this cannot be true!'

Ash's blood ran cold as he saw the trap ahead

of him. Guardian to a twelve-year-old child? Cutting out the child's mother? What on earth had John been thinking?

The lawyer paused, coughed, and looked directly at Fanny over his spectacles. Chastised, she subsided, but with a mutinous look. Mr Richardson then returned to the document and read to the end.

John explained in the will that Ash was to link closely with Fanny, so that together they might provide 'loving firmness' for Lady Cecily. *Loving firmness?* What did that even *mean*?

Ash's mind was reeling. Why on earth had John done this? Did he not trust Fanny to raise the child properly by herself?

The last thing Ash wanted was to be saddled with responsibility for a child! Fanny could easily have been named as guardian, with Ash and the lawyer as trustees. Indeed, it was normally expected that a child's mother would automatically be guardian.

The feeling of impatience and mild curiosity that had occupied him when Mr Richardson had begun his recitation had given way to shock and anger, barely contained.

Fanny, of course, then added to Ash's delight by indulging in a bout of tears. Cecily just looked bewildered. Ash met Mr Richardson's gaze briefly, sharing a moment of male solidarity, then he closed his eyes and brought his hand to his forehead. Would this nightmare never end?

Marianne emerged from Mrs Gray's registry hugely relieved. She glanced at the other two young ladies in the outer office. They were now seated together and had clearly been quietly chatting to each other. They looked at her now with similar expressions—curious, polite, questioning. She was unable to resist sending them what she hoped was an encouraging smile.

She patted her reticule as she stepped into the street, conscious of the paper within. This was her future. Governess to an unknown young lady, recently bereaved and living quietly with her mother. It sounded—actually, it sounded perfect.

For the first time since her decision to run away she felt a glimmer of hope. Perhaps, after all, things would work out. She had a situation and she would have a roof over her head. She would be living quietly in the country, far away from London. As long as Henry did not find her all would be well.

Of course she had no idea whether he was even looking for her. He might be content simply to let her vanish. On the other hand, that last look he had thrown her—one filled with evil intent—haunted her. Henry was entirely capable of ruthlessly, obsessively searching for her simply because she had thwarted his will by escaping.

She shrugged off the fear. There was nothing she could do about it beyond being careful. Besides, so far everything was working out well.

With renewed confidence, she set off for the modest inn where she had stayed last night. On Thursday her new life would properly begin.

'You are telling me that there is no way to avoid this?'

'Lord Kingswood, I simply executed the will. I did not write it.' Mr Richardson was unperturbed.

Fanny had gone, helped from the room by her daughter. Fanny had been gently weeping, the image of the Wronged Widow. Ash's hidden sigh of relief when the door had closed behind her had been echoed, he believed, by Mr Richardson. Fanny had not, it seemed, lost the ability to make a scene.

'You have not answered my question.'

There! The subtlest of gestures, but the lawyer had squirmed a little in his seat.

'Tell me how I can extricate myself from this and allow Lady Kingswood to raise her own child.'

'With your permission, Lady Kingswood can of course raise her daughter.'

'But her having to seek my permission is not right. She is the child's mother. Why should I be the guardian?'

The lawyer shrugged. 'Her father must have had his reasons. He did not clarify, and it was not my place to ask such questions.'

Ash decided to try another tack. 'What of Lady Kingswood's portion? How can I give my cousin's widow more than her husband did?'

'That part of the estate, as you know, is not entailed, which is how the Fourth Earl was at liberty to leave it to you. It is true that you do have the option of selling it or gifting it to someone. However—' he raised a hand to interrupt Ash's response '—after the death duties have been paid the estate will barely manage to break even. Lord Kingswood had been ill for more than a year, as you may be aware.'

'No. I was not aware.' Guilt stabbed through him. *Damn it!* Why had he not known about John's illness?

'During that time Lord Kingswood's investments suffered from a lack of attention, as did the estate. His steward was very elderly—he predeceased Lord Kingswood by only a few weeks—and the burden of management fell on the shoulders of Lady Kingswood. As…er…she had no previous knowledge or background in such matters…' His voice tailed away.

'But nor do I!' Ash ran his hand through his thick dark hair in frustration. 'If the estate has suffered under Lady Kingswood's stewardship, then how can I, equally inexperienced, be expected to do better?'

Mr Richardson eyed him calmly.

'Well?'

'I am afraid I have no answer to that question. What I do know is that if things are left to Lady Kingswood to manage…' Again his voice tailed off.

Ash reflected on Lady Kingswood. The young Fanny he remembered had been a beauty, a lively dancer and a witty conversationalist. He had no idea about the woman she had become.

'Are you suggesting that Lady Kingswood is *incapable* of managing?'

'I could not possibly comment.'

'Damn it!' Ash slammed his hand down on John's desk. *He was trapped.* A title, financial responsibilities, and now this. A twelve-year-old child to raise and a large estate to manage.

'Quite.' The lawyer indicated three large chests in the corner. 'Lady Kingswood informs me that documents relating to the estate and all of Lord

Kingswood's business affairs are contained in these chests.'

Ash opened the nearest box. It was full to bursting with papers, haphazardly stuffed into the chest. It would take at least a week to sort this box alone.

'Right. I see. *Right.*'

His mind was working furiously. This was going to take weeks to sort out. Weeks even to discover the extent of the commitment he had been left with. And his life was already full—friends to meet, parties to attend, an appointment to look at a new horse...

He came to a decision. 'I shall go to London now, as planned, and then return on Thursday, once I have dealt with my most pressing appointments.'

Inside, rage threatened to overpower him. *Why have I been given this burden? Damn it, John! Why did you have to die?*

Chapter Three

The inn at Netherton was similar in some ways to the Hawk and Hound. There was a stone archway off to one side, and Marianne had barely a moment to register the swinging metal sign before the coach swung into the yard.

See? Marianne told herself. *It is just an inn. The people here are no different from the people at home. I can do this.*

It was a refrain she had repeated numerous times in the few days since she had slipped away from the only home she could remember. Today she had survived the indignity of travelling on the public mail coach for only the second time in her life, sandwiched between a buxom farmer's wife and a youth travelling to visit his relations in Reading. The farmer's wife had talked incessantly, which had been both vexing and a relief, since no one could ask her any questions.

Grateful that the jolting coach was finally arrived at Netherton, Marianne descended, and pointed out her bandboxes to the coachman. He untied them from the top of the coach and passed them down to her, then he jumped down again, making for the warmth of the inn and its refreshments.

Marianne looked around the yard. The only other vehicle was a dashing high-perch phaeton, painted in an elegant shade of green, with green and black wheels. She had seen carriages like it before. They were all the crack among the London sporting gentlemen. Henry, of course, owned one—though his was a little smaller and painted red.

So where was the cart or the gig that would convey her to Ledbury House? Mrs Gray had said only that she would inform the family of her arrival. She had no idea who would be meeting her.

The other passengers had also dismounted and were going inside. Those who were travelling on would have a few moments here to relieve themselves, or quickly buy refreshments from the landlord.

Hesitantly, Marianne followed them into the inn.

The interior was dark, cosy and well-maintained. A fire burned in the grate, for the January day was chilly.

Marianne made her way towards the wooden counter at the far end of the room, where a woman who must be the landlady was busy pouring ale. As she walked Marianne found herself warily assessing the strangers in the room. Since the day and the hour she had left home she had not felt truly safe for even a minute. She had no experience with which to assess where danger might lurk, so found herself constantly on edge.

Her fellow passengers were already seating themselves in various parts of the taproom, and there were also two men who looked as if they might be farmers, each with a mug of beer in front of him.

Then she saw him. Her heart briefly thumped furiously in her chest and the hairs at the back of her neck stood to attention.

He was seated with his back to her, at the table closest to the counter. She could see his dark hair, swept forward in fashionable style. He wore a driving cloak with numerous capes. She could also see long legs encased in tight-fitting pantaloons and gleaming black boots. He looked like any one of a dozen London bucks.

Except this time, she reminded herself, *you have no reason to fear him.*

She kept walking, soothing herself with calm thoughts. As she reached his table she turned her head, compelled to confirm that it was no one she knew.

This man was a few years older than Henry—perhaps in his late twenties or early thirties. His hair was similar—thick, dark and luxuriant. But the face was totally different. This man was handsome—or at least he would be if he were not scowling so fiercely. His strong bones and lean features contrasted with Henry's slight pudginess and rather weak jawline. And now that she could see all of him she realised that his body shape was totally different from Henry's. He was lean and muscular, with no sign of a paunch. His clothing was similar to that favoured by Henry—and indeed by all the young bucks of London. But there the resemblance ended.

Sensing her standing there, he looked up from his mug and their eyes met. Stormy blue bored into her and Marianne felt a slow flush rise. My, but he was attractive! And she realised his gaze was doing strange things to her.

Breaking away from that endless, compelling contact, she bit her lip and took the final four steps to the counter.

'Yes, miss?'

Marianne summoned a polite smile. She felt slightly lost and shaky, and she could *feel* the man's gaze boring into her back.

Still, she managed to reply to the landlady. 'I am expecting someone to meet me here. I have travelled from London on the mail coach.'

'Who is it you are expecting, miss?'

Marianne's brow creased. 'I am not exactly sure.'

Inside, panic was rising. *What if there has been some mistake? What if there is no governess position?*

'I am to take up a position as governess at a place called Ledbury House. I was told to travel here by mail coach today.'

'Ledbury House? This gentleman—' the landlady indicated the fashionable buck '—is also travelling there. Perhaps you are expected to travel with him?'

Heart sinking, Marianne swung round to face him. His scowl had deepened as he'd listened to their exchange, and he now raised a quizzical eyebrow.

'Curious...' he mused. 'And to think I was unaware of the delights this day would hold.'

Marianne was taken aback. She was unsure how to take this. The man's words had been perfectly polite, but something about the tone suggested the possibility that he was not, in fact, delighted. Accustomed as she was to straightforward politeness, his words and tone felt disconcerting.

Something of what she was feeling must have shown on her face because, as she watched him, his expression changed to one of chagrin.

'I have no doubt,' he murmured cryptically, 'that this is a mess of Fanny's making and I am expected to fix it. Well, I shall do so this one time, but no more.' With this enigmatic statement he drained his mug, then stood. 'You'd best come with me.'

Not waiting for her reply, he swung away towards the door.

Marianne stood rooted to the spot, uncertainty bedevilling her. Should she go with him? A stranger? And she was to travel with him unaccompanied? Miss Marianne Grant, a lady, would never have done so. Miss Anne Bolton, a governess, could.

Conscious that all eyes were all on her, Marianne was surprised to find determination rising within her. Surprised because she did not often need to be brave. She was normally a placid, timid creature, most at home with a book in her hand and harmony and peace all around her.

This unknown gentleman was expecting her simply to climb into a carriage beside him—without any chaperon, maid or footman accompanying them. Perhaps he had a groom? Well, even if he didn't, it was clear that everyone expected the governess to go with him and be grateful for the ride.

Although he was handsome, and strangely compelling, she was almost relieved to be wary of him—being guarded would be much, much safer than being attracted to him.

Torn between the surprising temptation to sit down somewhere safe and wait for an unknown rescuer and the even stronger temptation to run, to get as far away as she could from the danger inherent in being alone in a carriage with a man, Marianne recognised that her best option was simply to get into the carriage and hope she would be safe with him.

She had very few options. She must get to Ledbury House, where she would have food and a place to sleep, and where she could perhaps eventually feel secure.

You are no longer Miss Marianne Grant, she reminded herself, *but a poor governess, and you need this situation.* Hopefully she would be safe and unmolested by this man for the last part of her journey.

Swallowing hard—she could almost *feel* the fear in the back of her throat—she gave the landlady a polite nod and followed him out to the yard.

There he was, barking orders at the ostlers, instructing them to harness his horses to the carriage as soon as they could find the time. Two men and a stable boy had immediately jumped to their task, apparently caught out by the gentleman's earlier than anticipated departure from the taproom.

Marianne walked slowly towards him. He glanced sideways at her, then turned his impatient gaze back to the ostlers. They stood like that, with Marianne feeling increasingly awkward and unsure, until the four beautifully matched greys were ready. The gentleman then held out his hand.

Confused, Marianne just looked at it.

'Your bandboxes?' he said mildly.

'Oh!' She passed them to him, and he stowed them in the back. One of the ostlers handed her up, and the gentleman got up beside her. He threw the men a couple of coins, and then they were off.

Marianne had never ridden in a high-perch phaeton before. It was high up, and there were no sides to speak of, and she was with a strange man who was taking her off to God knew where.

As a governess, this was now her lot. She had not the protection of any relative, nor even a servant known to her. Anything might happen to her, and no one would know or care.

It was not to be wondered at that fear, her constant companion these days, was now screaming inside her.

The carriage continued along the narrow streets of Netherton and onwards to the countryside beyond. Once free of the village the gentleman increased speed, driving his horses to what Marianne worried was an unsafe pace.

She wrapped her cloak more tightly around herself against the cold air and gripped the side of the carriage with her left hand. When they turned a bend in the road at what she felt was unnecessary speed, she could not prevent a small gasp.

Hearing it, he raised an eyebrow, but only slowed the pace slightly.

Marianne bit her lip. Between anxiety about being alone with a young man and driving too fast, she was all inner turmoil. Still, he had not so far shown any interest in her person. Except—Her mind wandered back to that first compelling gaze, when their eyes had been locked together and she had felt...*something*. Had he felt it too? Or had she imagined it?

The narrow seat was built to just about accommodate two people, with the result that he was seated uncomfortably close to her. His left thigh was aligned with her right leg, and she could feel his muscles tighten and relax as he concentrated on the exertions of driving. She could even detect his scent—a not unpleasant combination of what she thought was wood smoke and lye soap.

He seemed incredibly big and powerful and dangerous. And she had no idea who he was as he had not even had the courtesy to introduce himself.

They rounded another bend—to find a wide farm cart coming straight towards them! Marianne moaned, anticipating the inevitable collision. Their pace was too fast and the road too narrow to avoid it. She gripped more tightly and closed her eyes.

Seconds passed. *Nothing.* They were still moving! Opening her eyes, she was amazed to see that somehow they had passed the cart without collision. Twisting around, she saw that the cart was also continuing on its way. She sank back into her seat, unable to account for it.

'I apologise.'

Surprised, she looked at him.

He took his eyes off the road long enough to give her a rueful grimace. 'I was driving too fast. I have been taking out my frustration on you and everyone else.'

This was unexpected! She inclined her head,

unable to disagree with him. 'You were—and you have.'

His eyebrows rose and he chuckled. It was a surprisingly attractive sound.

'Shall we begin again?'

He slowed the horses to a walk and turned to half face her. 'Ashington—William Ashington. Also—since very recently—Earl Kingswood.' He bowed his head to her.

Warily, she nodded back. 'I am Miss Bolton.'

'A pleasure to meet you, Miss Bolton. I understand,' he continued politely, 'that you are to be the new governess at Ledbury House?'

'That is correct.'

She was as suspicious of his politeness as she had been thrown by his puzzling tone earlier. Still, perhaps he could give her some more information about the family.

She watched him closely. 'I am to be governess to a girl, or a young lady, who lives there with her widowed mama.'

'Lady Cecily, yes. Lord Kingswood died very recently.'

A flash of pain was briefly visible in his eyes. *Interesting.* So he was the new Earl and the previous Earl had been Lady Cecily's father.

'How old is Lady Cecily, do you know?'

He considered this, speaking almost to himself

as he thought it through. 'John and Fanny were married in ninety-four, and I believe their child was born a year or so after the wedding, so—' he turned to Marianne '—she must be twelve or thirteen.'

'Twelve or thirteen!'

Marianne had not been expecting this. She had, she realised, been hoping for a younger child, who might be easier to get to know. There was also the fact that a young lady of that age would soon be dispensing with the services of a governess anyway. So this position might not last for more than a few short years, regardless of how she performed in the role.

'Is that a problem?'

'Oh, no! Of course not. Just that I had somehow expected her to be younger.' She waited, but he had nothing to say to this. She tried another angle. 'Is Lady Cecily a quiet young lady, or rather more spirited?'

He snorted. 'I have met her exactly once—certainly not long enough to form an impression of her character.'

His tone indicated he was becoming uninterested in the topic, so she let it go.

'You are not, then, a regular visitor to Ledbury House?'

'I have been there twice in the past fourteen

years—once just before Lord and Lady Kingswood's wedding, and once this week for Lord Kingswood's funeral.' His tone was flat.

'Oh.' This was a little confusing. If he had been the heir presumptive, then why was he not close to the family, and why had he so rarely visited?

She stole a glance at him. Gone was the indulgent politeness of the past few moments. In its place was the hard jaw that she had seen before. She sighed inwardly. She had no idea why he was so frustrated, or whether any of it was due to something she had said. Still, it confirmed that she was right to maintain her wariness.

They continued on in silence for a few moments, with Marianne trying to think of something to say, and Lord Kingswood seemingly lost in his own thoughts. The road continued to twist and turn, and Marianne, despite herself, began to relax a little as she saw how deftly the Earl was handling the reins. She would not, it seemed, perish today at the hands of a breakneck driver.

After a particularly neat manoeuvre in which he negotiated a double bend with skill and ease, she could not help exclaiming 'Oh, well done!' Immediately she clapped a hand to her mouth. 'I do apologise! It is not for me to comment on your driving.' She held her breath as she waited for his response.

His brows arched in surprise. 'Indeed it is not. However, I shall indulge you, as you seem to have gone from abject terror to trusting my handling of the team.'

She blushed. 'Oh, dear! Was it so obvious?'

'Er—you were gripping the side as if your life depended upon it and gasping at every turn in the road. So, yes, it *was* fairly obvious.'

'I have never been driven so fast before, and have never sat in a carriage so far above the ground. It all seemed rather frightening. I would not presume to judge your driving skills.'

He threw her a sceptical look. 'Would you not?'

Her blush deepened. He knew quite well that she had been judging him.

'Miss Bolton, have you heard of the Four Horse Club, sometimes called the Four-In-Hand Club?'

'No? What is that?'

'Never mind.' He chuckled to himself.

'Well, I think that you are a very good driver,' she declared.

For some reason this made him laugh out loud. She could not help appreciating his enjoyment and noting how well laughter became him. Then she realised the direction of her thoughts and put an abrupt halt to them.

'Miss Bolton,' he stated, once he had recovered a little, 'I must admit I am grateful that fate brought you to Netherton today, for you have en-livened a dull journey. The Four Horse Club, by the way, is for those of us who have developed a certain level of skill at carriage driving. Now, here we are.'

He swung the carriage around to the left, en-tering a driveway via a set of iron gates. Ahead, Marianne could see the house. It was a broad, welcoming, two-storey building with tall win-dows, a wide front door, and ivy curving lovingly up the right-hand side.

'What a pretty house!' she could not help ex-claiming.

Lord Kingswood grunted. 'It may look pretty from afar, but it has seen better times.'

It was true. As they got closer Marianne could see signs of ill-use and lack of care. Some of the windows had not been cleaned in a while, it seemed, and the exterior was littered with au-tumn leaves and twigs—debris that should have been cleared away long since.

Her heart sank a little. What did this mean for her? Could they afford a governess? Would her existence be uncomfortable? Her pulse increased as she realised she was about to meet Lady Ce-cily and her mother. What if they disliked her?

Lord Kingswood glanced at her. 'You are sud-denly quiet, and all the vivacity has left you. Do not be worried—I have no doubt that they will be glad of your arrival.'

She gave him a weak smile. 'I do hope so.'

He pulled the horses up outside the house and jumped down. Immediately he came to her side of the carriage and helped her down. She could feel the warmth of his hand through her glove. It felt strangely reassuring.

She looked up at him, noting the difference in height between them. 'Thank you,' she said.

He squeezed her hand reassuringly, then let it go. She felt strangely bereft as he did so.

Turning, Marianne saw that the front door of the house was open and two ladies stood there. Both were dressed in mourning gowns, and one was a young girl of twelve or thirteen. This, then, was the widowed Lady Kingswood and her daughter.

Lord Kingswood strode forward and Marianne deliberately dropped back a pace.

'Good day, Fanny,' he said amiably. 'Good day, Lady Cecily.'

Marianne searched their faces and her heart sank. Neither looked welcoming. In fact both looked decidedly cross. Still, she was taken aback when Lady Kingswood's voice rang out, addressing Lord Kingswood.

'And so you have returned, as you threatened

to do! I wonder at you showing your face here again after what you have done to us!' She turned to Marianne. 'And who are *you*? One of his lady-birds, no doubt! Well, you shall not be installed in *my* home, so you should just turn and go back to wherever you came from!'

Chapter Four

Marianne's jaw dropped. *What? What is this woman saying?* She felt a roaring in her ears as all her hopes for a welcome, security, a safe place, crumbled before her. She stopped walking and simply stood there, desperately trying to fathom what was happening.

Lady Kingswood's face was twisted with raw fury—mostly, it seemed, directed at Lord Kingswood. Lady Cecily held her mother's arm, supporting her, and her young face was also set with anger. Both were white-faced, their pallor accentuated by their black gowns. Marianne knew that her own face was similarly pale.

Lord Kingswood kept walking, tension evident in every line of his body.

'Oh, for goodness' sake, Fanny, stop play-acting.'

'Play-acting? *Play-acting?*' Lady Kingswood's voice became shrill. 'You think this is some sort of *jest*, do you? Did you honestly believe that you could simply turn up here, with your lightskirt, and expect us to simply accept it?' She took a step forward into the centre of the doorway. 'You are not welcome here, and nor is she!'

'Dash it all, Fanny, you have become quite tedious. She is the new governess—not a lightskirt. And if you would pause these vapours for one second you would see that.' His tone was calm, unperturbed. 'Besides, you know full well that you cannot prevent me from entering Ledbury House. Nor do you have any say in who accompanies me.'

She gasped. 'That you should speak so to me! If John were here...why, he would—'

'Yes, but John is *not* here, is he?' He marched up to her and stepped inside.

Marianne felt a pang of sympathy for Lady Kingswood. Despite the woman's erroneous assumptions about her, Lady Kingswood was a recently bereaved woman who was clearly in distress.

The two ladies had turned to follow Lord Kingswood inside, and Marianne could hear the altercation continuing indoors. Behind her, a groom had taken charge of the horses and begun walking them towards the side of the house. The noise of hooves on gravel, combined with the jingling harnesses, prevented Marianne from making out the words, but she could hear Lady Kingswood's distress, punctuated by Lord Kingswood's deep tones.

The door was still open, but Marianne remained rooted to the spot. What on earth was she to do now? How would she get back to Netherton? She would have to walk, and some of her precious coins would have to be spent to pay for the next mail coach back to London—probably in the early hours of tomorrow morning.

She hurried after the phaeton and retrieved her bandboxes from the groom. He failed to meet her eyes and was clearly uncomfortable with the entire situation.

Marianne squared her shoulders, turned, and began trudging down the drive. As she walked, she carefully focused her attention on each step.

Don't think about reality. About the fact that you have no position. That you will be walking for the next hour just to reach the village. That you have no bed to sleep in tonight.

Could she afford to pay for a meal at the coaching inn? Once she had bought her ticket she would count her coins and decide what she must do.

Stop! She was thinking about *exactly* the things she should not be thinking about. *Just walk,* she told herself. *Just. Walk.*

'Miss Bolton!'

Surprised, she turned. Judging by Lady Kingswood's distress, she had not expected the argument between her and Lord Kingswood to end so soon. If she had thought about it at all, she would have said that neither of them would remember her existence for at least a half-hour.

Lord Kingswood was marching towards her, his face contorted with wrath. 'Where the hell do you think you are going?'

'To Netherton, of course.'

'Lord preserve me from melodramatic females!' He raised his eyes to heaven. 'Give those to me!'

Stupidly, she just stood there, trying to understand what was going on. He took the luggage from her.

'B-but...' she stuttered. 'Lady Kingswood—you surely cannot expect her to accept me as a governess, when she believes—' She broke off, unwilling to repeat Lady Kingswood's shocking assumption about her.

'I can and I shall!' he said through gritted teeth. 'Now, Miss Bolton, please come into the house and stop enacting tragedies. The day is too cold to be standing in a garden exchanging nonsense!'

He turned and began walking back to the house. As if tied to her precious bandboxes by an invisible thread Marianne followed, her mind awhirl.

The door was still open. Marianne followed

him inside. And there was Lady Kingswood, seated on a dainty chair in the hallway, sobbing vigorously, and being soothed by her daughter, who threw Lord Kingswood a venomous look.

'Now then, Fanny,' he said loudly, 'apologise to the new governess!'

'Oh, no!' said Marianne. 'There's really no need.'

'I think there is. Lady Kingswood has jumped to conclusions and insulted both of us. Fanny! Quit that wailing!'

Lady Kingswood sobbed a little louder. Overcome with compassion—for she could see how distressed the lady was—Marianne rushed forward and touched Lady Kingswood's hand.

'Oh, please, Lady Kingswood, there is no need! I can see your anguish. Is there something that can be done to aid you?' She looked at Cecily. 'Would your mama be more comfortable away from the hall?'

'Yes,' said Cecily. 'Mama, let us go to the sitting room and we shall have some tea.'

Lady Kingswood let it be understood that she was agreeable to this, and Marianne and Cecily helped her up. One on either side, they supported her through the hallway. Her sobs had quietened.

The Earl did not follow, but Marianne could still hear him, muttering under his breath.

Marianne could not help remembering her own grief in the days after her parents' death. She knew that she had been in a dark place, and that she had at times been so overwhelmed that, like Lady Kingswood, she had not been able to think straight. Whatever was going on between the widow and Lord Kingswood was none of her business. But she could not ignore someone in need.

Lady Cecily opened the first door to their left and they went inside. The pale February sunshine illuminated a room that was—or once had been—cosy. It was in need of a good clean, and perhaps the door could do with a lick of paint, but the sofa that they led Lady Kingswood to was perfectly serviceable.

She lay down, quiet now, and Marianne put a soft cushion under her head. 'Now, Lady Kingswood, should you like a tisane? Or some tea?' Marianne spoke softly.

'Tea...' The voice was faint.

Lady Cecily sat on the edge of the sofa and lifted her mother's hand. Marianne looked around. Spotting a bell-pull near the fireplace, she gave it a tug.

'It doesn't work.' Cecily rose from the sofa and opened the door. 'Mrs Cullen! Mrs Cullen!' Her voice was shockingly loud—and quite inappropriate for a young lady. 'Some of the bells work, but not this one.'

Oblivious to Marianne's reaction, the girl returned to her station by her mother's side. Marianne sat on an armchair near the sofa and took the opportunity to study both of them.

Lady Cecily was a pretty young lady, with blonde hair, a slim figure and distinctive amber eyes. She carried herself well and was clearly very fond of her mama. Lady Kingswood, still prostrate on the sofa, with her hand over her forehead and her eyes closed, was a good-looking woman with fair hair, beautiful blue eyes, and the merest hint of wrinkles at the sides of her mouth. She was, Marianne guessed, in her early thirties. If Cecily was twelve—which seemed correct— then Lady Kingswood must have been married young. Married young and now widowed young.

It was not uncommon, Marianne knew. Why, when she herself had turned seventeen, three years ago, her parents had offered her a London season—which she had declined in horror. Go to London? Where Henry did his drinking and his gambling and his goodness knew what else? She had shuddered at the very idea.

Her parents, themselves more comfortable in the country, had let the matter drop, but had encouraged Marianne to attend the local Assembly

Rooms for country balls and musical evenings. These she had enjoyed, and she had struck up mild friendships with some of the young men and women of a similar age. She had received two polite but unexciting marriage proposals, had declined both, and had continued to enjoy her life with her family.

Until the tragedy. That night when she had lost both parents at once.

Immediately a wave of coldness flooded her belly. *Lord—not now!*

Exerting all the force of her will, she diverted her attention from her own loss to the sympathy she felt for the bereaved woman and child in front of her. Gradually her pulse settled and the coldness settled down.

As she sat there, deliberately forcing her attention back to the present, she wondered where 'Mrs Cullen' was, and why she had not yet appeared. Lady Cecily was still sitting patiently, clearly unsurprised at the time it was taking.

Eventually Marianne heard footsteps in the corridor and the door opened, admitting a woman who must be Mrs Cullen. She was a harassed-looking woman in her middle years, with reddish hair and a wide freckled face. She wore the simple grey dress of a servant, covered with a clean white apron. Her arms were uncovered, her hands red and chapped from kitchen work, and there was a trace of flour on her right cheek.

She bobbed a curtsey to Lady Cecily. 'Yes, miss?'

'My mother is unwell. Could we have tea, please?'

'Of course. Right away, miss.'

'Oh, and Mrs Cullen, this is my new governess. Miss...' She looked expectantly at Marianne.

'Miss Bolton. Anne Bolton,' Marianne said confidently. The lie was coming more easily to her now. *That is not a good thing.* 'I arrived a short time ago.'

'Yes, Thomas said so. Welcome, Miss Bolton.'

Marianne automatically thanked her, then frowned in confusion. *Who is Thomas?* she wondered.

Mrs Cullen must have noticed her confusion. 'Oh—Thomas is the groom and the gardener, and I am the cook.' She flushed a little. 'I apologise for rattling on. It is nice to meet you, Miss Bolton. Now, I shall go and make that tea.'

She left in a flurry, but Marianne was relieved to feel that at least one person had welcomed her in a perfectly natural way.'

'Thomas is married to Mrs Cullen's daughter, Agnes. Agnes is our maid of all work.' Lady Cecily was speaking shyly to her.

Marianne gave her an encouraging smile. 'Mrs Cullen… Thomas… Agnes. I shall try to remember all the names. How many others are there?'

'None. We used to have a housekeeper and a footman, and two housemaids, but they have all gone. And our steward died. He was old—not like Papa.'

'None?' Marianne was shocked.

A house of this size, an earl's home at that, with only three servants?

From the sofa, a low moan emerged.

'Mama!' Lady Cecily was all attention.

'Help me up.'

Assisted by her daughter, Lady Kingswood raised herself into a sitting position. Her face was blotched from her recent tears, but she was still an extremely pretty woman, Marianne thought. She could not help but notice the fine silk dress that Lady Kingswood was wearing. Cecily's gown looked similarly expensive—the finest fabrics and the expert cut indicated that considerable expense had been laid out on both mourning dresses.

So why, Marianne wondered, *have the staff all gone? And why is the house so dilapidated?*

Lady Kingswood took a deep breath. 'Miss Bolton,' she began, fixing Marianne with a keen eye, 'while I appreciate the kindness with which you responded to me just now, there are certain questions I must ask you.'

Marianne's heart sank. 'Of course.'

'I contacted a London registry to find a governess, but they sent me no word that they had appointed someone. I had no notion of your arrival.'

'They appointed me only two days ago, but assured me they would write ahead to let you know I would arrive today.'

'No letter has been received.' Her eyes narrowed. 'So how did you manage to arrive with A—with Lord Kingswood?'

Haltingly, Marianne explained how it had come about. Lady Kingswood listened intently, but Marianne had the feeling that she was not convinced.

'I assure you,' she said earnestly, 'I had never met Lord Kingswood before today.'

'Hmm...'

Lady Cecily, Marianne noted, was looking from one to the other, her expression one of mild confusion. Lady Kingswood noticed it too.

'Cecily, please pass me my shawl. It is positively freezing in here!'

It was true, Marianne thought. Still attired in her cloak, bonnet and gloves—and how rude she was to be so—nevertheless could tell that the sitting room was only a little milder than outdoors.

Discreetly, she removed the gloves and stowed them in the pocket hung under her cloak.

Cecily passed an ornate shawl to her mother, commenting as she did so, 'The fire has not been lit in here, Mama. And Agnes will be helping Mrs Cullen with dinner. We shall have to wait until afterwards for her to set the fire in the parlour again.'

Lady Kingswood looked a little uncomfortable. 'I should explain,' she said, addressing Marianne, 'that we have had to make certain economies during my husband's illness. Temporary, of course.'

'Of course.' What else could she say?

Thankfully, Mrs Cullen then reappeared, with hot tea and delicious-looking crumpets. Marianne, who had eaten nothing since yesterday evening, felt her stomach cry out for the food.

'Dinner will be ready in about a half-hour, my lady,' the cook said to her mistress. 'What with the new Earl and Miss Bolton arriving, I've added a few extra vegetables and put a pie in the oven.' She looked at Marianne. 'Once you've finished your tea I'll show you your room, if you wish.'

Marianne thanked her, noting that with the mention of Lord Kingswood the tension in the air had increased again.

The Dowager Countess Kingswood served the tea and they all drank and ate in silence. Marianne loved the freshly baked crumpets. If these were any indication, then Mrs Cullen was a fine cook.

'Mama,' said Lady Cecily suddenly, 'can Lord Kingswood really bring whomever he wishes into Ledbury House?'

Lady Kingswood frowned. 'Yes,' she said bitterly, 'and there is nothing that either of us can do about it. The law allows it. He is master here now.'

'But,' said Cecily, 'that is not fair!'

Marianne reflected on this. Like her, they were victims of the law. Men wrote things in wills; women suffered them. As if it was not enough to lose a loved one through death, they then had to be subject to whatever the law said must happen next. In the Kingswood ladies' case that meant subjecting themselves to the arrogant Lord Kingswood. For Marianne it had meant the arrival of Henry and his friends into her peaceful existence.

She shook her head slightly. Well, she would do all she could for Lady Kingswood and her daughter, as Mrs Bailey had done for her.

'This is the room used by Lady Cecily's previous governesses. As I didn't know you were coming I haven't had time to make up the bed or clean the room, but I shall get on to it as soon as I can.'

Mrs Cullen stood back, allowing Marianne to enter first. The room was fairly small, but it had a fireplace, an armoire and a chest of drawers, as well as a solid-looking bed with a clean mattress. The place needed dusting, and the window was grimy, but all in all, it was a pleasant room.

Marianne crossed to the window. The view was delightful—she could see the drive, the overgrown garden and the woods beyond.

'It is a lovely room. Has Lady Cecily had many governesses?'

'Oh, well…' Mrs Cullen flushed a little. 'We live very quietly here, and rarely go to London, so people sometimes move on to other positions. Not just the governesses.'

'But you have stayed—and so has your daughter?'

'Ah, but my mother and father both lived here all their lives. My mother was cook for the old Lord and Lady Kingswood, him being the Third Earl, and then for Master John and his wife—the present Dowager Countess—until I took over. She worked here for over forty years. I was born in this house, and so was my Agnes. This is our home too. We could never leave it, no matter how bad— That is to say we have a fondness for the place, and for the family, and they have always been good to us. Although, now—' She frowned. 'But that is of no matter. Now, would you like some warm water for washing?'

Marianne had listened to this rambling speech in some astonishment. Only loyalty to the Earl's family, Mrs Cullen seemed to suggest, had prevented them from leaving. So why would they think of leaving in the first place? Were they not being paid? Were they badly treated? They certainly seemed to be burdened with overwork.

Mrs Cullen was waiting for her response. 'Oh, thank you! But I know you are busy preparing dinner. If you will show me where to go, I shall fetch a jug of water myself.'

'Indeed, you will not!' Mrs Cullen looked shocked. 'A gently bred lady such as yourself, fetching and carrying like a scullery maid? No, Aggie will bring it to you directly, for I shall replace her in the kitchen.'

She bustled off, leaving Marianne with much to think about. She was beginning to understand why she had been given this position. Without a character reference she could not afford to be over-particular. And with a high turnover of staff—including, it seemed, governesses—Lady Kingswood could not be over-particular either.

Which meant that they were all tied together—herself, the ladies, the staff. And the new Earl Kingswood.

Chapter Five

Marianne ventured downstairs again with some trepidation. Aggie had informed her, when she had brought the water, that dinner would be served in twenty minutes, so Marianne had had a hasty wash, brushed as much dust as she could from her gown, then gone in search of the dining room.

The house was a similar size to her own home, though the layout was different, but she had tried two or three wrong doors before she'd eventually found the correct room. No one was there, but the table was laid for dinner.

In her head she was counting the number of servants they had at home. Seven—and that was just the indoor servants. In contrast Ledbury House, which was probably larger, was surviving on two—hence the dilapidation.

A small fire was burning in the dining room grate, and Marianne crossed to the fireplace to warm her hands. After the cold ride in the carriage she had not as yet warmed up.

Behind her, the door opened and closed, sending smoke from the fire billowing into her face and causing her to cough helplessly.

'Oh, Miss Bolton—that is the draught! We do not stray too close to the fire unless we know that no one will open the door.'

It was Cecily.

'The smoke comes into the room and can make you cough if you are too close.'

'Miss Bolton will soon learn our ways, Cecily.' Lady Kingswood had followed her daughter into the room. 'Now, do tidy your hair, child. It is becoming unpinned.'

Obediently, Cecily raised her hands to her hair, which was, in fact, loosening a little at the back.

'Can I help?' Marianne, having recovered from her coughing fit, stepped towards her. 'It is this pin which has become loose—there, now I have fixed it!'

'Thank you, Miss Bolton,' said Lady Cecily.

Her mother had already turned away, and now seated herself at the foot of the table. Marianne waited to see which side Lady Cecily would sit, then moved towards the other. That left one place setting—the head of the table where, presumably, Lord Kingswood was expected to sit. Lady Kingswood, noting it, pressed her lips together.

The door opened again, behind Marianne, and she realised from the other ladies' sudden stiffening that it must be Lord Kingswood. He seemed to pause, then walked silently to his place at the head of the table.

'Good evening, Fanny, Cecily, Miss Bolton.'

He looked every inch the gentleman, Marianne had to concede. He wore the knee breeches, snowy white shirt and superfine jacket that were currently *de rigueur* for evening wear. His cravat was tied in a complicated knot and he was fiddling absently with a beautiful pocket watch.

The fashionable clothing showed off his fine, muscular figure to advantage, and Marianne could not help again contrasting his appearance with that of Henry and his friends—some of whom were thin as a lath and others, like Henry, who were inclined to carry extra weight. Lord Kingswood somehow *filled* his clothes. Their clothing was similar, but there the resemblance ended.

'Good evening,' she murmured politely, reminding herself that appearance meant nothing. Lord Kingswood, though a few years older than Henry, was clearly part of the London set. Perhaps he even knew her brother! A wave of fear washed over her at the thought.

Cecily also replied to him, but Lady Kingswood merely inclined her head. Mrs Cullen and Agnes then appeared, with a selection of dishes, and the tension in the air dissipated a little as they all helped themselves to various delicacies.

Feeling she must say something, Marianne managed to engage Lady Cecily in a conversation about foods that she liked and disliked, and as the meal went on she felt Cecily warming to her a little.

The food was delicious—Mrs Cullen was clearly an expert cook. Marianne thanked heaven for small mercies. The house was cold, and run-down, and its occupants were at each other's throats, but at least there was decent food.

Strange that she had taken her life so much for granted. Until a few days ago she had never had cause to question where her next meal was coming from. Although she had not actually run out of money, she had worried about doing so during the past few days. Now she appreciated the food before her as she never had before. She savoured every bite and was grateful.

'This is delicious,' she said aloud. 'I must compliment Mrs Cullen on the meal.'

'I agree.' Lord Kingswood had unexpectedly

decided to join in the conversation. 'I admit I had assumed that with everything else in this house going to rack and ruin the food would be appalling. I admit to being pleasantly surprised.'

Lady Kingswood threw him an angry look. 'How dare you insult my home?'

'I was complimenting your cook.' He eyed her evenly.

Marianne felt the tension rise. *Oh, dear!* It was all going to start again.

'Rack and ruin, you said.' She glared at him.

'True. I have not been in Ledbury House for many years, and I am saddened to see how run-down it has become.' His tone was unapologetic.

Oh, why did I compliment the cooking? Marianne thought.

'Yes, you have not been here for fourteen years. And I wish you had not come now.'

Lady Kingswood's voice quivered, and she had stopped eating. Cecily was looking anxiously from her mother to Lord Kingswood and back again.

Do something! Marianne was thinking to herself.

'I have often thought,' she said, her tone deliberately relaxed, 'that pretty, comfortable houses remain beautiful through the ages, no matter the ups and downs of the families living within them.'

Is that enough?

Lady Kingswood looked at her. 'This *is* a pretty house, isn't it?'

'*Very* pretty.'

Her hostess reached for a dish and spooned some potatoes and leeks onto her plate. At the other end of the table the Earl was glowering, and he seemed to be getting ready to say something. Something unhelpful, Marianne was sure.

She tapped her fingers on the table, considering. Then decisively she raised her hand to her face, hoping to catch his attention. It worked. He glanced at her and she gave him a level stare. She did not look away, but simply maintained the gaze.

His eyebrows flew upwards, then he flushed slightly and broke the contact. But he did not say whatever it was he had been preparing.

Marianne returned to her own meal, feeling that she had at least prevented all-out war at dinner.

What a managing, impudent young woman! Ash was thinking. *How dare she presume to check my behaviour!*

He had no doubt that was what Miss Bolton intended. The level stare she had sent him had left him in no doubt as to her meaning. He was to bite back his retort and allow Fanny to continue to play the injured widow.

Well, it will not do!

He no more wanted to be here than Fanny wanted him here. He had never asked to be Earl. John's father and his own papa had been twin brothers, and his father had constantly talked of the lucky chance of being the younger son.

'Just think!' Papa used to say. 'If I had been born just twenty minutes earlier my life would have been made a prison by the responsibilities of the Earldom! It would have been farms and quarter-days and conscientiousness, with no time to enjoy my life.'

He had instilled in Ash an abhorrence of responsibility, convincing him as a boy that John's life would be unending dreariness and care. Ash had maintained that conviction, and even now was wary of anything that smacked of responsibility. He relied on himself and nobody depended on him. He was free to come and go as he pleased, and he liked it that way. What was more, he was determined to ensure that the Earldom would not trap him into conventionality or duty.

He might be Earl in name, but he was damned

if he would be sucked into spending his time here, in this run-down, isolated house!

Only his obligation to John had ensured Ash's temporary return. That and the knowledge that if he absented himself or passed responsibility to Fanny the place would be bankrupt within six months.

He had gone through John's financial affairs with the lawyer, and had seen enough to know that with care and attention and some of his own money he should be able to restore the accounts to good health in a year or two. Only John's illness—and his inability to manage his affairs as a result—had led to the downturn in fortunes. Wages had not been paid, good staff had left, and everything had gone downhill from there.

Ash had been busy in London these past two days. His valet and coachman were to follow him here tomorrow with his trunks, and he had charged his secretary with finding a good steward. He had found time to visit his closest friends to explain that he would likely be absent for a while. Most of them had thought it a great joke.

'But, Ash!' one had said, punching him light-heartedly on the arm. 'You have never had any cares! I give it a month, then you will tire of this diversion!'

'I only wish that were true, Barny,' he had replied, somewhat sadly. 'But I cannot see a month being long enough to fix this dashed mess!'

Barny had been right about one thing, though. Ash had indeed never carried any responsibility. Nor had he ever wished to. He was blessed with a decent fortune from his mother's family, which enabled him to live comfortably as a single man. He rented a house near Grosvenor Square, over-paid his servants to ensure he would avoid the inconvenience of hiring and training new ones, and spent his life entirely at his own leisure.

He was at no one's beck and call, he had no ties and he liked it that way. Responsibility meant limits and not being in charge of one's own course.

Wistfully, he reflected that if not for John and this confounded mess he would be at White's right now, enjoying good company and fine wine. Instead of which—

'We shall retire to the parlour and leave you to your port.'

Belatedly he realised the table had been cleared and the three ladies were departing. Rising swiftly, he nodded politely, then sank back into his chair with relief when they had gone.

Although a favourite with the ladies—one of his tasks in London yesterday had been to bid farewell to the dashing high-flyer whose company he had been enjoying for nigh on two months—he was nevertheless unused to domesticity, families and, frankly, histrionics. His life was normally calm, devoid of drama and well-organised. And he liked it that way.

His mama had died when he was young, leaving her entire fortune in trust for Ash, and when he'd come home from school and university he and Papa would enjoy good food, fine wine and a wide range of male sports. Ash was a skilled horseman, boxer and fencer, and Papa had ensured he had access to all the best clubs.

And always, *always*, Papa had ribbed his brother, the Third Earl, teasing him about his dullness and domesticity.

John, Ash knew, had been raised from babyhood to be the next Earl Kingswood, and had taken his responsibilities seriously even in childhood. He would obediently leave Ash playing in the woods or fishing to go off with his father and his father's steward to inspect a broken bridge or visit a tenant farmer, leaving Ash perplexed at John's dutiful compliance.

Ash had a sneaking suspicion that he would not be up to filling John's shoes, and that thought scared the hell out of him.

There! He had admitted it.

Remembering that there was no manservant to

appear with the alcohol that he suddenly craved, Ash rose and began searching in the rosewood sideboard. Success! Two bottles of port and some dusty glasses. Blowing into a glass to clear the worst of the dust, he then wiped it with his kerchief and filled it with port.

Lifting the glass, he made a toast to his cousin, then sampled the ruby-red liquid.

Not bad, he thought. *A pity you aren't here to share it with me, John.*

Not for the first time he thought with regret on the distance between himself and John since his cousin's marriage. If they had been closer perhaps he could have helped during these last months—prevented John's home from deteriorating, his financial affairs from spiralling downwards and his family from becoming distressed. Perhaps he could have learned a little about what he was supposed to *do.*

And you are still adding to his family's distress, a small voice in his head reminded him.

He sighed. He knew it. Somehow, though, when Fanny was being Fanny his reason went out the window and it seemed he became eighteen again.

Fanny had always been impractical, he recalled. Of course his eighteen-year-old self had not seen further than her deep blue eyes and blonde curls.

Like John, he had become completely infatuated with Fanny when she and her family had moved to the district. Spending the summer at Ledbury House that year had been ecstasy, agony and ultimately a severe lesson. For of course she had chosen John.

And he and John had fallen out over it.

They had both said words intended to hurt the other and, stupidly, had never put it right. Ash had attended their wedding—as John's cousin he had been obliged to—but afterwards had avoided him. At the time Ash had not been able to bear to see John and Fanny together. In his youthful mind he had thought that what he was experiencing was heartbreak, and the only way to recover was to cut Fanny out of his life—which had meant it was easier not to make the effort to repair his relationship with John.

Somehow years had gone by, and then had come the message that John had died, following a long illness.

His thoughts drifted back towards Fanny again. How did he feel about her now? Despite the momentary echo of his former infatuation when he had first encountered her in the library, it was clear that now he saw her differently. She was an attractive woman, certainly, and yet neither his heart nor his loins showed any interest in her. In fact, his predominant mood when he found himself in Fanny's company was one of irritation.

And *she* had known it—had seen straight through him. The governess—*Miss Bolton.*

He pictured her in his mind's eye. Now, *there* was a woman to stir him! She was gently bred—that much was obvious—and somewhere in her early twenties. She was also extremely pretty, with dark hair, gentle brown eyes and a pleasantly plump figure.

His connoisseur's eye had assessed her at the inn as she had stood there gaping at him. Miss Bolton possessed an indefinable quality that had attracted his attention. At the time he had felt as though something significant had passed between them, but had dismissed the notion as fanciful. Had the circumstances been different, he believed he would have tried to strike up a conversation with her.

Today, though, filled with irritation at having had to leave London and come to this godforsaken place, Ash had not been in the mood to charm unknown young ladies. He had not followed up on his attraction towards her but instead had been consumed with the frustrations of an earldom, an estate and a ward that he had never wanted.

When he had discovered he was to be forced to convey Miss Bolton to the house his annoyance had increased. And that had been *before* she had criticised his driving! Oh, he had heard her gasp, seen how she gripped the side of the phaeton. For goodness' sake—did she think him a cow-handed amateur? Why, he was known as one of the best drivers in London!

To be fair, he had warmed towards Miss Bolton a little as they'd neared the house—her innocent approval of his driving skills had amused him, and he had felt sorry for her when he'd heard Fanny call her a lightskirt. As if he would be so crass as to bring a paramour to Ledbury House!

But then he recalled that Fanny had never been known to show insight. Or common sense. Suddenly the qualities that had attracted the eighteen-year-old Ash—particularly Fanny's flightiness and love for drama—seemed much less attractive in a thirty-year-old Dowager Countess.

And Fanny had never *read* him as the governess had tonight at dinner. Somehow Miss Bolton had known that he was about to react to Fanny again—that he was prepared to keep the argument alive. Her still, calm gaze had discomfited him.

He shifted uncomfortably. What right had she—an almost-servant in *his* employ—to behave so towards him? Miss Bolton, he decided, was much too presumptuous.

Draining his glass, he set it down with a thump and went in search of the ladies.

Chapter Six

Thankfully the fire in the parlour was high, and the room was actually warm. For the first time since arriving in Ledbury House a few hours ago Marianne felt warmth getting through to her bones. The excellent food had helped, of course—though the frosty atmosphere had somewhat spoiled her enjoyment of the best meal she had had since leaving home three days ago.

Frowning, she reflected on the difficult situation she had found herself in. Lady Kingswood and the Earl were at loggerheads, and likely to remain so. And Lady Cecily, she thought, was caught in the middle—loyal to her mama but disliking the conflict. Surely Marianne's first duty was to her charge? It was not in Cecily's interests for her to witness what might prove to be an ongoing open battle.

Marianne herself hated quarrels, and often acted as peacemaker between her friends, and even occasionally between the servants at home. She knew that sometimes even difficulties that seemed intractable could be resolved, and wondered if that might be the case here.

She also knew that if people were *determined* to hurt others—if they genuinely had no care for others—then walking away was the only safe option. Which was why she herself had left home. There was no *misunderstanding* between her and Henry. In fact, it was the opposite. She had finally realised who he truly was, and the fact that he had no compassion or morality left within him.

Gazing into the fire, Marianne reviewed what she knew of the situation here at Ledbury House. Lord Kingswood had inherited the estate and the law allowed him to do as he pleased with it. Lady Kingswood and her daughter had no choice but to submit to the law, and to his mastery.

As he was, apparently, also Lady Cecily's guardian, he had invited the Dowager Countess and her daughter to remain living in the main house for now. Lady Cecily had confessed that the Dower House was in a bad state of repair, so she and her mama were relieved to be still living there.

Since Ledbury House itself was in no great condition, Marianne shuddered to think how bad the Dower House must be. However, although the estate seemed to be in financial difficulties, and had lost most of its staff, they had still hired her to be governess to Lady Cecily, and both Cecily and her mother had elegant clothing. So Cecily's future and current needs had been a priority when economies were being made.

Other governesses had left—perhaps because they had not received their wages, or perhaps, as Mrs Gray had reported, because Ledbury House was simply too quiet, too remote for those used to the bustle of London. But had there been other reasons?

Knowing that a number of footmen and maids had left their positions in her own home after Henry had become master, she wondered if perhaps something similar was at play in Ledbury House. Was someone or something making the servants' lives difficult in Ledbury House?

From what Marianne could tell so far, Lady Cecily seemed to be calm, polite and unassuming. Lady Kingswood's conduct had been challenging today, but then, she was a newly bereaved widow, experiencing the powerlessness and frustration of the law's preference for men. It was too soon for Marianne to judge whether she was habitually demanding.

So had some of the staff left because of Lord Kingswood's manner? She could well believe that! But, no—he had stated clearly that he had not been at Ledbury House for many years prior to this week. So whatever had been occurring it was not due to him. And yet his arrival looked to have increased tensions within the household.

The thought recalled her to the present. Lady Kingswood was sitting peacefully in an armchair near the fire, while Lady Cecily busied herself with some sewing. Unlike the sitting room they had sat in earlier, this parlour was clean and comfortable. Mrs Cullen and Agnes had clearly had to choose which rooms would receive attention. Although Lady Kingswood seemed outwardly serene, Marianne noted with concern the slight crease in the woman's forehead and the fixed way she was staring into the fire.

Tentatively, Marianne offered, 'This is a beautiful room.'

Her hostess lifted her head and looked at her blankly before focusing on what Marianne had said. She smiled slightly. 'Thank you. I had it redecorated just before John—just before my husband became ill.'

Keen to prevent Lady Kingswood focusing on her bereavement, Marianne began asking her about the various furnishings, the colours chosen and the layout of the room. She complimented her on her good taste and commented on the warmth and cosiness of the room, highlighting how welcome it was after her cold journey earlier.

The air thawed a little between them, and the conversation began to flow with something approaching a natural rhythm.

Until the door opened and Lord Kingswood joined them.

Lady Kingswood's reaction was immediate. She drew herself up in her chair, raised an imperious eyebrow and stated generally, 'Is it that time already?'

The implication—that Lord Kingswood had not tarried long enough over his port—was evident to all present. The air was positively bristling with tension. Yet the Earl, ignoring it, made for the fire. Holding his hands to it briefly, he then turned to face the room, allowing the fire to warm his back and legs.

'Finally!' he pronounced. 'A decent fire!'

'Indeed.' Lady Kingswood fixed him with a steely glare. 'The room was warming up nicely until your arrival. Please do not block the heat from the rest of us.' She glanced down at her hands, addressing no one in particular. 'I have often thought that consideration for others is a virtue sadly undervalued.'

He snorted. 'I myself have often bemoaned the

loss of *politeness* in society. An important virtue, sadly lacking at times, would you not agree?'

Lady Kingswood's hands became fists in her lap. 'Are you accusing me of rudeness?'

'Not at all,' he replied urbanely, moving to seat himself in an armchair. 'I was speaking generally. Surely you do not see *yourself* as being rude?'

Lord, here they go again! thought Marianne.

She decided to intervene. 'I have often noticed,' she offered, 'that what seems acceptable to one person may seem unacceptable to another. Surely there are individual differences that must be allowed if people are to get along with each other?'

He turned his head and deliberately, coolly, looked at her. And kept looking at her. She could feel her colour rising. Had she said something wrong? Surely he could see that she was simply trying to help?

Lady Kingswood had stood up, and now retrieved a book of sermons from a side table. Deliberately, she opened the book and pretended to read, ignoring everyone around her.

'Sermons, eh, Fanny?' Lord Kingswood chuckled. 'From what I recall you were never one for sermons when *I* knew you.'

'That,' she snapped back, 'was nigh on fourteen years ago—when I was but a child myself. You know nothing about who I am now.'

'Oh,' he said, making a careful study of his signet ring, 'I suspect you are not much changed, Fanny. At heart, you are as you ever were.'

Marianne frowned. Lord Kingswood's comment had reminded her of how she had agonised over Henry's character. Was there *any* good in her stepbrother? Could she do *anything* to help him behave better towards the people around him? She had often asked herself these questions—until that last night, when he had showed himself to be beyond redemption.

Henry had never accepted his father's second marriage and had tried his best—even as a child—to make Marianne's life miserable. He had always been careful not to let his papa or Marianne's mama see his true self. Marianne had tried to speak to him about it once, when she was aged about ten and Henry had been fifteen. He had simply laughed at her.

'Your precious mama,' he had sneered, 'should not even *be* in this house. It is *my* mother who is the true mistress, and she should never have been replaced. I cannot wait for the old man to die and then I will throw *both* of you out! Oh, how I long for that day!'

Shocked, Marianne had decided not to tell Mama about it, for fear that she would be upset.

But she had spoken to Mama about Henry in general terms. 'Why is Henry so angry, Mama?'

'Hush, now, child,' Mama had responded. 'He is angry because he misses his own mama, and that is a sad thing, is it not?'

'If you and Papa die, where will I live?'

'You will always have a home here if you want it. Now, do not worry about things that may never happen!'

Yet it *had* happened, and Henry *had*, in fact, forced her to leave her home simply by making her life intolerable if she stayed. She would be twenty-one in April and, in theory at least, might have had more freedom after reaching her majority. However, she did not understand enough about the law to be certain, and there had been no one she could ask.

She shivered. Despite the tension of today's events, at least here she was not in imminent danger of any assault upon her person. And her bedroom door, she had noted, had a lock and key.

She really must be careful about confusing Henry with other men. Yes, she needed to be wary of any man, yet there was nothing to suggest that Lord Kingswood was anything like Henry. He was gruff, yes, and seemed miserable—but, she judged, there was no badness in him.

Her heart went out to this little broken family. She looked at each of them in turn. They all looked unhappy. All three of them. And they were all bound together here. She would have to help them make the best of it.

Marianne shook out her dresses and hung them in the armoire. The hour was late, but she did not feel like sleeping. The hostile atmosphere in the parlour had persisted until at last Lady Kingswood had announced that she would retire. All the ladies had risen with her, leaving the Earl to his solitary enjoyment of the fire.

Marianne had received a cordial goodnight from both ladies as they'd climbed the stairs, and a request to meet with Lady Kingswood after breakfast to discuss Cecily's learning. Cecily had looked a little anxious at this and Marianne, remembering what it had been like to be twelve, had felt some sympathy for her.

And now she was in her room, alone at last, with time to reflect on the events of the day. There was no denying the comfort of knowing that this was to be her own room for some considerable time, that she had a roof over her head, food to eat, and a position that gave her some security. Temporarily, anyway.

During the evening her room had been given a

cursory clean by Agnes, Mrs Cullen's daughter, who had also made up Marianne's bed. She had promised to set a fire in the grate from tomorrow, but had not had the time to do so tonight. Marianne had thanked her and asked her to leave her basket of cleaning materials. Agnes had eventually left, after talking incessantly at Marianne for quite half an hour.

Having sat down with relief when Agnes had finally left, Marianne had now forced herself to get up again and unpack. She had never before had to perform this task for herself—yet another luxury she had taken for granted. She shook out and hung up her few other items of clothing and stowed her bandboxes—with Mama's jewels still safely inside—on top of the armoire.

Afterwards, picking up a duster and cloth, she began cleaning the main surfaces of the room herself. It was surprisingly satisfying to see the grime come away. The tallow candle was burning down surprisingly quickly, so she gave the window panes a quick wipe, vowing to herself to do more in the morning, with clean water. Closing the curtains, she quickly undressed and climbed into bed. The room was so cold that she could see her breath.

She blew out the candle.

Lying there, in a strange bed, far from home,

Marianne could not help shedding a tear for all she had lost. Not only her happy life with Mama and Papa, but her home, her security and now her identity. She was Miss Anne Bolton now, and she would do well to remember it. *'Marianne...'* she whispered to herself. But Marianne was gone.

Ash stood outside, enjoying the cool freshness of the air and reflecting on his first full day as master of Ledbury House. The night was cold, clear and quiet, and the silent stars wheeled across the night sky in a slow dance. Here he was, stuck in a forlorn, miserable, rustic house, far from the civilisation, lights and busyness he was used to. He was trapped with three emotional females—who of course had all bonded together at the least provocation—and the prospect of congenial company was weeks, if not months, away. He generally avoided females—apart from his *chères-amies*, of course—preferring the company of his male friends. He missed their company— the eating and drinking, the card parties and horse racing, and the innocuous repartee that characterised his interactions with them.

He sighed and turned to go inside. As he did so his eye was caught by a light coming from a first-floor window. A candle on the sill illuminated

Miss Bolton, vigorously cleaning the window panes, her breath clearly visible in the cold air.

He stood watching for a moment. The light shone upwards, giving her pretty face a warm glow. He could not help a sneaking admiration for the woman. Governesses did not normally perform menial work, yet there she was, cleaning at midnight, oblivious of his presence.

Ash could not help feeling a little ashamed—as master, it was *his* responsibility to ensure that the house was suitable for its occupants.

But you have only just taken the place on, he reminded himself.

Still, the onus was now on him. He had gone from having no cares to suddenly having to work out how rooms were cleaned, chimneys swept and fires lit.

For a moment he considered what Miss Bolton's first impressions must be. A dirty, rundown house, a master and mistress constantly arguing, a lack of staff and a cold room with grimy windows. Despite his earlier irritation with her, he felt a pang of guilt, and a feeling of what felt strangely like warmth towards her.

It was entirely new to him to feel anything like it. He was used to considering only his own comfort, and could not recall the last time he had given any consideration—beyond common courtesy—for anyone else. It was an unsettling feeling, and he did not like it.

Deliberately, he put Miss Bolton out of his head and went inside. Locking the main door, he could not help but compare it to a prison. Except that he was imprisoning himself.

Chapter Seven

Marianne sat stiffly, feeling a degree of pressure, as she repeated some of the responses she had given Mrs Gray in the registry. In response to Lady Kingswood's questions she had outlined her level of knowledge on the main subjects that Lady Cecily would be expected to learn. Despite apparently losing a series of governesses, Lady Kingswood was being very thorough, and Marianne could feel her anxiety rising in response. She *needed* this position.

Lady Kingswood nodded. 'That all sounds satisfactory. I expect high standards from Cecily—but I warn you, do not make a bluestocking of her.'

Marianne raised her eyebrows questioningly.

'I was married at sixteen, Miss Bolton. I should like my daughter to be prepared for an early marriage also. She must be accomplished in all the arts—she needs to improve her skill on the harp, and her painting and drawing. She must behave with decorum and propriety at all times, and she needs to know how to go on in society. I have noticed that—so far—your manners are excellent, and I hope that, as our...our *situation* improves there will be opportunities for Cecily to begin to go out in society, in preparation for her debut in a few years. Once we are out of black gloves she will need to experience a range of social events so that she learns how to behave in company.'

Marianne nodded—none of this was unusual.

'But,' Lady Kingswood continued, 'Cecily is not destined to be a governess. Therefore, she must be *accomplished* without being *bookish* or too knowledgeable. It would be sure to put off potential suitors, for no man wants a wife who claims to know more than he does.'

Marianne's shock must have shown on her face.

'Trust me, Miss Bolton, I know what I am talking about and I insist on this. Do I make myself clear?'

'Yes, Lady Kingswood.'

Well, what else could Marianne say? Her employer must be obeyed. She had never before considered learning to be a bad thing—she had been encouraged by her parents to develop her own mind and her own opinions. Still, she thought, it was certainly true that society expected young ladies to be 'demure'—which often, Marianne believed, meant vapid and insipid.

In her mind, she told herself off. Her role was to make Lady Cecily into whatever Lady Kingswood believed was appropriate for a young lady—not what *she*, Marianne, believed. Marriage had never been more than a vague idea in her own mind, and she had not come under any pressure from her own parents to marry young. They, like her, had been content to wait for a suitable husband to come along. But he never had. Indeed, she had never met any man who had touched her heart…

She pondered this for a moment. If she had been safely married when her parents had died she would have been protected from Henry, from having to run away—and from poverty and the need to take paid employment.

That would have been nice, she thought wistfully, before mentally shaking herself. An invisible husband who did not exist was no good to her. And she had never been one of those who sought marriage as soon as they were of age. Like Lady Kingswood, evidently.

'What was it like, to be married so young?' she wondered aloud, then bit her lip. Was that an impertinent question?

'Romantic,' said Lady Kingswood, with a short

laugh. 'At first, anyway. I had more than one suitor, and I had thought the most difficult part would be choosing the best husband.' Her eyes became unfocused. 'I often wonder what would have happened if I had made a different choice...'

Her voice tailed away for a moment, then she seemed to gather herself.

'But the hardest part was adapting to my life as a wife, and soon after as a mother, while living here with my husband's parents. Still, I survived. I still survive.'

Marianne nodded. 'You have great strength, if you do not mind my saying so.'

Lady Kingswood's face lit up. 'Thank you. Strength of character is one of the things I admire in myself. I only wish Cecily was similarly strong. But I fear she is too often led by her soft heart.'

'A good heart is a different kind of strength, surely?'

'Indeed it is not!' her employer replied sharply. 'Now, go to where Cecily awaits you in the sitting room. I shall expect an update each day as to her progress!'

'Yes, Lady Kingswood.'

Was this how Mama had behaved towards Marianne's governesses? She rather thought not. Mama had been too kind, too gentle, to be so determined. She had trusted Marianne and her governesses to work together in the best way possible, and somehow it had worked out. Lady Kingswood, it was clear, took a different approach. And she had strong expectations of her daughter.

As she left the room, Marianne hoped she could navigate what might prove to be choppy waters.

A few hours later, Marianne closed her book. 'That will do for now, Lady Cecily. I think I have a good idea about your level of French,' she said in that language. 'Let us have a break, then later you can play a piece on the harp for me.'

Cecily grimaced. 'Very well.'

'You sound reluctant. Do you not enjoy playing?'

'Oh, I do! Or, at least, I *did*. But Mama expects me— At least, my progress is not what Mama wishes. I must practise harder!'

'I am sure your mama only wishes the best for you.'

'Yes, of course.' Cecily's tone was flat.

'Lady Cecily! Miss Bolton! Come and see what has arrived!' Agnes exploded into the room in a flurry of excitement.

Cecily perked up. 'What is it, Agnes?'

'Only the finest carriage I have ever seen. And the horses are as like as twins—all four of them!'

Marianne was confused. 'Do you mean Lord Kingswood's phaeton? That we travelled in yesterday?'

'Lord, no, miss—though that's a fine carriage too. This one is enormous! And I don't know where Thomas will put *another* four horses!'

Lady Cecily had already risen and moved to follow Agnes into the front hall. Her curiosity piqued, Marianne followed. Mrs Cullen had opened the front door and was frantically trying to tuck loose strands of hair beneath her cap.

'Who is it, Ma?' asked Agnes.

'The new master's personal servants, bringing his luggage,' her mother returned. 'You'd best get out of the way before they come in, though.'

As she spoke, the carriage door opened and a personage emerged. He was a young man in his late twenties, of slim build and noble carriage, and he paused on the step to look around him.

'Lawd!' gulped Agnes. 'Look at 'im! Look at his clothes! His hair!'

The man's clothing was, in fact, neat and restrained. Dark trousers, a plain waistcoat with no seals or fobs, and a plain black coat of excellent cut. But he carried it with such an air that even Marianne could not help but stare.

Recovering herself, she stole a glance at Agnes. The maid's jaw was hanging open.

'Is it a duke, Ma?' she breathed.

Mrs Cullen shook her head. 'No, Aggie. It's worse than that. It's a *valet*. Lord Kingswood told me yesterday he would come this afternoon.'

'Lawks! A real-life valet…right here in Ledbury House!' Aggie considered this. 'What's a valet, Ma?'

'A manservant. Lord Kingswood's man. Lord, the state of the house!'

A second man was descending from the carriage, and Thomas had now appeared to help the coachman with the horses. As they watched the valet moved to the back of the carriage in order to supervise. Thomas began to unload various trunks.

'A *servant*? He's never a servant!'

Agnes's incredulity meant that her voice rose a little, and she jumped when a deep voice behind them interjected.

'He'll be an *ex*-servant shortly, if he causes you all to continue hanging around the hallway, gaping like urchins at a circus!' Lord Kingswood's tone was scathing.

They all whirled round, as if caught stealing sweetmeats.

'Miss Bolton,' he continued, in the same manner, 'I am surprised to see you here. Might I help you with something?'

Marianne flushed, and stammered something incoherent.

'Quite,' the Earl replied with deadly politeness.

He stalked past them through the open door, where he greeted the second traveller. 'You are Cronin, I presume? Good. I shall expect to see you in Lord Ki—in *my* study in ten minutes.' He turned to the valet. 'Loveday—I shall never travel without you again! You are required to make my life here bearable.'

The valet bowed serenely and exchanged a few quiet words with his master, before returning to Lord Kingswood's numerous trunks.

Marianne felt fear ice through her—she might lose her position. She had to get away from the hallway before the Earl stepped back in!

'Come, Lady Cecily.'

Outwardly calm, she led her pupil back to the parlour, but inside she was berating herself. Lord Kingswood was quite right—it was her job to instil a sense of decorum into Lady Cecily. Her first day and she was already making a mull of it!

Relieved that Lady Kingswood had not witnessed her lapse, she reached the safety of the parlour and closed the door.

Lord! She groaned inwardly as she recalled

Lord Kingswood's cool comment and angry expression. Knowing that he had the power to throw her out on a whim, if he so decided, was frightening enough. Realising that she had given him *exactly* the sort of ammunition he needed to do so was worse.

But would he? She tried to review the situation with a rational eye. Lord Kingswood had the air of a man exasperated, it was true, but the arrival of his own servants might calm him down.

The second man who had emerged from the carriage—Mr Cronin—had had the look of an administrator, or a secretary, perhaps. He had been called to the study, which made sense. Perhaps the Earl wanted to meet with him about matters of business. Her own father had used to spend long hours with his man of business, poring over lists and accounts and documents. Hopefully Lord Kingswood would be distracted long enough to forget her lapse.

She picked up a book from the side table and pretended to read. It would not do. In her mind she saw scenes of disaster playing out—imagined him ordering her from the house, berating her for being the worst governess ever, telling her that he would immediately seek a proper governess, one who was actually capable of carrying out the role. She would end up going back to Mrs Gray with an admission that she had served for only one day.

She pictured Lord Kingswood's angry face as she had seen it earlier. Did he dislike her?

Stop it! she told herself. Not since her first foray into the Assembly Rooms in Middleton on her debut had she worried so much about other people's opinions of her. Of course everyone had turned out to be most amiable at all the balls and assemblies, and Mama had admonished her for her foolish fancies and for letting her imagination get the better of her.

And now she was doing so again. Really, she did not know enough about the Earl, or Lady Kingswood, to say whether they liked her or not. And as the governess surely it mattered not. So long as she performed her duties to their expectations she would remain.

Ah, but you want him to like you! a little voice whispered in her mind.

Nonsense! she retorted.

Lord, now she was having arguments with herself!

She focused on her book again, and this time managed actually to read.

Ash stifled a yawn. Papers were scattered all over John's desk, with some piles on the floor. He and Cronin had, he thought, made some headway in understanding the various tasks to be done in terms of the estate. But the doing of it, he knew, would take weeks, if not months.

He glanced to his right, where Cronin was adding to the largest pile—the unpaid bills. It seemed that Lady Kingswood had not paid so much as a single bill in the past six months. She and Mrs Cullen had continued to order supplies from all the local tradesmen, as well as—he perused the document in his hand—expensive dresses. Had Fanny not thought about how the bills were to be paid?

Ash foresaw that he would have to throw substantial amounts of his own money into setting it all to rights.

He sighed, resentment once again bubbling up inside him. He should be in London right now, enjoying a drink with his friends, not sitting with his new steward sorting out dull papers. This was not his life.

'You may be interested in this one, my lord— it apparently arrived the day before yesterday.'

Cronin handed him a letter, which Ash quickly scanned. It was a note of introduction for Miss Anne Bolton, the new governess. It outlined the wages to be paid to her, and her expected arrival on the mail coach.

The day before yesterday.

If it had arrived two days ago then Fanny should have seen it. Should have known to expect Miss Bolton. Should have sent Thomas to meet her. But she had not done so. And her anger against Miss Bolton had seemed genuine.

Ash frowned. 'How do you know when it arrived?'

'A maid told me. She handed the letter to me as I came in.'

'That would be Agnes. As I mentioned, she is currently the only maid here.'

Cronin's eyebrows raised a little at this. 'I took the liberty of questioning her further. She said that she had instructions to open all the letters arriving at the house.'

Now it was Ash's turn to be surprised. 'What— *all* of them?'

Cronin nodded. 'Agnes explained that she cannot read well, but knows a little. She reports that her mistress has instructed that all letters are to be opened, and anything containing— er—*numbers*—is not to be given to Lady Kingswood. Instead, Agnes has been putting them in this room.'

Ash shook his head in despair. *Anything containing numbers.* So that was Fanny's way of dealing with overdue accounts.

Cronin, averting his eyes, returned to his task. Absentmindedly, Ash read the rest of the letter. It explained that Miss Bolton was recently bereaved, and that her father had been a lawyer. It was signed Mrs Gray and gave the address of a registry in London. There was no mention of a reference.

Ash did not have occasion to hire staff very often. He lived simply, and Tully, his coachman, Loveday, his valet, and Mr Hart, his secretary, had been with him for a number of years now. His landlord in London organised the female servants for the building, and Ash had never particularly been aware of them.

Of course, now that he thought about it he understood that his world was full of serving maids and housemaids, and others that he didn't see—kitchen maids and scullery maids and laundresses and seamstresses. Somehow he had never really *noticed* them before, nor thought about the work they did.

He sat there, with the letter about Miss Bolton in his hand, and realised that he had no clue how to go about hiring female servants, nor what attributes he should consider. And he probably also needed more male employees. At least one footman. And possibly another groom.

He reviewed Ledbury House's current staff. Thomas the groom seemed reasonably skilled— the horses had been well cared for and the stables were neat and well looked after. Tully would sort him out, no doubt.

And Mrs Cullen was a decent cook, thank goodness. If the grocer and the butcher and the other merchants had their bills paid he trusted that she would continue to cook good food and he would not be forced to think on the matter any further.

Agnes… He frowned. Too garrulous, too pert, and entirely too visible. Perhaps she could be given a role that kept her below stairs? And how many housemaids were needed for a house of this size?

Next, Miss Bolton. Now, *there* was a woman who would not be kept below stairs.

He pictured her in his mind's eye, recalling large brown eyes, which showed something akin to nervousness at times, a cloud of dark hair, pinned into a fierce hairstyle from which a tendril had escaped last night at dinner. His connoisseur's eye had, of course, swept over her form on more than one occasion. A good figure—tall, proud and with curves exactly where he liked them.

It was a pity, he mused, that she was a governess in his household. He was having to admit that he was drawn to her and he would have to exercise self-discipline to prevent his thoughts about her from becoming improper. Of course *some* improper thoughts could not be repressed, but he must not allow himself to continue to dwell on them.

He considered what he knew about her. *Recently bereaved.* He frowned, feeling a little guilty about his curt treatment of her earlier. Deliberately, he shrugged it off. *She'll get over it. And she shouldn't have been gawping in the hallway, anyway.*

Cronin cleared his throat, bringing Ash back to the present.

'Might I suggest, my lord, that I continue this task alone? Now that we have established the basics, the next step is for me to calculate the sum total of the debts, and then you may consider what to do about it.'

'Well, I shall have to pay them, of course!'

There was no other option. As a man of honour, he would not stand by and see the family name criticised, or for John's widow and child to be dunned by tradesmen. No—that was inconceivable!

'Yes, my lord. And—'

'Yes?'

'I should like to tour the estate in order to have a better idea of how things stand.'

'That's a good idea, Cronin. I shall accompany you.'

It *was* a good idea. How was he to be master of—of all this—when it had been fourteen years since he had even visited and he had never had a thought of being master here? It would likely be extremely tiresome, but he counted it a necessary evil.

'Miss Bolton shall also accompany us. And Lady Kingswood, of course.'

'Miss Bolton?' Cronin's surprised expression mirrored his own.

Now why did I include the governess in my plans? I must be unhinged!

'The new governess. She will wish to know her way about, no doubt, as Lady Kingswood will expect her to—to instruct Lady Cecily in matters relating to care of the tenants. One can never begin these things too soon! The governess only arrived this week. It's all in here, you know.' He handed Cronin the letter from Mrs Gray's agency.

'Ah, yes. The document with the numbers.' Humour gleamed briefly in Cronin's eyes.

'Indeed. Please ensure that Miss Bolton is paid whatever wage she is due.' For some reason that was important to him. 'I shall leave you to your work.' He rose. 'And—Cronin…?'

'Yes, my lord?'

'Thank you.' The man nodded.

As Ash left the study and made his way to the parlour he was conscious of a sense of relief. Cronin, hired just yesterday by Hart, his secretary, came with good references, and he had previously worked as a steward on an estate of a similar size. The man clearly knew his work, and Ash hoped that he would help ease some of the burden associated with these new responsibilities. The sooner he could be sure things were financially stable here, the sooner he could leave and get back to his real life. Unlike John, he refused to bury himself in the country.

Chapter Eight

Opening the parlour door, Ash was surprised to find only Miss Bolton inside.

'Ah! Miss Bolton! The very person I wished to speak to!' He would be damned if he would let her know that she had caught him unawares. 'Where are the others?'

She eyed him warily. 'Lady Kingswood has informed me that she normally has a lie-down in the afternoon and that Lady Cecily also sleeps then. It is a longstanding tradition, she tells me.'

There was a short silence.

Miss Bolton seemed to gather herself before asking, 'What did you wish to speak to me about?'

Ash had no idea how to respond to this. In fact, he was finding himself all at sea in her company. Fanny he knew of old. The child, Cecily, was of no matter. But how did one behave with a governess—particularly such an attractive one?

Her large, fine eyes were gazing at him evenly, causing an unfamiliar flutter in his chest. Lord, never say he was developing a *tendre* for her! Knowing he should not, yet unable to resist, he said the only thing he could think of that would ensure he could have the pleasure of her company for the next half-hour.

'You and I, Miss Bolton, have arrived here just recently, and the territory—the house, I mean—is unfamiliar. I wonder if you might accompany me on a tour of the—of it.'

She looked a little perplexed but set aside her book. 'Very well.'

'Good. Right.'

He held the door open for her, and the edge of her sleeve brushed against his arm as she passed.

Ignoring the unexpected and unwanted reaction from his body, he added brusquely, 'My new steward, Mr Cronin, will organise a tour of the estate at some point. It might be useful for you and Lady Kingswood to accompany us.'

'Of course.'

She was frowning. Why was she frowning? Had he erred in some way? Was his request inappropriate—might she think that it was because he wanted to spend time with her? That would never do—even if it was true.

He caught himself up short. Why should he care what she was thinking, for goodness' sake?

'The former steward died and no one had appointed a new one.'

She nodded but had nothing to say to this. Silence thickened between them.

'Let us begin at the top and work our way down,' he suggested, leading the way to the hall and the main staircase.

'Do you have the keys?'

Unconsciously, she tilted her head to one side as she addressed him. It drew his attention to the line of her neck and shoulder.

'Keys? What keys?' What was she talking about?

'The keys for any locked rooms—normally they would be kept by the housekeeper, but we have no housekeeper, so I assume that Mrs Cullen has them.'

'Oh! I had not thought— Well, let us view what we can for now. I can always come back later with keys if needed.'

She nodded in acceptance and they mounted the stairs together. He was intensely conscious of her, by his side. Strangely, his mind was suddenly filled with things that he might say to her if the situation were different.

He was usually only in the company of attractive young women in one of two situations. If she had been a young lady of society he would right now be entertaining himself with a gentle flirtation, in the hope of being rewarded with a smile, a blush, or even—eventually—a kiss. Alternatively, if she had been a high-flyer or a game widow, he would have had seduction on his mind.

But she was neither a flirtatious debutante nor a potential lover, and so the warm looks and 'accidental' touches that his mind was suggesting had to be ignored. Conversation, too, was proving difficult—for what did one discuss with a governess?

'How has your first day at Ledbury House been?' he finally blurted out, without much foresight.

Her eyes flew wide open in alarm. 'My lord, I apologise for allowing Lady Cecily to stand in the hall when the carriage arrived. I know it was a lapse on my part, and it will not happen again.' Her voice shook a little.

What would a governess's employer normally say to something like this? Having already forgotten the incident, he brushed her words aside with a stern 'I should hope not.' Surely that was adequate?

Lord, stop worrying! he told himself. He had no idea why he felt so disconcerted.

They had reached the upper floor and now he opened a narrow door, which he guessed would lead to the attics. He was suddenly genuinely curious about this house he had inherited—even if it *had* brought him nothing but work and frustration so far.

'Unlocked!' he exclaimed, opening it wide.

Behind the door was a steep, narrow staircase. With a gesture, he indicated that Miss Bolton should precede him.

This proved to be an error of immense proportions. Following a few stairs behind, he was rewarded with eyefuls of Miss Bolton's perfectly formed rump, the curves of which were imperfectly concealed beneath her fine black dress. Ash groaned inwardly.

Reaching the top, he avoided her gaze as he steadied his breathing. There were four small bedrooms, none of which looked inhabited.

'These were probably used by menservants,' Miss Bolton mused softly. 'They need a good clean but are basically sound.'

Ash had to agree. There was no sign of damp, which was a relief. The last thing he needed to add to his growing pile of financial commitments was roof repairs. Though he should get Cronin to have it checked, regardless. *Lord!* Never in his life before had he been bothered with roof repairs!

Miss Bolton led the way back down to the main upper floor. Thankfully, this time he was spared the temptation of her curvaceous behind. They checked numerous bedrooms, some of which were, according to Miss Bolton, in need of re-decoration, and all of which needed to be cleaned.

Ash was glad of her common-sense responses—she clearly knew much more about these things than he did. It was like the thought of roof repairs. To him, rooms were for *using*—he had never had to consider how they came to be furnished or re-decorated.

The only rooms they avoided were the master bedroom—formerly John's, and now his—and those belonging to Lady Kingswood and her daughter.

'This next one is my room,' offered Miss Bolton tentatively.

'May I see it? he asked politely. 'Just to check what work might need to be done.' He hoped she would agree, as he was struck by a sudden strong sense of curiosity about her.

'Very well.' She led him inside, leaving the door ajar, then stood in the doorway as he looked about him.

Ash scanned the room, careful to behave in a

similar way here to the way he had elsewhere. He deliberately eyed the ceiling and the walls, looking for cracks and flaws, then took a few steps deeper into the room and looked about. It was a small, stark, cold space—literally cold. The other uninhabited rooms were equally cool, but this was different. He could not feel easy about Miss Bolton having to sleep in such a chilly place. There was a small fireplace, he noted, but no kindling. He himself had been grateful for the fire in his own room, these past nights.

'Have you no fire?' he asked.

She shrugged. 'I believe the chimney works, but Agnes has not had the time to lay a fire for me.'

His jaw hardened. This was one responsibility he could do something about. 'I shall instruct her to do so.'

'Oh, no, please do not!' Her brow creased.

'Why on earth not?' He was conscious of confusion, and with it mild irritation. Why did this woman persist in rejecting his attempts to help her? He had practically had to force her not to run away yesterday, and now this!

'She is too busy. This should not be a priority for her, and I should hate to add to her burden of work!'

'Nonsense!' he exclaimed. 'No doubt she is

paid for her work, and as master I shall not allow her to avoid tasks that are rightly and reasonably hers!'

'As master,' she retorted, 'you should know already that she is terribly overworked—as is Mrs Cullen. And I am not certain that they *have* been paid!'

She clapped a hand to her mouth, as he had seen her do before.

'Oh, Lord Kingswood, I do apologise! It is not my place to comment on such things.'

Ash was aware of sudden anger. *How dare she speak to me in such a way?*

'It is not!' he snapped. 'If I should need your opinion on managing my household I shall ask you for it!'

'Yes, my lord,' she replied demurely, and then seemed to consider the matter. 'Of course it is not actually your *fault* that you do not know. Why, no one could expect it!'

Somewhat mollified by her acknowledgement that he was not at fault—though still feeling a marked sense of injustice, along with unaccustomed uncertainty, he nevertheless could not help asking, 'What do you mean?'

'Well,' she offered slowly, 'it seems to me that you have not had to manage a household of this size before. And you have inherited a situation where there are undoubted…challenges.'

He snorted. 'I admire your perspicacity. But it hardly takes a genius to come to that conclusion. I have, after all, been perfectly frank about my recent inheritance.'

She flushed. 'You think me rude. I am sorry.'

He made an exasperated sound. 'Not rude. Simply…frustrating.'

She blinked. 'Frustrating?'

'Yes. Mostly because I have the sneaking suspicion that you have the right of it.' Sighing, he set his pride to one side. 'Tell me about Agnes and Mrs Cullen.'

Her eyes narrowed, then she nodded to herself. 'Well,' she began, 'Agnes is the only maid here. We had—I mean there should be at least seven indoor servants for a house of this size.'

We had what? he wondered. *What had she been about to say?*

'My valet and new steward have arrived today. Will that help?'

'Not at all,' she returned earnestly. 'Two more mouths to feed, two more bedrooms to clean, and no doubt the valet will make demands of Aggie—water for washing, that sort of thing. If I were you I should—' She broke off, flushing.

'Pray do continue,' he drawled, leaning against

the cool wall and crossing his arms. 'You have begun my instruction. You cannot stop now. Why, as a governess, you should always complete the lesson!'

'You are jesting with me!' she returned snappily.

Seeing her cross face made him abruptly forget his own frustrations. Despite himself, he laughed.

She eyed him in bewilderment. Somehow this increased his humour. He laughed, and laughed, and laughed some more.

Gradually her bafflement was slowly replaced by an appreciation of his humour. Eventually, seemingly despite herself, she joined in. It was the first time he had seen her so much as smile. Her face lit up as she laughed along with him— and yet he knew she had no idea what had triggered his fit of helpless hilarity.

Their eyes met, and they enjoyed for an instant a sense of connection.

After a time, and conscious of his station, he reined in his mirth. 'Miss Bolton, I thank you. You have enlivened the day for me!'

'But I still do not understand what I said that was so amusing!' There was a crease in her brow.

'You misunderstand me. It was nothing you *said*—more your obvious frustration with me as an inept pupil!'

'I should not *dream* of expressing frustration towards you, Lord Kingswood,' she said stiffly. 'As my employer, you are naturally above criticism.'

'Now, now, Miss Bolton—just when I thought we might be reaching an understanding. If I were truly above criticism it would mean that you would have avoided commenting on my carriage-driving ability?

'I did not then know that you were my employer.'

She was unbending, remote, but he knew that he was besting her.

'That is true. Very well, I shall discount that particular episode.' He paused. 'I imagine that you would also have avoided commenting on my decisions as master, nor sought to advise me?'

She nodded regally, though she looked a little uncomfortable. 'Yes, my lord. That is correct.'

'And yet not five minutes ago you were about to tell me what you should do if you were me! Ah, I see by your blush that I have scored a hit! Now, no matter. I am still agog to hear what you would do in my shoes.'

'I am sure I cannot say, my lord.'

'Now then, Miss Bolton, do not get into a miff with me! We were discussing the number of servants needed for an establishment such as this.

And I had made the unpardonable error of suggesting that the arrival of Cronin and Loveday might alleviate the situation—'

'Oh, no!' she interjected. 'Not *unpardonable*!'

'Unpardonable!' he repeated. 'Now, are you going to reveal to me how I can get myself out of this hobble?'

'Very well,' she said, 'though I am not sure you deserve my help now.'

'Not *deserve* it? Why, how can you say such a thing when all I have done is try and understand how I might get a fire in your room!'

She eyed him with some scepticism. 'I suspect, my lord, that you are still laughing at me!'

'I would not dare to do so!'

She snorted.

'Well, what an unladylike sound! I am reasonably confident that Lady Kingswood would not wish Lady Cecily to trumpet like a farmyard animal.'

'Trumpet? I did not trumpet!'

'Well, how would you describe the sound?' He mimicked her snorting sound—exaggerated for full effect—and was rewarded by a glint of humour in her eye.

His appreciation however, was short-lived. With a visible effort, she bit back the saucy retort that was clearly on her lips.

A pity, he thought. *This is the first bit of entertainment I've had since leaving the capital. Apart from the similar entertainment she offered me during the carriage ride yesterday. Hmm...* Twice in two days he had come alive in her company.

'A house of this size requires a housekeeper, at least three housemaids, two footmen, a kitchen maid and a scullery maid,' she offered evenly. 'You already have a cook, and Aggie is currently acting as a maid-of-all-work. The house is simply too big for her and her mother, which is why only the main rooms are clean—and even they are not cleaned frequently enough. To ask Aggie to do more would be unfair.'

He considered this. 'What role should Aggie play if I employ more household staff?'

'I believe,' she said tactfully, 'that Aggie would be an ideal scullery maid. It means that she would work alongside her mother, rather than above stairs. But that decision would be up to the housekeeper.'

Aggie not work above stairs? he thought. *Good!*

'You are very wise in these matters,' he noted. 'Have you worked in many large households?'

'Oh, no!' she replied, visibly flustered. 'Not at all! But I—my friends—ladies—sometimes speak of these things.'

With this he had to be content. But his instincts

were aroused. She was keeping something back from him. *Interesting*. There was more to Miss Anne Bolton than met the eye. And it would be amusing to find out exactly what it was she was not telling him.

As they left her bedroom he could not resist one final look back. The window panes had been cleaned—by Miss Bolton herself, as he well knew. There were no personal knick-knacks on the table or the nightstand. Just a hairbrush and some pins.

He glanced at her bed, neatly made. There she slept. Tonight she would undress in this very room and lie in this bed, wearing only her shift or a nightgown. The picture in his mind's eye was entirely inappropriate for him to hold as her employer and yet he could not deny the compulsion.

Miss Bolton intrigued him—in more ways than one.

Chapter Nine

Marianne walked down the main staircase at her employer's side, glad that they had finally left her bedroom. Despite their shared laughter, the anxious voice in her mind was already sowing seeds of doubt again. Her heart was now racing as she considered how close she might have been to losing her job. Not only had she failed in her duties to Lady Cecily earlier, she had then had the temerity to criticise Lord Kingswood.

To his face.

Repeatedly.

She groaned inwardly, just thinking about it. How foolish she had been! Her difficulty lay in the fact that—despite Lady Kingswood's assertions—she had been raised as a *lady*, not a *governess*. Oh, she knew how to behave in polite company, how to address people from different walks of life, how to speak Latin and write with a neat hand. All these were qualities one would want in a governess. But they were also attributes expected of a lady.

The difference—one of the key differences, she now realised—was that a governess was not expected to speak her mind. Under any circumstances. Lord Kingswood—who presumably had had limited contact with governesses—might not have realised it. *Yet.* But Lady Kingswood would.

I must be on my guard, she thought. *I might reveal too much without even realising I am doing so.*

This was an unexpected challenge. She had anticipated that lying about her background would be her greatest concern. She had not realised that she might betray herself just by expressing her true thoughts about something.

Thankfully, something about the situation had amused him. She felt a strange warmth in her belly as she recalled his unguarded laughter. His handsome face, creased with amusement, was undoubtedly attractive. She pictured him, seeing in her mind's eye how he had thrown his head back and given into his mirth. She had been compelled to laugh with him, so genuine and infectious had been his enjoyment. It had led to a brief moment of unexpected harmony between them.

She frowned. It would not do to be too much at ease with him. She must remain guarded.

Afterwards, his tone had turned teasing, but she had rebuffed him with what she hoped was a suitably professional demeanour. And he had seemed genuinely to listen to her advice. Whether he would take it, she did not know.

They had both already visited all the rooms on the main ground floor so, after a cursory glance at the serving room that adjoined the dining room, they made for the dimly lit back stairs. As they walked they discussed in a companionable way the obvious differences in the rooms that Aggie cleaned—the dining room and parlour—and the others, that had been abandoned to dust, dead spiders and unpolished silver.

'The chimneys all need to be cleaned,' he noted, 'and some of the servant bells are broken.'

'Your steward will find tradesmen who can do that,' said Marianne unthinkingly, then bit her lip.

Every time she spoke she risked revealing that she had grown up in just such a house, and that she had been trained by her own mother and Mrs Bailey in the management of a large household.

'I should think that would be logical, in any case,' she added, in an attempt to make it seem that she didn't know exactly what she was talking about.

'Hmm…' he agreed absentmindedly as they began to descend the servants' stairs. 'Where do we get the staff *from*? In London, my secretary would approach a register office—such as the one you used—but will it be the same for household staff here, in rural Berkshire?'

This was something a governess *would* know about. 'I should think,' she offered, 'that a register office could help. There may also be local families with young people wishing to go into service.'

Her own mama had deliberately recruited junior staff from among their tenants and the local village in order to give them a start.

He flashed her a grateful look. 'A good suggestion.'

Her heart skipped a beat. It was a fine feeling to know he appreciated what she said. The impact of that dark blue gaze made her toes curl deliciously and her pulse skip.

Stop! she told herself. *Do not be distracted by his kindness!*

For that was all it was. He was the first person to show her any true warmth or kindness since she had felt Mrs Bailey's farewell embrace. Further back there had been endless unappreciated warmth, kindness and love from Mama and Papa. Unappreciated only because she had had no expectation of it being taken away. That carriage accident had deprived her, in an instant, of the two people she had loved most in all the world.

For an instant she recalled her mother's warm hugs and a wave of grief and loss and loneliness washed over her. She stumbled on the stair and would have fallen, but Lord Kingswood caught her elbow and steadied her.

'Did you trip on something?' he asked solicitously. 'Is this something else I must add to my list of repairs?'

'Um…no—just my own clumsiness,' she replied.

Dash it! She'd heard a slight tremble in her voice.

She looked at him. Monumental error. He was on the stair below and had turned towards her. His face was only inches from hers, and she found herself frozen and helpless by his proximity. He was dangerously attractive—and, *Lord*, her senses knew it!

Her breath caught in her throat and her arm tingled where she felt the warmth of his strong hand through her thin sleeve. She knew that she should move away, knew also that he was not in any way preventing her. Yet she was incapable of movement or speech. The only reality was his compelling gaze.

Abruptly he turned away, seeming to shake

himself. 'I am relieved to hear it,' he said tersely, continuing his passage down the last few stairs. 'I shall stay in front of you, in case you should stumble again.'

Stumbling again, thought Marianne, *is just about the worst thing I could do right now.*

Deliberately, she diverted her thoughts away from what had just happened. Away from him. Away from her lost parents.

She reached the bottom, took a breath, and looked around her. The narrow passageway was similar to the one at home. No fancy paintwork or expensive floors here—just whitewashed walls and flagged stone floors.

Lord Kingswood had already begun walking, and she half skipped to catch up with him. Systematically he opened the various doors on either side as they went. Empty storage rooms, mostly. One had a pile of root vegetables inside, another had a side of beef and a couple of chickens.

'At least we have been paying the butcher,' Lord Kingswood murmured to himself.

Marianne was a little shocked. Were things so bad with the debts here? Could they even afford to keep her?

I would stay here, she thought fiercely, *without wages. Just to have a place to sleep, and guaranteed food.*

Her own vehemence surprised her. Yet she reasoned it was entirely logical. She had no immediate requirement for money. More pressing was her need for stability. Her cold little room here in Ledbury House felt infinitely more secure than the notion of traipsing back to London, back to the register office, to seek another position.

They continued along the passageway.

Suddenly, up ahead, a door opened to their left and a dark figure emerged. He seemed to be carrying something—a box, which clinked and rattled as he walked. Lord Kingswood froze, laying a hand on her arm in an unspoken command for her to do likewise.

The man continued up the corridor, leaving the door ajar, and Lord Kingswood silently followed.

Marianne was intrigued. What was going on? She paced quietly after her employer, conscious that he was trying to move stealthily. Not that the shadowy figure ahead seemed aware of their presence. Nor did he seem to move furtively. In fact, he was whistling!

They were now level with the room from which the man had emerged, and they both looked inside. It was the wine cellar! Not much wine inside, though—most of the shelves were empty.

'As I thought,' said Lord Kingswood grimly.

He increased his pace to keep up with the

man. Ahead, the passageway ended with an open doorway, revealing a large kitchen beyond. Lord Kingswood and Marianne followed swiftly through the kitchen, outside and into the kitchen yard. A cart was waiting, its single horse harnessed and ready to go. The man stowed the box in the back of the cart, then continued, jumping up onto the driver's bench.

Lord Kingswood made his move. Striding out, he called loudly, 'Thomas!'

Thomas wheeled around, shock apparent in his expression. 'Oh, Lord Kingswood—my lord! You surprised me! I did not expect you to be there!'

'I am quite sure you did not,' murmured the Earl menacingly. He strode forward. 'Can I ask you where you are going with—' he looked into the box that Thomas had been carrying '—nine bottles of fine French wine?'

Thomas looked confused. 'To the village, my lord.'

A female voice intervened. 'Leave those there for now, Thomas. I shall speak to the new master.'

It was Mrs Cullen, emerging from what looked like a henhouse, Agnes by her side. They were each carrying a small basket of eggs.

Mrs Cullen placed hers in the back of the cart, next to the box of wine. 'Go you and see to the other horses.'

Thomas shrugged, jumped down from the cart, and set off towards the stables.

Lord Kingswood had switched his attention to Mrs Cullen. He looked thunderous, and Marianne was glad his anger was not directed at her.

'Thomas is acting under your instructions, I gather?'

Mrs Cullen flushed. 'Well, yes, I suppose… Though it could be said that he is acting under the instructions of the mistress.'

'Explain!' His exclamation was terse, his tone that of a man about to lose his temper. 'Tell me why my own servants look to be stealing my property!'

Marianne was quaking for poor Mrs Cullen. She had been present on many occasions when Henry had boxed the ears of some unfortunate servant when he had displeased him. Though Lord Kingswood, as she was realising, was a different sort of man to Henry, still she feared that he would upset the poor cook.

'It is not stealing, my lord, and I shan't take such an accusation from you or anybody else!' Mrs Cullen was pale, but with two spots of colour, one on each cheek. 'We are doing what we must to put food on the table—on *your* table, my lord!'

Beside her, Agnes burst into noisy tears. 'Stealing? *Stealing*, Ma? He says we're stealing!'

'I heard him, Aggie—and, like I say, no one shall call me or mine a thief! We are honest, God-fearing folk as have tried to do our best for Ledbury House and for the family, and if he thinks he can come in here and call me a thief, well—'

Anxious to prevent the words of resignation that were surely coming, Marianne—with all her years of training coming to the fore—knew she had no choice but to intervene. 'Now, then, Mrs Cullen, I am sure this is naught but a misunderstanding. Like Lord Kingswood, I am new here, and we do not yet understand how things are done in these parts.'

Mrs Cullen looked a little mollified. 'That's as may be, miss, but you heard him call me a thief. And what's more he called Thomas a thief! And he called my Aggie a thief!'

Aggie's sobs grew louder.

'Quit that infernal racket!' bellowed Lord Kingswood. 'If there is some justification, then let me have it, but for the life of me I cannot see how you can explain nine bottles of Lord Kingswood's—of *my* best red wine being removed from this house and stowed in a cart!'

Marianne threw him a darkling look. This was

not helping! He raised his eyebrows at her, but halted his tirade for the moment.

'Mrs Cullen,' she said in a soothing tone. 'This must be very distressing for Aggie. Could she perhaps go and make us all some tea? I suspect we shall need some. And is there somewhere indoors where we can go to discuss this properly?'

Mrs Cullen nodded. 'Yes—go you and make some tea, Aggie. Put those eggs in the pantry—I shall need them for tonight's dinner.' She turned to Lord Kingswood, adding stiffly, 'Please follow me, my lord. We can discuss this in the housekeeper's sitting room.'

He nodded, lips pursed. His bearing was that of a man sorely tested.

'Not that we *have* a housekeeper, of course,' the cook added darkly, turning to walk back towards the house. 'If we had, we would not be in such a hobble!'

On this pronouncement, she went in through the kitchen door.

Lord Kingswood turned towards Marianne. 'Well?'

'Well, what?' She was all confusion.

'You might as well come too, since you are master of all of us, it seems!'

She flushed. 'I apologise, my lord. I should not have interfered—'

'No, you should not!' he agreed tersely. 'But you did. Again. Now, let us go and hear whatever it is that Mrs Cullen has to say!'

He stomped off, leaving her to follow in his wake.

'And so we sell the eggs, and whatever extra vegetables we have, and sometimes we pay them with wine. And what's more Lady Kingswood knows about it!'

Mrs Cullen sat back, having completed her tale.

Marianne was not sure she should even be here. The revelations had been uncomfortable to hear—particularly the fact that the local trades-men had not been paid in almost a year because there was no money. The other staff—including the previous governess—had left, having not received their wages, just as Marianne had sus-pected. And Mrs Cullen had kept food on the table by bartering and selling Ledbury House's only assets—the meagre supply of eggs, turnips and cabbages they harvested and the contents of Lord Kingswood's wine cellar.

She stole a glance at the new Lord Kingswood. He looked stunned. The door opened, admitting Aggie, with a pot of tea and a mismatched col-lection of cups. As she laid them out on the table Lord Kingswood stood wordlessly, walked to the door, and left without so much as a backward glance.

Marianne was conscious of a feeling of disappointment. She had not realistically expected him to apologise to his staff—very few gentlemen would do so, even when exposed as blatantly as Lord Kingswood had been. But she had hoped he might say something conciliatory to Mrs Cullen and Agnes, who still seemed rather distressed.

She set out to charm and calm them, listening with genuine sympathy to their distressing tale. Staff had left gradually, it seemed, with harsh words being spoken in some cases. Once the housekeeper had gone the burden of supplying food had fallen upon the cook, and she had hit upon the plan to trade what they could.

'Mrs Cullen, I must say I admire you for doing what you did.' Marianne touched the older woman's hand. 'And I think it was extremely clever of you to barter with the wine!'

'Well,' the cook explained, 'none of us likes wine. Thomas prefers my beer what I brew, and apart from a little sherry at Christmastide I never touch alcohol. So it seemed as how nobody would need it!' She preened a little. 'I know I'm a good cook—not that I'm guilty of the sin of pride, because all I know I learned from my own ma—but I was never bookish or smart. But I've kept this house fed, I have, and not a shilling in the place 'cept what Thomas can get for the eggs and the cabbages!'

Ash slammed his fist against the door. Safe in the sanctuary of his room, he finally gave free rein to the anger and frustration within him. *What in hell is wrong with these people?* John had become ill and civilisation had vanished from the entire house!

Fanny, it seemed, had no common sense whatsoever, and was not in the least way able to manage a house. She had failed to ask John to tell her how to apply for funds, had failed to collect rents from the tenants, had failed to pay the servants, and had even failed to ensure that there was money for food! Lord, when he had known her before he had suspected she was bird-witted, but he had not known the extent of it! Why on earth he had ever thought himself to be in love with her he could not now understand.

He knew that he himself had never held such responsibility as this before, but at least he was trying to make the best of it. Fanny, it seemed, had avoided making any decisions and simply relied on others to find solutions.

Today, when he had finally realised that John's prized case of Grenache wine was to have been bartered for ten shillings' worth of meat and some spices—a fraction of its true value—Ash could happily have smashed every piece of china in the house!

Truly, he could not blame Mrs Cullen, her lachrymose daughter *or* the beef-witted Thomas. They had no idea of the true value of the wine they had been happily giving away for trinkets these past months. The local merchants did, though.

And Miss Bolton had angered him, too! He reflected on this, for really he could not immediately say why. Like him, she had been in the dark about the shenanigans that had taken place. And her intervention, he had to admit, *had* had a calming effect on the other servants, and had ultimately helped him discover the truth.

He reviewed the incident again, and this time he identified what it was that she had done. She had…she had *managed* him—as if he were a schoolboy or a recalcitrant toddler!

By God, and he had let her!

He shook his head in bemusement. Then, with a sigh, he took what he needed from his strongbox and went in search of his steward.

Finally, Mrs Cullen and Aggie had calmed down. Over tea, Marianne had engaged them in discussion on a range of topics aimed at reassuring them that they were valued. She'd praised their hard work, sympathised with the difficulties they'd faced trying to run the house alone, and marvelled again at their ingenuity in bartering with the local tradesmen. She had also persuaded Thomas to remove the wine from the cart until Lord Kingswood indicated what he wanted to do.

In recent years, at home, Mama had encouraged her to intercede in issues with the servants, and that training had stood her in good stead today. A gem like Mrs Cullen—such a good cook, and one whose loyalty to her post was unquestionable—could not be allowed to walk out. Marianne dared not think about Lord Kingswood's response if he were told there was to be no dinner.

The door opened abruptly and there he was. They all started, almost guiltily, though they had done nothing wrong. He filled the doorway with his height and his breadth, simply his *presence.*

'Mrs Cullen...' he began.

She eyed him warily. 'Yes, my lord?'

Oh, I do hope he does not say something unhelpful! thought Marianne.

She took a quick breath, as if to say something herself—she knew not what.

Immediately that blue gaze swivelled towards her. 'You have something to say, Miss Bolton?'

'No, no. Nothing at all,' she mumbled.

His eyes narrowed, but after a moment his attention moved back to the cook. Marianne let out a grateful breath.

'I apologise for my misapprehension earlier.' His tone was clipped, but it *was* an actual apology. 'I had no idea,' he continued, 'of the situation with regard to the local tradesmen. I wish to make it clear, though, that from now on there is to be *no* bartering, and that none of my wine is to leave this house without my permission. Is that clear?'

'Yes, my lord.'

He placed a roll of banknotes on the table. Mrs Cullen's eyes grew round.

'You will purchase whatever supplies are needed and you will keep a ledger of all the costs. Cronin, my steward, will deal with this until a housekeeper is appointed.'

'Oh, I have a ledger already,' said Mrs Cullen cheerily. 'I wrote down everything we gave away, and what we got for it. Would you like to see it, my lord?'

His eyes closed briefly, as if he were in pain. 'No,' he said faintly.

'Can we still sell the extra eggs to the village grocer, though?' asked Aggie daringly. 'Only, we don't need them all, and we may as well make a few shillings from them, my lord.'

Lord Kingswood looked taken aback. 'I suppose so,' he said. 'You may discuss it with Cronin. Now, with regard to the nine bottles of prime Grenache currently resting outside in the back of a cart—'

'Oh, Miss Bolton has already instructed Thomas to return them to the wine cellar,' offered Mrs Cullen, in a mistaken attempt to be helpful.

'Has she, indeed?' he asked, a deceptive mildness in his tone.

Marianne could feel herself flushing. 'That wasn't quite how it happened—' she began.

Lord Kingswood crossed his arms and leaned against the doorjamb. 'Really? Do enlighten me. How *did* it happen?'

'I merely thought that Thomas should not take it away until after— I mean until you had decided— I mean—'

'Is it normally a governess's role to direct the house servants, Miss Bolton?'

She dropped her eyes. 'No.' There was a short pause. Then she looked up at him again defiantly. 'But this is not a normal situation.'

That elicited a bark of laughter from him. 'I confess you have me there! Very well, I shall indulge you—this time.'

He turned and departed, leaving an awed cook and her even more awed daughter, exclaiming over the roll of banknotes before them, and a governess feeling confused, relieved and unexpectedly charitable towards him.

Chapter Ten

The next two weeks saw changes at Ledbury House. Mr Cronin, the new steward, arranged for a chimney sweep, as well as for workmen to come and make the necessary repairs. The sound of hammering, sawing and off-key whistling filled the house, and Marianne and Cecily struggled to complete their lessons in peace. Cronin also employed three village girls to help in the house, and Marianne, quite without Lord Kingswood's knowledge, found herself directing them.

There had been no option, she felt, but to take matters in hand. Lady Kingswood was uninterested, though mildly pleased that her comforts—and Cecily's—would be seen to. Mrs Cullen was willing, but found herself unable to say which tasks should be tackled first and how.

After being called to pass judgement on a heated debate between the new maids as to which of them was to clean the dining room—Mrs Cullen had accidentally given them all differing and confusing instructions—Marianne had taken charge. It was rather more involvement than she would have liked—for she was used to working with a competent housekeeper—but she managed to get them working co-operatively, and the main parts of the house began to look a little better.

Mr Loveday, the Earl's valet, was as particular about his master's dress, needs and comfort as he was over his own appearance. He would allow no one but himself to wash or mend any of Lord Kingswood's clothes, and his appearance in the kitchen always caused consternation among the maids, who eyed him with awe.

Aggie confined herself to the kitchen and scullery, helping her mother with the cooking and expressing relief to all who would listen that she no longer was forced to go above stairs.

The village girls were hardworking and polite, and knew how to clean and tidy. They were unpolished, however, and needed the guiding hand of a good housekeeper to help them develop additional skills and understand correct behaviour. Marianne did her best, but it could not substitute for the intense training that she knew they required. And even the three of them still were not enough.

Tentatively, she decided to speak to the steward about it.

She came away feeling impressed. He seemed to be a man of sense. He had thanked her for her assistance with the maids and indicated that Lord Kingswood's London secretary had been tasked with finding a housekeeper, a footman, a groom and two more maids. Marianne had been relieved to hear it.

He had also confirmed that Lord Kingswood had indeed requested a tour of the estate and had asked that she accompany them. He himself was becoming acquainted with the wider property, meeting the tenants and poring over paperwork, and he now felt well-informed enough to lead the tour—if Miss Bolton might be free to accompany him and the master after nuncheon? Lady Kingswood, unfortunately, would not accompany them, having given him to understand that she could not possibly forgo her afternoon rest.

Marianne had agreed, and now looked forward to the trip with a little trepidation. She and Lord Kingswood had reached an unspoken truce in the past two weeks, and she had found herself adapting to her new life with surprising ease.

No one seemed particularly interested in her past, which was a relief. One of the benefits, she thought wryly, of being a governess was that she was, in a sense, a nonentity. The servants did not presume to question her, as she was above their touch, and the family did not question her as she was below theirs. She sat perfectly in the shadow world between upstairs and downstairs, free to move across both worlds, yet not fully belonging in either.

Dinner times had become a little less fraught, as Lady Kingswood seemed to have become gradually reconciled to her fate—on the surface, at least. Marianne had enjoyed a few light conversations with her, and with Cecily, and Lord Kingswood occasionally joined in with suitably bland comments.

Lady Kingswood was not a person of information. She enjoyed talking of fashion and hairstyles, and whether Gowland's Lotion or Catharmian Water was best for the complexion. She was fascinated by the fashion plates in *La Belle Assemblée* and *Ackermann's Repository*, and was itching to commission more dresses for herself and her daughter,

'For, depend upon it,' she had declared, 'we shall be into half-mourning before we know it, and I shall need at least four grey dresses. Of course now that I have money of my own I shall go to London and organise it myself!'

Marianne thought that Lord Kingswood had

rolled his eyes briefly at this, but he had made no comment.

The chimneys had all been cleaned, so they were now able to sit in relative comfort in the evenings. There was a decent library in the house, although Lady Kingswood was herself not a reader, and seemed to disapprove of books. Marianne had nevertheless persisted, enjoying conversations with Lord Kingswood about books they had both read, and exciting Cecily's interest in reading some of the books discussed.

Last night, though, Lady Kingswood had decided to put her foot down, and it had not ended well.

'I really must insist,' she had said to Marianne, 'that you do not allow Cecily to read too many books. Why, she could end up with brain fever!'

Marianne had been taken aback. 'Brain fever?' she had repeated foolishly. 'From *reading*?'

'Nonsense!' Lord Kingswood had responded. 'How could she get brain fever from reading, Fanny? The idea is preposterous!'

Marianne found herself in the unusual situation of agreeing entirely with Lord Kingswood, while also wishing he had not said what he had.

'But, Ash!' Fanny had replied. 'You must know the dangers of overthinking—especially for the female mind. Why, I declare if *I* have to think too hard on anything it quite wears me out!'

Lord Kingswood had uttered a bark of laughter at this. Catching his eye, Marianne had realised that they were of one view on the supposed dangers of reading, and of Lady Kingswood's ability to think. But she knew he ought not to say so.

Unable to help herself, she had sent him a warning look. This time, instead of responding with anger or resentment, he had twinkled humorously at her and allowed Lady Kingswood's comment to go unchallenged.

Yes, thought Marianne now, *if we are all careful we can get along together quite nicely.*

Cecily's education was proceeding well. Without Lady Kingswood's knowledge, and in addition to the gentle arts that Lady Kingswood favoured, Marianne was teaching Cecily about the topics the girl was actually interested in—including the basics of politics and history. She had also started introducing brief lessons on household management and budgets. Lady Cecily would not be completely at a loss on these matters when she grew up—not if Marianne could help it!

Surprisingly, Lord Kingswood had developed an easy friendship with the girl—forged over Cecily's love of horses. He encouraged her to canter, to gallop and even to take fences—despite her mama's fears.

Marianne, herself a competent horsewoman, enjoyed seeing Cecily's increasing confidence— and her more relaxed relationship with her guardian. She liked Cecily, seeing in her a reflection of her younger self, devoted to her mama and with a good heart.

Marianne picked up on the girl's sadness at times, too—it was important to remember that bereavement was still playing its part for all of them in different ways.

Half-mourning.

Marianne reflected on society's traditions as she donned her cloak and bonnet for the ride out with Lord Kingswood and Mr Cronin. Black cloak over her plain black dress. Her bonnet simple and unadorned. She had not thought to change from black to traditional grey when Mama and Papa had been dead six months.

Soon, she realised, it would be a year, and under normal circumstances she would be expected to take up her old life again—to wear whatever colours she wished, to socialise and laugh and act as though her world had *not*, in fact, fallen apart on that fateful day. It would be her twenty-first birthday in April, and if Henry had been a caring, generous guardian she might have enjoyed a special celebration aimed at replicating what her parents might have given her.

Thankfully, as a governess, she could continue to wear drab colours and fade into the background and no one would think anything of it.

She remembered her younger self with some bemusement. Who *was* that happy, merry girl? The one who had occasionally danced and laughed and flirted at the Assembly Rooms, her evenings there filled with dancing slippers and curls and ball gowns? It seemed like another life, another person. Yet truly she did not miss that life. The only parts she did miss were Mama and Papa. And the feeling of being loved.

'And this is the third and final farm, my lord.'

Mr Cronin drove the gig down a leafy lane towards a farmhouse of warm red brick and thick thatch. As well as the house itself Marianne could see outbuildings and labourers' cottages. The whole estate was not dissimilar to home. It was, perhaps, slightly larger in acres, so it surprised her that many of the labourers' cottages looked uninhabited, and that some were in poor condition.

As with the other two farms, the farmer had been warned in advance of their arrival, and he and his family were waiting to greet them. As had also been the case at the previous two farms, Lord Kingswood handed her down from the gig before striding forwards to introduce himself—this time to Mr and Mrs Harkin and their numerous offspring.

The next half-hour followed the same pattern as before. Marianne drank tea with the farmer's wife and learned what she could about her family and the farm, while Lord Kingswood and Mr Cronin dealt with matters of business with the farmer over home-brewed ale. Mr Cronin had already collected the rents—although Lord Kingswood had apparently told him not to request the full amount.

'For which we are most grateful, miss, as you may imagine!' declared Mrs Harkin. 'My husband has set aside every penny that is due, of course, but now that we haven't to use it all it means we can buy our William—he's the fourteen-year-old, miss—an apprenticeship with Mr Calvert the wheelwright. He's a good lad, our William, and it will make me so proud to see him with a trade.'

'I am sure,' agreed Marianne with a smile. 'And what a lovely home you have made for your family!'

'Well,' said Mrs Harkin confidentially, 'we were worried when the other Lord Kingswood died and it looked like all would go to rack and ruin, but now the new Earl is here and he shall no doubt set all to rights!' She leaned forward to touch Marianne's hand. 'And what a handsome gentleman he is, do you not think?'

Marianne had no answer to this, though her heart had developed the most inconvenient habit of thundering and racing whenever she was in his company. Awkwardly she felt her colour rise, and she murmured something about not having noticed particularly, while pretending to be distracted by choosing which sweetmeat to have.

Later, she repeated a carefully edited version of the conversation to the two men, as they returned to Ledbury House.

'Their most pressing need, according to Mrs Harkin, is seed for this year's crop and labourers to sow it. Their fallow fields are due to take grain, and last year's grain fields to be used for pasture, and Mr Harkin, according to his wife, has neither the workers nor the seeds he needs.'

Lord Kingswood nodded. 'That fits with what Mr Harkin told us, and with the stories of the other farmers, too. Cronin, please let me know how much this is to cost me!'

Marianne listened with admiration as the men discussed the finer details. It was clear that Lord Kingswood was investing his own money so that the farmers could sow their grain. There was no guarantee of a profit in the autumn, as that would rely on finding labourers both to sow and, later, to harvest the crops. Still, it seemed as though the new Earl was going to support the farmers—for this year, at least.

Greatly daring, Marianne chimed in occasionally with comments or suggestions of her own. These were well received by both men, who treated her with an easy respect. It had been a long time since Marianne had felt so valued by others, and she hugged the feeling to herself. Perhaps this life she had created for herself would work out after all.

Increasingly, Lady Kingswood's plans for a journey to London dominated her conversation, until at last she fixed a date for the trip. As Cecily's governess, Marianne was to accompany them, as she might 'come in useful' on Lady Kingswood's planned shopping expeditions.

Mr Cronin wrote to Grillon's Hotel to reserve a suite of rooms, and then the packing began.

If Marianne had thought about it she would have said that two ladies—one only twelve years of age—and a governess, travelling to London for a stay of less than a week, all three attired in simple mourning gowns, would require very little organisation and preparation.

Not so.

Lady Kingswood had the entire staff in uproar as she decided what she would take, and then changed her mind every half-hour. She had rarely visited London when her husband was alive because, as she said, John had disliked the capital.

In the end the carriage was laden with four full trunks containing every single item that Lady Kingswood might conceivably need during her trip to the capital. The lady was flapping like a distressed hen over all sorts of imagined disasters—such as forgetting the curling irons.

Marianne, who had her own reasons for disliking and fearing London, could not understand Lady Kingswood's particular anxieties, most of which seemed to her to be entirely imaginary.

'My poor nerves!' her mistress declared, climbing into the carriage. 'This is why I so rarely travel to London! And, of course, my dear husband always used to arrange everything for us, so that I did not have to carry these worries myself. Come and sit beside me, Cecily,' she added. 'But now,' she continued, as Marianne took the facing seat, 'I am a poor widow, and all alone in the world.' Her sad tone and harassed air were in great contrast to the excited gleam in her eye as she contemplated the joys of shopping that awaited her. 'At least now I am in control of my own money, though...'

Lord Kingswood had travelled ahead the day before—neatly avoiding the pleasure of Lady Kingswood's conversation in a closed carriage the whole way to London. He was planning to meet with his secretary who, he said, had been experiencing some difficulty in hiring additional staff.

'I shall be busy with my own engagements while in London,' he had informed them, 'although of course you may call on me if needed.'

'Thank you,' Lady Kingswood had responded, 'but I do not anticipate the need.'

No, thought Marianne wryly, *you are each glad to be away from the other.*

Surprisingly, she herself had quite missed Lord Kingswood's company since he had left yesterday. Quite without realising it she had come to enjoy his presence these past weeks.

With a start, she realised that she had now been at Ledbury House for exactly two months.

The journey was long, but uneventful. Marianne spent most of it trying to respond appropriately to Lady Kingswood's chatter, while inside worrying about being found by Henry once they were in London.

Grillon's Hotel was all that Lady Kingswood

had wished, and the ladies settled into their luxurious suite with little ceremony.

Then the shopping began.

Marianne had never been one for shopping. Oh, she loved beautiful dresses as much as any young lady, but found it difficult to become excited over dove-grey silk versus dark grey crape. Lady Kingswood, however, insisted that it mattered hugely. As did the type of sleeve, lace trim and button that would be used on the many dresses she planned to order for herself and her daughter.

Marianne spent her days carrying parcels, looking at fashion plates and sitting waiting, while Cecily and her mother went for fitting after fitting in five different dressmakers'.

It occurred to Marianne that she must be a sad disappointment to the female species, for she had been more interested in farm management than she was in fashion. It was true that she was now becoming a little more accustomed to the bustle, dirt and noise of London, and the fear that she would inevitably run into Henry somewhere was lessening as she realised just how huge the city was. Still, it was with a great deal of relief that, on their fourth day in London, she heard that Lord Kingswood had asked to meet them.

'What can he possibly want?' asked Lady

Kingswood crossly. 'Can't he stay away even for a week?'

They were soon to find out. In a polite exchange of notes, Lord Kingswood was invited for tea in their suite at Grillon's. Marianne found that thinking about seeing him again led to a strong sense of pleasure and anticipation. Probably because she was suffering from a lack of challenge to her thinking mind, she decided.

And then he was there!

Marianne's eyes ran over him with an intensity that was almost like hunger. He wore a blue coat that moulded itself to his frame over a stylish waistcoat, a snowy white shirt and neckcloth. His breeches clung tightly to his strong thighs and his boots shone with a polished gloss. He was greeting her, his blue eyes smiling slightly as they exchanged the conventional platitudes.

Marianne was conscious of her pounding heart, slightly sweaty palms, and a terrible fluttering in her stomach at his presence. *It must be nerves, of course.* He was still her employer. It would not do to think of him in any other light.

Once tea had been served, and the usual topics had been discussed—yes, the weather *was* disappointingly cold, although it was March— Lord Kingswood came to the point. The register offices had been unable to find suitable staff for

Ledbury House—most likely because previous employees had not been paid.

Lord Kingswood's estimable secretary had managed to track down most of the former servants, and paid their lost wages, but unfortunately all the reputable register offices had politely but firmly indicated that they had no suitable candidates at this time.

Therefore his secretary had turned to a different agency, run by a Mrs Gray, who offered potential servants who came with no references.

At this point he sent a piercing glance in Marianne's direction. She blushed, wondering if he would question her, but thankfully he moved on.

'So,' he said to Lady Kingswood, 'given that we have no idea of their skills, character or aptitude, and that they are female servants, I should like you to accompany me to the register office tomorrow morning to meet the different candidates.'

Lady Kingswood was not impressed. 'That will be quite impossible! Cecily and I have appointments at three respectable dressmakers' for fittings. And besides,' she added candidly, 'I care not who you employ. It makes no difference to me.'

Lord Kingswood's jaw tightened. 'Do you take no responsibility at *all* for the household?'

She shrugged. 'I like it when things run smoothly—and I should like to have a personal maid who can dress my hair well. Cecily is almost thirteen now, and I should like to experiment with more grown-up hairstyles for her.' She bit into a delicate cake. 'Mrs Gray... That was, I recall, the agency that found Miss Bolton. Miss Bolton!' Her attention turned to Marianne. '*You* should go! I am sure you can be of assistance!'

Pleased with herself, she sat back as if it were all settled.

Lord Kingswood frowned. 'But it is not Miss Bolton's responsibility,' he pointed out gently.

'Oh, fiddlesticks! She will not mind. Will you, Miss Bolton?'

What was Marianne supposed to say to that? Of course it was not her responsibility, but she *wanted* to do it.

Lord Kingswood turned to Marianne. 'If it would not inconvenience you too much...?'

Marianne flushed and stammered her agreement. Such a prosaic task, interviewing maids and a housekeeper. Yet after three days of fabrics, ribbon and fashion plates it would be a welcome relief.

The fact that it would mean spending a few hours in Lord Kingswood's company had nothing whatsoever to do with it.

Chapter Eleven

'Lord Kingswood, you are most welcome. And Miss Bolton. Do, please, be seated.'

Mrs Gray was just as Marianne remembered her. The same dark skin, iron-grey hair and serene demeanour. What was different, though—so *very* different—was Marianne's feeling on entering the register office.

Although it had been only a little over two months since she had sat in this very room, answering the other woman's questions, so much had changed! She had adapted so well to life at Ledbury House that it was hard to remember how anxious she had been about it all.

Yes, Lady Kingswood could be irritating, and it was hard at times to escape Aggie's prattling, but all in all Marianne had settled into her new world perfectly well. She was growing in confidence by the day, and Cecily, Mr Cronin and

Lord Kingswood were becoming some of her fa-vourite people.

She had found a rhythm in her days that quite suited her. She taught Lady Cecily in the morn-ing and then in the afternoon, while the ladies napped, she met with Lord Kingswood and Mr Cronin to share in their discussions on matters of business. They accepted her as an equal, and Marianne had come to enjoy those afternoon meetings.

Evenings were taken up with the formalities of dinner, and then after-dinner conversation with Lord Kingswood and the Kingswood ladies. Cec-ily was gradually finding her voice in these con-versations, and Marianne deliberately drew her out, knowing it would be good preparation for her come-out in a few short years.

All in all, Marianne realised, she was eager to return to Ledbury House. It was beginning to feel like home—and she had never thought that she would feel she belonged anywhere again.

And she knew why.

It was because of the Earl.

Being back in his company after a few days apart made that entirely clear to her. Finally she had met a man she favoured—but there was no possibility of a marriage between them. Earls did not marry penniless governesses. She must be sensible and not allow her thoughts to wander in that particular direction.

'I have six possible housemaids for you to meet,' Mrs Gray was saying, 'but only two candidates for housekeeper. As you will know, experienced housekeepers are hard to find.'

Marianne forced her attention back to the present as they discussed the various servants they hoped to appoint.

'The first possible housekeeper is already waiting outside,' explained Mrs Gray. 'I shall invite her in as soon as you are ready. If you do not mind, I shall ask her the usual questions.'

'Of course,' agreed Lord Kingswood. 'Your experience gives you proficiency and authority here. I confess I am a total amateur, but…' he smiled '…a willing scholar.' He glanced briefly at Marianne. 'Besides, you selected Miss Bolton, who has turned out to be a perfect fit for us.'

Marianne flushed a little at this unexpected praise. Being in his company was causing all sorts of flutterings within her, and seeing his respectful manner towards Mrs Gray was warming her heart. A woman in business could face many obstacles—a woman whose family had clearly come to England from somewhere in Africa would be shunned by many.

Marianne, of course, was profoundly grateful

that Mrs Gray had sent her to Ledbury House. Despite a challenging start she had learned to feel safe there. Here in London...not so much.

She shivered, a sudden sense of foreboding assailing her as she realised she had been lulled into forgetting that she was in London. *Henry's* London.

'Shall we begin, then, if you are ready?'

Lord Kingswood agreed, and Mrs Gray brought the first woman in.

The next twenty minutes were strange for Marianne. Knowing how nervous the poor housekeeper would be, she tried her best to offer reassuring smiles as Mrs Gray asked a series of questions. Unfortunately, after only a few minutes, it became clear that while the woman had *assisted* a previous housekeeper, she had never held the responsibility herself.

She would make a good upper housemaid, Marianne thought, and a good housekeeper in years to come, but she was patently not ready to manage a team of servants and help with household budgeting. They thanked her politely, but as soon as she had left all agreed that she was not the right person.

'The other candidate for housekeeper should be here by now,' said Mrs Gray, rising. 'I shall fetch her.'

'I do hope this one is suitable,' murmured Lord Kingswood with a worried look.

'Me too,' agreed Marianne fervently.

'Thank you for assisting me with this, Miss Bolton,' he said softly, looking at her intently. 'I really appreciate it.'

Something about his tone, and the look in his eye, was making Marianne's heart sing. He *meant* it—she just knew he did. And in that moment she felt an affinity towards him which was unlike anything she had ever experienced before.

They looked at each other for an inappropriately long moment, then the door reopened, breaking the connection between them.

'Here is your next possible housekeeper,' Mrs Gray announced, leading a woman into the room. 'This is Mrs Bailey.'

Mrs Bailey! Marianne looked up—into the shocked eyes of her own former housekeeper!

Ash was—surprisingly—quite enjoying the process of engaging staff. He never would have thought he would find himself in this situation—and no one, least of all himself, would have expected him to be *entertained* by it. Yet it was surprisingly stimulating to discuss with Miss Bolton and the register office owner the intricacies of the mix of servants they hoped to employ, and think how they might fit in with the existing Ledbury House staff.

He was, of course, relieved and delighted to be back in London, and had taken up with his friends as if he had never been away. For the past few days he had enjoyed boxing, fencing and fine dining, as well as an evening of wine and cards at his club—which had continued until five bells and left him with a headache and a pile of winnings.

Yet when his secretary had anxiously told him of the difficulty in hiring staff for Ledbury House Ash had responded with equanimity—with enthusiasm, almost. Perhaps a part of him had become accustomed to using his brain on a daily basis, and perhaps he thought the experience might be amusing.

He had, of course, anticipated that Lady Kingswood would not be interested in assisting him. Although two months ago she had made the effort to write to a register office to employ a new governess for her beloved Cecily, Fanny had not, as far as he could work out, had any involvement in the actual selection of Miss Bolton. And since, Ash mused, Miss Bolton had turned out to be a person of good mind and an excellent governess—if a little managing—perhaps this agency was the right one to use in his next step in the search for decent servants.

When Fanny had suggested that Miss Bolton should help he had felt a sense of satisfaction—as if he had planned it so. Miss Bolton had proved herself a valuable and sensible helpmate, and he knew Mr Cronin valued her opinion. As did he.

It had been a joy to see Miss Bolton again. After five days away from home—from Ledbury House—he had welcomed the sight of her pretty face and merry smile when he had arrived for tea at Grillon's. And now she was next to him, and he was feeling a delicious warmth in her company.

It was unlike anything he had experienced before. There was lust in it—that was clear—but it was mixed with a sense of friendship. This was unexpected. Ash had never been *friends* with a woman before. The heat he felt for her was intense—perhaps on a par with his youthful passion for Fanny all those years ago. But had he ever truly known Fanny? Or, more accurately, had he blinded himself to her true nature?

Miss Bolton he believed he *knew*. He could read her moods—could tell when he had irritated her, knew when she was feeling sad...most likely as a result of her bereavement. Occasionally he had been tempted to ask about her deceased father, but had known that it would not be appropriate. As her employer, he must not cross that line.

Even having lustful thoughts about her felt wrong. He had always despised those men who took advantage of their servants—particularly the women—and yet he knew it was seen as acceptable behaviour among some of London's young bucks, and some older degenerates.

Putting his preoccupation with Miss Bolton to one side for now, he focused on the woman accompanying Mrs Gray into the room—hopefully the woman who would be Ledbury House's new housekeeper. He liked what he saw. She was a short, slightly rounded, middle-aged woman, with an air of neatness and quiet competence about her. Just now she was looking a little pale and distressed. She was looking fixedly at Miss Bolton, but recovered with a start when Mrs Gray introduced them both.

Mrs Gray bade her sit, then began asking the same questions she had asked the previous aspirant.

Thankfully, after a shaky start, Mrs Bailey seemed to gather herself, and gave solid answers to Mrs Gray's questions. She was clearly an experienced housekeeper who knew her work.

Something about her was nagging at Ash, though he could not for the life of him work out what it was. He focused his mind, and observed her more closely, and soon worked out what was bothering him. She seemed *too* anxious—much more anxious than he would have expected, given her experience and competence.

He leaned forward. 'Mrs Bailey, I have a question for you.'

'Yes, my lord?'

Her hands were shaking a little in her lap.

'Can you tell me why you have no reference from your last employer?'

Her eyes flicked to Miss Bolton, then back to him. 'It is,' she said slowly, 'a distressing tale.'

Intriguing.

'Let us hear it, then.'

She paused, then seemed to gather herself. 'I was housekeeper in a sizeable house, and my daughter, Jane, was a housemaid there. Jane is here today—I hope to find positions for both of us in the same household.'

'Yes...? Do continue.'

Mrs Bailey's lips tightened. 'Unfortunately Jane came to the attention of the— Of a young man.'

She paused again. She seemed to be struggling to speak. Beside him, Miss Bolton was twisting a handkerchief over and over.

Mrs Gray intervened, asking bluntly, 'Is your daughter with child, Mrs Bailey?'

'No! Thankfully not that. I was able to rescue her from the young man before—before he had... No, she is not with child. But I could not continue to live there, with him so determined and my poor Jane so upset and frightened. So we left. He will never give either of us a reference now.'

Beside him Miss Bolton gasped, and he looked at her. She was pale and trembling, clearly aghast at Mrs Bailey's tale. He felt a wave of compassion wash over him. Sometimes Miss Bolton seemed so self-contained it was easy to forget that she had led a fairly sheltered life. He was surprised by an almost overwhelming compulsion to take care of her.

'Thank you for telling us, Mrs Bailey,' he said evenly. 'I should like you to wait in the other room for a few minutes.'

The woman nodded, thanked them, and went outside.

'Miss Bolton?' he said immediately, turning towards her. 'Are you well?'

She did not look well. Her eyes seemed huge in her pale face and she looked at him uncomprehendingly. Instinctively he reached for her hand. She clung to it tightly, as if he were her anchor. He felt an unexpected lump in his throat.

Mrs Gray stood and went to a cabinet in the

corner of the room. She poured some amber liquid into a glass and offered it to Miss Bolton.

'Brandy,' she said calmly.

Miss Bolton released his hand and reached shakily for the brandy. She coughed a little as she drank it, but after a few moments some colour had returned to her cheeks and she was able to assure them that she was quite well.

Ash allowed this to pass without contradiction, and gently asked if she wanted to leave.

'Oh, no!' said she. 'I assure you I am perfectly recovered. It was just—the shock—Mrs Bailey and her Jane—I—'

'Hush, now, child,' said Mrs Gray kindly, giving Miss Bolton a speaking look.

Miss Bolton, seeing it, subsided.

The older woman turned to Ash. 'My recommendation, my lord, for what it is worth, is that you should appoint Mrs Bailey as your housekeeper and her daughter as personal maid to the ladies. I met Jane earlier, and I believe her to be of good character, as well as a competent housemaid. She also, she says, has some skill as a dresser, having previously served a young lady.'

Miss Bolton choked again, and when she had finished coughing Ash confirmed that he would indeed appoint the two women.

'I should say, Mrs Gray, that I can now see that

you are a woman of sense and discernment, so I shall leave the rest of the process to you. I will happily accept your list of recommendations from among those you have registered. Right now I wish to take Miss Bolton back to her hotel, where she may recover properly.'

'A wise decision, my lord,' agreed Mrs Gray.

Ash was unclear if she was referring to his new staff or his concern for Miss Bolton.

He rose, offering Miss Bolton his arm.

He had much to think about.

Marianne was still shaken by her unexpected encounter with Mrs Bailey and by hearing the housekeeper's tale about Jane. It had to have been Henry, of course. Although some of his friends were just as lacking in character as he, and might force themselves on an innocent maid, only Henry would have the opportunity to *persist*, necessitating Mrs Bailey's removal from her home and her living.

Mrs Bailey was right about the lack of references, Marianne reflected bitterly. Henry's vindictiveness at being thwarted would make him determined to harm Mrs Bailey and Jane in any way he could. He would be uncaring of the potential damage done—in fact he would revel in it.

Hearing what had happened to Jane had brought

back Marianne's own difficult memories of her terror at Henry's hands. The healing effect of living at Ledbury House had had a soothing influence on her. In addition, she acknowledged that getting to know men like Lord Kingswood and Mr Cronin had contributed to having her faith in the male species somewhat restored. Now she found herself shaken by Mrs Bailey's tale.

Jane had, of course, been *her* personal maid— Mrs Bailey had been so proud of her daughter's elevation to that role. And now they had been made homeless by the same evil that had forced Marianne into leaving home. Thankfully Lord Kingswood had agreed to employ them, giving them, too, the chance of a new start at Ledbury House.

Marianne frowned. How would they endeavour to keep their former connection secret? It would surely be nigh on impossible. She had almost blurted out her knowledge of them while she had held the brandy glass in her hand, and Lord Kingswood had looked at her with such concern. With a look and a word Mrs Gray had cautioned her, and so she had remained silent.

She knew not whether she had done the right thing. Being dishonest did not come easily to her. And yet she had obeyed Mrs Gray's warning. The register office owner had probably dealt with

many similar situations, Marianne knew. She had
clearly worked out that Marianne and Mrs Bailey knew each other, and that they had come to
her agency for similar reasons.

*And of course Mrs Bailey was always going to
try Mrs Gray's agency first*, thought Marianne.
After all, it was she who recommended it to me.

'You are remarkably quiet, Miss Bolton. It is
unlike you. Normally you are full of opinions.'

Marianne came back to the present with a jump.
Lord Kingswood, seated opposite in the carriage,
was regarding her intently.

She flushed. 'Oh! I was thinking of—of Mrs
B-Bailey, and of what happened to her daughter.'
She had stumbled over Mrs Bailey's name, her
mind checking for an instant whether she was
'allowed' to know it.

'A distressing tale, for sure.' He leaned back
and brushed a speck from his immaculate sleeve.
'Had you come across Mrs Bailey before?' he
added casually.

'Um—well, not really.'

Miss Bolton had not. Miss Marianne Grant certainly had.

She squirmed uncomfortably.

He raised his eyes from his sleeve to pin hers.
'I see.' His fingers drummed lightly on his thigh.
Marianne watched, helplessly fascinated. 'Miss

Bolton, would you be willing to travel back to Ledbury House early—if Fanny can spare you, that is?'

'I should like it above all things!' Marianne responded honestly, and quite without thinking. 'That is, of course, I am happy to support Lady Kingswood in whatever way she needs me...' Her voice tailed off.

He grinned. 'Quite.'

As he watched her his smile slowly faded, to be replaced by something powerful and compelling.

Leaning across the carriage, he surprised her by taking her hand. 'Miss Bolton—I wish you to know that should you ever have need you can come to me for assistance.'

Marianne could not breathe. His hand was warm, but the look he was sending her was, she felt, piercing right through her to her deepest secrets. Her heart pounded mercilessly. Time seemed to stand still as she gazed helplessly into those eyes.

Should she tell him?

But what if he sent her away without reference for dishonesty? Oh, it didn't bear thinking about! The notion of him being disappointed in her was too much to contemplate. It must not happen. She could not leave this life that she had so carefully built—a life in which she had a home, a place in it. Her little room, her afternoon meetings with—with *him*.

The look he was giving her was warm, measured, compassionate. Perhaps she could trust him?

She wavered, considering, and then the moment was abruptly broken when the carriage suddenly swerved, coming to an abrupt halt seconds later. Marianne found herself hurtling forward, but Lord Kingswood's strong arms closed on her shoulders, bracing her. Their faces were inches apart.

With a strangled groan Lord Kingswood closed the small gap between them and kissed her.

Chapter Twelve

Instinctively, and quite without thought, Marianne parted her lips and returned his fire with flames of her own. He groaned again, and Marianne felt the sound reverberate through her bones. It fanned the conflagration inside her to new heights.

She was lost in sensual wonder. His hands gripped her shoulders, gentle enough not to hurt, yet firm enough so that she could feel each finger through the fine silk of her black dress. His thumbs were caressing the soft skin over her collarbones, sending a delightful tingling through her. His mouth tasted delectably sweet.

Not sweet like a sweetmeat, she thought stupidly. *More like honeyed wine.* He was delicious.

Dimly, she heard the coachman jump down, and realised he was about to appear at the carriage door to check that they were uninjured. When Ash released her she automatically sat back in her seat, adjusting her bonnet and trying not to look as if she had just been thoroughly kissed. Her heart was pounding, senses tingling, and there was a delectable warmth in the pit of her stomach.

My goodness! she thought. *What a kiss that was!*

'Apologies, my lord!' The coachman's head was at the window. 'There's been an accident up ahead. Looks bad.'

Ash frowned. 'Can we be of assistance, perhaps?' He reached for the door.

The coachman lowered the step and he descended.

Pausing, he turned back to look at Marianne. 'Stay here,' he commanded softly.

Marianne, who was still busy trying to deal with all the sensations, feelings and thoughts he had just created within her, nevertheless knew her duty.

'Absolutely not!' she retorted, rising from her seat and moving to the step.

She reached out her hand for his assistance and, after the briefest of hesitations, he gave it.

'You are a headstrong, stubborn, wilful woman, Miss Bolton.' There was a glint of humour in his eye.

'I know it!' she rejoindered, not without a little pride.

He squeezed her hand, then released it, and they turned to the scene of the accident ahead.

It was shocking. A high-perch racing phaeton had overturned, its axle clearly damaged. Both horses were screaming in terror, but as they approached it became clear that they were physically unharmed.

Ash's coachman ran directly to the second carriage horse, which was desperately trying to free itself from the traces. Showing great courage, he managed to get close enough to take hold of the bridle, and began soothing and quieting the distressed animal and its mate.

At the same time Marianne hurried towards the overturned carriage to discover how the driver fared. Two others—a man and a woman both dressed in the plain clothes of servants—were ahead of them, and the woman gasped as Ash and Marianne approached.

'Lor', 'e's broke 'is head, 'e has!' she proclaimed.

It did look bad, Marianne conceded. The man had been thrown from the carriage and had injured his head on landing. He was lying awkwardly on his side, and blood was emerging in a fast flow from a wound to the front of his head. His face was obscured by dirt mixed with blood, and for a moment Marianne feared that he was dead.

Was this how it was when Mama and Papa had their accident?

The thought would not be denied. Marianne had struggled each time she had wondered about the reality of their deaths last summer. Carriage accidents happened all the time. Hardly a week went by without the announcement of some new death in the newspapers. But her own parents should never have been counted among the victims. Nor should this man, whoever he was.

Thankfully, at just that moment he moaned and stirred.

'Fear not,' Ash said calmly, moving to bend over him. 'You have taken a spill, but you seem to be in one piece.'

The man moaned again and opened his eyes. 'What? Where—?'

'You are on Jermyn Street.' Ash peered closer. 'Why, I think I have met you before. Mr—Mr Grant, is it not?'

Marianne could see the man clearly now too. Her heart seemed to stop. *Henry!* It was Henry! There was no doubting it! First Mrs Bailey, now Henry. Her old life was determined to find her today, it seemed.

Fear threatened to overcome her as Ash's words

sank in. Her heart, having stilled in shock, was now racing. Her palms were sticky, there was a roaring in her ears, and her knees felt as though they might not support her weight. She stumbled slightly as blackness briefly threatened to overcome her.

Taking a deep breath, she looked again. Yes, it was Henry—of that there was no doubt. The nightmare was real.

But he had not seen her. *Yet*. He was still rather confused and rubbing blood away from his face.

Carefully, Marianne shuffled behind Ash, out of Henry's eyeline.

Oh, why did I leave the carriage?

Thankfully, more bystanders were joining all the time, keen to see the spectacle, and Marianne shrank further back. She glanced to the carriage. If she walked towards it would she be even more noticeable? Perhaps she should stay here, behind the six or seven onlookers who had now gathered.

She waited.

'Definitely her...' Henry muttered to himself a couple of moments later as he sat up. He was looking around him, slightly dazed. 'Think they can just go like that? Make a fool of me? Marianne and the others...'

He mumbled something else unintelligible. Marianne was now paralysed with fear. Any sec-

ond now he would see her, and *name* her, and her
world would fall apart.

'Yes, yes…' Ash was saying soothingly. 'We
shall get you to your home and call a doctor for
you.'

He turned to the man who looked like a servant, saying quietly, 'Could you perhaps procure
a hackney for Mr Grant? He is foxed, and will
have a sore head on the morrow, but otherwise
there is little seriously wrong unless I mistake
the matter.'

The man nodded. 'Foxed for sure, my lord!
I can smell the brandy from 'ere. Shouldn't be
allowed—these young bloods thinking they can
drink what they like then tool about in a carriage at top speed on the public thoroughfare!
Tried to overtake that cart, 'e did—when anybody could see there wasn't space for 'im!'

'Nevertheless,' said Ash evenly, 'the quickest
way we can sort this out is by removing Mr Grant
from the scene.'

The man flushed. 'Yes, my lord.'

He disappeared off to secure a hackney, and
within only a few moments one had arrived. Marianne remained hidden behind the now substantial crowd, who were ogling and exclaiming about
the young man with blood all over him. The ser-

vant helped Henry to his feet and supported him as he walked slowly to the hackney.

Amid the commotion the horses were freed from the tangled traces, then a crowd of burly men began securing the carriage with ropes, with which they would move it off the road. The carriage horses were tied behind the hackney.

Having seen Henry safely stowed inside, Ash turned and began scanning the crowd, clearly looking for Marianne. She knew the moment he discovered her. His eyes found hers—a connection which seemed more than just a gaze. It was an acknowledgement, a recognition…a *knowing*.

It shook her as much as any of the other extraordinary events of this day.

'And so,' Ash continued smoothly, 'I should like to ask for your indulgence in releasing Miss Bolton from London early, so that she might assist Mrs Cullen and Mrs Bailey in dealing with the other new staff.'

They were seated in Grillon's, drinking tea with Lady Kingswood and Cecily, who were returned from another hectic day of shopping. Ash had walked Miss Bolton there from the scene of the accident, it being only a short distance away.

Marianne's pulse had now returned to a more reasonable speed and she was, she felt, managing to look reasonably calm. Inside, she knew there were things she needed to think about, but right now she was focused on her tea, and on Ash's request to Lady Kingswood.

'But I need her *here*, with me!' replied Lady Kingswood, a hint of petulance in her tone. 'Why, she has been so helpful in fetching and carrying for me!'

Ash's eyebrows rose. 'I am sure you would agree, Fanny, it is not a governess's duty to fetch and carry.'

Lady Kingswood had the grace to flush a little. 'Well, no one *forced* her to do it. It is her nature, I believe. She is simply kind and helpful.'

She sent Marianne an insincere smile. Marianne looked into her teacup and wished she were a hundred miles away.

Grillon's footman re-entered their comfortable sitting room, this time bringing a platter of bread, cold meats and cheese. Once he had left conversation resumed.

'I *might*,' said Ash, 'consider hiring a footman for you during your remaining days in the capital.'

A gleam lit Lady Kingswood's eye. 'Would he wear full livery? And would you pay for the whole?'

Ash nodded. 'Yes—and yes! You are ever audacious, Fanny! So we are agreed, then?'

Lady Kingswood glanced at Marianne, then back to Ash, and her eyes narrowed. 'One more thing, Ash. Are you also returning to Ledbury House early? You seem much more *interested* in our quiet home than you said you would be.' There was an edge to her voice.

Ash's eyebrows rose. 'My dear Fanny, you may accuse me of many things, but an *interest* in farming and managing house servants is *not* among them. I am unspeakably jaded by the entire enterprise and mean to make the most of my time here in London before I am forced to return to the countryside.'

He gestured firmly to emphasise the point.

'Why, one of my acquaintances has this day suffered a carriage accident—Miss Bolton will share the details with you—and I intend to stay long enough to ensure that he is fully recovered.' He rose. 'No, I shall adhere to my plan and remain here until next week. Now, if you'll forgive me, I have had more than enough of domestic matters today—enough, in fact, to last me a lifetime—so I shall take my leave of you. You shall have your footman!'

He rose, his air that of a man jaded beyond endurance, bowed curtly and left.

'Well!' uttered Fanny, after the door had closed behind him. 'I asked only a civil question. It is not *my* fault that he has the running of the estate!'

Marianne barely heard her. It felt to her as though the floor beneath her feet had turned to quicksand. In her mind she listed the various shocks of the day: Mrs Bailey's appearance at the register office. Her tale about Henry attacking Jane. The carriage journey with Ash. That kiss. The accident. Seeing Henry. That sense of connection she had felt to Ash.

Ash? When had she begun calling him Ash in her mind? Some time today, certainly.

And now two further shocks. First, he found his life at Ledbury House *tedious*, and had no true interest in running the estate. And second, he knew Henry.

Chapter Thirteen

Ash strode through Berkeley Square on the way back to his lodgings, glad now that he had directed his coachman to return without him. He needed the walk to clear his head and try and work out what on earth was happening to him. His fixation with Miss Bolton was fast becoming an obsession.

Today he had betrayed all his higher instincts and kissed her. And, while he revelled in the memory, he regretted succumbing to his baser nature. Although notionally in Fanny's employ, Miss Bolton was in a real sense in *his* power, and today he had abused that. He had seen enough over the years to understand that women sometimes co-operated out of fear, and had sworn never to step over such self-imposed lines.

Until today he had managed to keep to that vow. Until today he had never had to wonder why a woman kissed him. Until today his relationships had always been fairly distant, unambiguous—almost businesslike. Until today.

He literally had no idea whether Miss Bolton had genuinely welcomed his kiss or whether she'd felt compelled to pretend so for fear of losing her situation as a governess in his household. She had *seemed* to enjoy his attentions, he reflected, remembering the enthusiasm with which she had returned his embrace. But had it been genuine, or had it been feigned?

He had no way of knowing, and no way of finding out in future.

His uncertainty was partly fuelled by another concern. He was sure now that she was hiding something from him. Today at the register office he had noted her reaction to Mrs Bailey and to the story she had told about her daughter Jane. Did Miss Bolton know them? Or had the story triggered something she had seen or heard about before?

Her reaction had reminded him of the anxious, fearful Miss Bolton he had met at the inn at Netherton two months ago. That lady had gradually disappeared, to be replaced by a relaxed, quick-witted, managing woman who challenged his mind and tested his sense of authority.

Initially he had accepted her tale about it being her first post as a governess and that she had decided to take up the role after her father had died, leaving her without independent funds. Now— now he simply did not know what to believe.

Fanny's observation had also rocked him. The fact that Fanny, not known for her insight, had realised he was interested in the governess had caused him to act decisively.

He hoped his pretence about Henry Grant being his friend and his words about being tired of es- tate management and desiring only to stay in London for as long as possible had dented Fan- ny's notion that he might be attracted to Miss Bolton. For he knew that was *exactly* why she had asked if he, too, was planning to return to Ledbury House early.

And what was the truth?

He *had*, he admitted, been tempted to break his engagements and travel back to Ledbury House early. If only to discuss with Mr Cronin and Mrs Bailey—and Miss Bolton, of course—the works to be completed in the house. He wanted Mrs Bailey's assurance that the London servants would work co-operatively with Mrs Cullen and the village girls. It was nothing to do with miss- ing Miss Bolton. Of course it was not!

Miss Bolton herself, he had noted, had only looked mildly confused. She seemed not to have grasped the implication of Fanny's words, thank goodness.

Now, he decided, *I must be resolute. I must put all thoughts of Miss Bolton and Ledbury House out of my head. I am back in London, where I belong. The rest matters not.*

Two days later Marianne waited anxiously in the sitting room at Grillon's for the arrival of Mrs Bailey and her daughter. Her luggage rested by her feet, for she was packed and ready to return home to Ledbury House.

Ash had made his travelling carriage available to them—an unexpected and unlooked-for privilege. Ledbury House's new housekeeper and her daughter had been instructed to present themselves here at ten o'clock, to meet Lady Kingswood, after which they would set out for Ledbury House with Marianne.

Lady Kingswood, however, had been somewhat distracted by the arrival, an hour before, of her new footman—a superior-looking, confident young man in magnificent livery. She was still preening herself at this boost to her consequence, and hoping she would be seen by as many ladies of her acquaintance as possible, when the footman who was stationed outside the door of their suite opened it to announce the new housekeeper and her daughter.

'Allow them to enter,' intoned Lady Kingswood dramatically, 'for I am quite at my leisure!'

Mrs Bailey and Jane entered, looking a little anxious. Marianne exchanged a glance with the housekeeper, giving her what she hoped was a welcoming smile. She had not seen Mrs Bailey since that day at the register office, and of course had not seen Jane since she'd left home.

If they were anxious, their anxiety did not last long. Within a very few moments it became clear that Lady Kingswood had already tired of the conversation, and before long she had dismissed the three of them.

They made their way silently to the carriage, and then finally they were inside and the door closed. As the carriage left all three women expressed their relief, and Marianne hugged both Mrs Bailey and Jane fiercely.

'Oh, Miss Marianne!' Mrs Bailey cried, wiping away a tear. 'It is so good to see you again and to see that you are safe. I thought I should pass out when I saw you in that register office!'

'Me too!' said Marianne fervently. 'I had no expectation of seeing either of you—though of course when I heard what had happened with Henry I understood it all immediately!' She

turned to Jane. 'I am so, so sorry that he importuned you. Are you—are you still unwell?'

Jane looked at her steadily. 'I was at first. But
I am much recovered now and I am determined
to be well.' She smiled shyly. 'It is a relief to be
away from—from him, and to be working for
you again, miss!'

'Oh, no! You are not working *for* me, but *with*
me,' said Marianne. 'You must not forget that
I, too, am an employee at Ledbury House—the
governess only. I eat with the family, it is true,
but I have friends among the servants. It is most
gratifying!'

Jane looked shocked. 'Friends with the servants—
oh, miss! And you such a fine lady!'

'I was born a lady, that is true, but we are both
women, are we not? And we are nearly the same
age. My changed circumstance means, I hope,
that we can be friends. What say you?'

Jane's mouth fell open. She looked to her
mother, who nodded.

'I think it will serve very well. You two have
always rubbed along together nicely—and do
not forget, Jane, that your father was the son of
a gentleman, though my family were all servants. These are unusual circumstances, and
we need people who care for us. And people to
care for.' She thought for a moment. 'Tell me of

Lord Kingswood. He holds you in high regard, I think?'

For some reason Marianne felt a slow blush rise in her cheeks. 'Oh—um…he is most considerate.'

Mrs Bailey was eyeing her keenly.

Marianne rushed on. 'He is not happy to have inherited the title, I think. In fact he has said, very recently, that he is tired of the entire thing and will only return to Ledbury House when forced to by the pressure of business.'

Mrs Bailey's gaze dropped to Marianne's lap, where she was desperately screwing a handkerchief into a crumpled mess. 'I see. He said this to you? Directly?'

'He told Lady Kingswood. I was there.'

Mrs Bailey tapped a finger against her cheek, considering this. 'Interesting… What is his relation to Lady Kingswood?'

'Cousin by marriage. She is the Dowager Countess.'

Mrs Bailey nodded thoughtfully, then changed the topic, asking about the house, the other servants, and the work to be done.

Marianne answered as well as she could, and spoke plainly about the challenges ahead. 'So A—Lord Kingswood has begun spending money on staff and repairs, but there is still much to be done.'

'Good,' said Mrs Bailey firmly. 'I enjoy a challenge.'

A little later, with the ease of long acquaintance, they lapsed into a comfortable silence. Marianne could not resist just *looking* at both of them from time to time. Their faces were so familiar, had been part of her life for so long...and she had taken them—taken her whole life—for granted.

Never again. From now on she would count all her blessings and be grateful.

She pictured her plain little room at Ledbury House. Tonight she would sleep there again— would close her own curtains and her own chamber door and rest, secure in the knowledge that now she had allies and friends around her.

She thought back to her earlier comment. Mr Cronin was her friend too. She was looking forward to seeing the steward again and hearing his news about the work that had begun on the farms—especially his efforts to repair the outbuildings and labourers' cottages.

Lady Cecily was, she reflected, also a positive part of her life. Although her charge was almost eight years younger, Marianne enjoyed her company. She would miss her in these next few days.

Guiltily, she realised that she felt a measure of relief that Lady Kingswood was remaining in

London until the end of the week. It would allow Mrs Bailey and Jane to settle in, and Marianne to have a quiet, peaceful few days.

Finally, she allowed herself to think of Ash. Immediately an image of him sprang into her mind's eye. Ash, smiling at her. Then another. Ash telling her she could come to him in need. What had he meant?

Does he know, or suspect, that I was lying to him?

Her thoughts moved on to the kiss they had shared. Immediately her heart stilled, then raced as her body relived the delightful sensations she had felt when his lips had been pressed to hers. She closed her eyes and the memory strengthened. Oh, but she had had no idea that a kiss could leave you feeling blissful, shaken and frightened all at the same time.

Frightened? Why did she feel frightened?

She opened her eyes again. Mrs Bailey was sleeping and Jane was looking out of the other window. In truth, she acknowledged, she had felt no fear at the time—only excitement, and passion and a wish for the kiss to continue and continue.

The fear had come since. She had always been too trusting. Her life, she knew, had been sheltered, and her parents had kept from her much of the reality of life. But she knew things, too.

She had been the first to visit a sick tenant, or to insist her father pay for some need she had discovered in a groom or a retired servant or a wounded animal.

And she had seen animals mating at times—it had always struck her as strange and almost comical.

Her fear of Henry was acute—but then, he had singled her out. She knew what could happen to maidens who were unwary. And since Henry's attack on her she'd had knowledge of how a man could force himself on an unwilling maid.

What she was now learning was that sometimes a maid was *willing*. She had known of maids who disappeared from service with whispers that they were with child after a willing liaison. She had often wondered why such girls would allow themselves to be ruined in that way. Why would they risk their position for a dalliance?

Some of those girls never married, and their mothers and aunts helped them raise their offspring. They would tut and complain about 'feckless young men' and 'philanderers,' but were ultimately powerless to make the fathers take responsibility for their children.

Marianne had never thought about this before—about the difference between men who took what they wanted by force and those who got their way through seduction. If an uncaring man achieved his goal through sweet words and tender kisses, rather than by force, and the outcome was the same, was he really any better than Henry?

She squirmed uncomfortably. *Yes. Yes, he was. Of course he was. Lord, there was no comparison between someone like Henry and someone like Ash!*

And yet there were similarities too. Ash had claimed to be Henry's acquaintance. She was still shaken by that. Ash had never, Marianne was sure, visited her former home, for she surely would have remembered him. But they wore similar clothes, were part of the same set, and enjoyed the same pastimes in London. Drinking. Gambling. Betting on boxing and horse racing.

Lady Kingswood had been frank about Ash's reputation with women. 'Always a high-flyer in his keeping, my friends tell me!' she had confided to Marianne just last night. 'Well, that might suit his wife—if he should ever marry—for once he has sired an heir he will perhaps not bother her any more.' Her eyes had taken on a faraway look. 'I wonder…' she had said thoughtfully. 'There may be possibilities there…'

Marianne had waited patiently for some explanation, but it had not come. Lady Kingswood had retired early, leaving Marianne frowning and confused.

All in all, it had reinforced Marianne's fears. Ash? A libertine and a seducer? Remembering that kiss, she could well believe it, and it served only to strengthen her resolve that it must not happen again.

The danger was not that he would force her, as Henry had tried. The danger was that he might not need to. The danger was in her own traitorous body, her own heart.

Ash sighed and sipped his wine. Once again he was overwhelmed by a feeling of *ennui*. His friends were—as they usually were—currently trying to outdo each other as to who could drink themselves into oblivion soonest. He had left the card tables an hour ago, and was now listlessly contemplating his wine in solitude, in a quiet corner of his club. There was a group of young cubs in the far corner, but no one was bothering him.

Really, he could not account for his feeling so unsettled. It was with him constantly. He was back in Town, living the life that he had built for himself—the life that his father had helped him build before his death. And yet Ash could not shake a feeling of restlessness, of waiting for some other life to claim him again.

All his usual pleasures seemed flat. He had enjoyed his time in Jackson's earlier, and had taken his stallion for a long gallop this morning. But the drinking, gambling and easy repartee that had until recently been his habit had somehow lost its flavour.

'Lord Kingswood?'

Ash looked up. One of the young cubs had approached him. He looked familiar, but Ash, with wine-induced sleepiness dulling his wits, could not immediately place him.

'Yes?'

'I am Grant. Henry Grant. You came to my assistance a few days ago and I wish to thank you.'

Ash remembered him now. The man in the carriage accident—the one he had lied to Fanny about, saying he was an acquaintance. In truth, he barely knew him.

He waved the man's thanks away. 'Think nothing of it. I'd have done the same for anyone.'

'Nevertheless, it was me you assisted and I am truly grateful.'

'Never mind that,' said Ash, feeling a little uncomfortable, 'how is your head?'

Grant smiled. 'I had the devil of a headache for a day or so, but I am fully recovered, I assure you. One of my horses, however, remains lame and may not improve.'

'Glad to hear you are recuperated. I am sorry about your horse.'

Grant shrugged. 'It is of no matter. I will buy another.'

Ash frowned slightly. *A man should have more care for his horses than that!*

He drained his wine glass and stood up. 'I am glad you are on the mend. Now, if you will excuse me…'

'Er—there is one thing I wish to ask you.'

Grant put a hand on Ash's sleeve, as if to prevent him from leaving. Ash looked pointedly at it and Grant removed it with alacrity.

'Well?' His tone was curt.

His friends would have read the danger signs. Grant, however, was either oblivious to Ash's irritation or uncaring.

'My memories of that day are a little hazy—' he began.

'Yes—that would be because you were bosky.'

Grant looked startled.

'You know,' said Ash, who was beginning to enjoy himself a little. 'Foxed. Drunk as a wheelbarrow.'

Grant had the grace to flush. 'Yes, well, everyone has too much to drink once in a while.'

But not at one o'clock in the afternoon, Ash was

tempted to retort. *And not when trying to drive a high-perch phaeton through Jermyn Street!*

Henry Grant was only a few years younger than Ash, but Ash felt a hundred years older than him. He let the man's defensive words pass unchallenged, however, and waited for Grant to say whatever it was he was so determined to say.

'There was a young woman with you. I only saw her for an instant, and afterwards wondered if I might have imagined her.'

'Yes?' said Ash tersely.

'Well, I wondered—um—that is to say I was curious about who she was and how she came to be there.'

'Why?'

This was unexpected, and Ash was suddenly entirely awake. *What is his interest in Miss Bolton?*

Grant looked uncomfortable. 'I thought I knew her, that is all.'

Interesting. Grant might have some information on the mysterious Miss Bolton's past. 'How do you know her?'

'Oh, I—she was a friend of—of my sister. If it is the same lady.'

Ash eyed him speculatively. 'What is the name of your sister's friend?'

'Oh!' He flushed. 'Come to think of it, I cannot remember. But the lady who was with you did not seem to have a maid accompanying her, so I wondered if—'

Ash was more than a little taken aback. 'Mr Grant, are you asking me if the lady was in fact my mistress?'

Grant's flush deepened, and something like anger flashed briefly in his eyes. He made haste to deny it, but it was clear that was exactly what he had been asking.

The nerve of the man, Ash thought. *How dare he pry into my personal life?*

Ash wanted nothing more to do with him. 'I am going now, and I shall forget that we had this conversation, Mr Grant.' He dipped his head slightly, disdain evident in the coolness of the gesture.

Grant, looking frustrated, had no choice but to retire to his friends, whatever other questions he had going unanswered.

Ash made his way to the hallway and asked for his hat, cloak and cane. As he waited, he tried to work out what the connection was between Grant and Miss Bolton. How would a young woman who lived quietly in the country with her lawyer father ever have come into contact with one of the young bloods of London? Where was Grant's family from, and how old was this sister he'd mentioned?

He had no doubt that Miss Bolton was genuinely country-bred. Her reactions to the noise, smells and busyness of London, as well as her witty and shocked observations, had brought him considerable amusement each time he'd called to Grillon's to see her—to see *them*. So was Grant lying? And, if so, why?

Perhaps, Ash thought wryly, *he has an eye for Miss Bolton for himself!*

Although the governess did not have the showy beauty of the various incomparables that were being paraded around town, she had a quiet beauty that was stunning in its impact.

Well, if that is the case, I shall allow him this: he shows good taste in women.

Suddenly he was glad that Miss Bolton had left Town. The thought of Grant pursuing her sent anger flooding through him. His heart thundered, coldness filled his belly and his hands balled into fists.

The poor footman who had just that moment returned with Ash's cloak, hat and cane looked decidedly startled by Ash's demeanour.

Ash smoothed his features into an acceptable mask, thanked the man, then set out on the short walk to his rooms. As he walked down St James's Street he lifted his head to feel the freshness of the rain on his face. It was barely there—more mist than rain—but he felt the need to cool down, and to shake off the unexpectedly strong reaction to his conversation with Henry Grant.

He pondered the matter all the way to Upper Brook Street, but could not for the life of him figure out whether his response was provoked by antipathy towards Grant or a sense of protectiveness towards Miss Bolton. Both options were unprecedented.

Although frequently irritated by fools, he tended not to actively dislike people—particularly when it was early in their acquaintance. He had met Grant once or twice, had recognised him when he had lain injured after the accident, but would have had difficulty in many circumstances in distinguishing him from any of his raucous friends.

A wild lot, that group, he mused, piecing together various bits of gossip he had not previously bothered to think about. Tales of gambling debts and wild parties came back to him.

He curled his lip in disgust. Yes, he and his own friends liked to gamble, and to bet on the horses and at the fives court, but they knew not to go beyond the bounds of respectability.

Grant and his friends were, he believed, close to being ostracised by polite society. And if their behaviour was anything like the forward manner of Henry Grant tonight he could see why. They were probably less than five years younger than his own group, but even in their wildest days he and his friends had not done anything to shame their families or their names.

His thoughts turned again to Miss Bolton. Perhaps he had been right in thinking that Henry Grant was seeking to seduce her. He certainly could not imagine a cock of the walk like Grant *marrying* a governess!

And surely it was not unreasonable to feel protective towards her? She was, after all, in his employ.

Ah, but would you have had the same concern for Aggie, if it had been she whom Grant wanted?

The quiet voice within his mind taunted him to look closer into his own heart. This was more than the concern he would have for any woman at risk of being pursued by a selfish young buck like Grant. The fact that it was Miss Bolton gave his emotions an edge that was more than plain chivalry.

Almost he finished the thought—then pushed it away with an instinct born of preserving his equilibrium.

'Of course I would protect Aggie too!' he exclaimed aloud, his voice sounding extremely noisy in the darkness.

Glancing around to make sure no one was there, and feeling extremely foolish, he quickened his pace and made for his lodgings.

Chapter Fourteen

'Grant? Henry Grant?'

Barny's voice was hurting Ash's head. They were in their usual spot, downstairs at White's, and Ash had tried a casual query about the young man who had irritated him so much last night.

'That's him. But, Barny, keep it down a bit, will you?'

Barny nodded sagely. 'Thought you'd sloped off a bit early last night... Bad wine, was it?'

'Not the wine, no. More like a distaste for my own company.'

And an arrogant young man who made me focus on the uselessness of my existence.

Aloud, he added, 'Do you ever get tired of London, Barny?'

'Tired? Of London? Course not!' Barny eyed him suspiciously. 'You're not turning soft, are you, Ash? These months you've spent rusticating and starved of good company have turned your brain, eh?'

'Actually, I've quite enjoyed it. The rusticating, I mean.'

And the company. Especially—

Barny goggled at him. 'Never tell me you are become a *farmer*! Why, next you shall turn as dull as old Moreton—always prating on about corn and livestock and whatnot!'

'Moreton? I had forgotten about Moreton's fascination with farming methods. I shall certainly seek him out.'

'Are you gammoning me? You will *seek out* Farmer Moreton? *Deliberately?* Lord, I never thought to see the day!' Barny searched his face, adding dubiously, 'He's upstairs, you know. Moreton, I mean. Not Grant. He and the other young bloods don't show their faces before dinner.'

'Ah, yes, Mr Grant... Tell me what you know of him.'

Barny frowned. 'Not much. Cambridgeshire, I think. Came into the property less than a year ago, when his old man died.'

'What of his sister?'

Barny looked at him blankly, then his eyes widened. 'That's right—there *is* a sister, apparently. Freddy said he met her at Grant's house party last Christmas. I think she's younger than Grant.

Never comes to town. Nor did the parents, come to that. Country types, you know.'

Ash nodded. Things began to make more sense. Perhaps Miss Bolton really had been friends with Mr Grant's younger sister—she could certainly be described as a 'country type' herself.

'He's part of that gin-hell set,' Barny added. 'Up for every lark, and some of it not…you know… not quite the thing.'

'What sort of lark?'

'They play deep at the hells—gambling for huge sums. There are rumours of debt. Plenty of drink, of course—but we all drank too much at their age.'

'What of women?'

'Ah, well—' Barny helped himself to some snuff. 'There's an entry in the wagers book that says they'll have a by-blow each by Christmas!'

'Really? But many men father children in temporary liaisons. Do they look after them?'

Barny leaned forward. 'Here's the thing. It's said that the families of these ruined girls don't come looking for aid—they want nothing more to do with the gin-hell boys. Most unusual.' He looked round, to check that no one was in earshot, then added, 'Rumour has it that some of them prefer their women unwilling.'

Ash raised his eyebrows.

'Quite. But there was something about Grant in particular—some tale or other. Can't remember what, though. It'll come to me.'

'Barny, as always, you are a fount of knowledge.' Ash heaved himself upright. 'Now I shall leave you, as I am going to talk to a man about crops.'

Barny shook his head sorrowfully. 'Lost!' he said mournfully. 'Another good man, succumbing to the evils of responsibility.'

Ash laughed and left him.

As he mounted the stairs in search of Mr Moreton—a man hitherto of no interest to him whatsoever—he reflected that he had, as Barny had noted, changed. He stood stock-still as the realisation hit him like a thunderclap.

When had he changed? And why?

It had been coming for a while, he mused. Town was losing its appeal, and the rounds of sport and socialising no longer satisfied him as they had when he was younger. But the real catalyst was Ledbury House. That burden, which he had cursed so bitterly on the day of John's funeral, now fired his imagination and his energy. He was positively *enjoying* having a purpose—a notion that he would have laughed at two months ago.

Of course his real life was still here in London—the Ledbury House project was a passing fancy, no more. Perhaps he should seek out some other purpose to occupy his mind when he was in Town. There was nothing special about Ledbury House...

Unbidden, an image came into his mind. Miss Bolton, her eyes sparkling with merriment as she rebuked him for some perceived slight. Again Miss Bolton, pensive as she considered a matter of business in Cronin's office. And finally, and most potently, Miss Bolton as she had looked when they had ended their kiss. Her eyes had been heavy with desire, her face beautiful in unguarded passion.

He almost groaned, so strong was the memory.

Really, he ought to stop thinking of Miss Bolton in such a way. She was his ward's governess, nothing more. Yet as he approached Mr Moreton the decision was made. He would return to Ledbury House as soon as he was able. There were matters of business to discuss with Mr Cronin.

Marianne's life was almost perfect. She was back at Ledbury House, and this time she had Mrs Bailey and Jane by her side. Before sunset on that first day Mrs Bailey had already been through the house like a gale, a flock of awed and willing housemaids in her wake, and the great clean-up had begun.

The workmen and chimney sweeps had been set to work and Mrs Bailey had taken charge. Aggie and the village girls had been joined by three new housemaids and a footman from London, as well as Jane and Mrs Bailey herself.

Now, three days later, the house had emerged from its cloak of dust, dirt, soot and grime. Brasses and silver had been polished, windows washed and floors cleaned. Mr Cronin was delighted with Mrs Bailey's achievements and gave her such fulsome praise that she blushed like a girl.

Jane, who was to be personal maid to Lady Kingswood and Cecily when they returned, had insisted on washing and mending Marianne's second gown.

'For I am only darning pillowcases and table-cloths at present anyway, miss, and I prefer to be busy.'

Marianne had gratefully handed it over and gone back to mending petticoats—a task much more within her abilities.

Aggie had told her that while she had been away a fox had taken one of the best hens, that Mr and Mrs Harkin's baby was sick and that an old nest had been discovered in one of the chimneys. 'Which probably explains, miss, why that fire would smoke the room out every time we'd light it. Now that the chimneys have been cleaned we can have fires in every room if we like.'

But there was no need for fires as spring had finally, it seemed, decided to come to Ledbury House. Everywhere Marianne could see signs of life. Pale green foliage began to adorn bare branches, turning the slope from a slant of angles and lines into a swaying mass of verdant beauty. Birds flew past with twigs in their mouths and small insects began to appear, buzzing through the air or scuttling in the undergrowth.

In the garden, a few flowers were bravely poking through, struggling to breathe among overgrown bushes. Marianne, determined to contribute to the rejuvenation she felt all around, found a trowel and a knife and set them free.

It was backbreaking work, for each time she finished one part of the garden she noticed more areas in need of care. But there was something so satisfying in clearing every little patch of land, trimming every overgrown bush and shrub and discovering the hidden beauty of what had once been a stunning garden.

She fell into bed at night exhausted, yet feeling more satisfied and content than she had done in a long, long time.

On the fourth day Lady Kingswood and Cecily returned, with the news that Ash was to follow them on the morrow. Marianne's heart leapt at this news, though she scolded herself inwardly for her foolishness.

Really, she ought to know better!

Yes, he had kissed her—and her insides still melted at the memory—but it had probably meant nothing.

Ash was a young buck, like Henry and his friends, although he was a few years older. He lived the same lifestyle as they did. He acknowledged Henry as an acquaintance—although Marianne recalled that at the time of the accident he had not seemed to know Henry particularly well.

Perhaps, she thought, *that is how they behave in the gentlemen's clubs and social circles they mix in. Perhaps 'friendship,' as I understand it, is unknown to them.*

What she *did* know was how Henry and his coterie behaved towards women. They acted as if they were entitled to kiss whomever they wished, to speak to servant women in whatever manner they wished, and certainly Henry had no qualms about attacking women—both she and Jane had experienced that ordeal.

With Henry the signs were there, in terms of how he spoke about women when they were *not* present. He seemed to hold women in general in disdain. And Marianne had heard both him and his friends make rude and coarse comments about women during their raucous revelries.

Of course Henry was polite and respectful in polite mixed company, and any ladies of his acquaintance would think him a perfectly amiable young man. Knowing what he truly was, Marianne felt that made his behaviour in private even *more* reprehensible.

The question was, how alike *were* Henry and Ash? Just because they followed the same fashions and enjoyed the same pastimes—boxing, gambling, horses and drinking parties—that did not mean they were the same.

Certainly during the last two months she had felt as though she had come to really *know* Ash. She could read his moods, could sometimes almost *see* his thoughts flash across his mind like ripples in a pool. And he behaved—usually—perfectly well with her.

Amiable. He seemed *amiable*. Actually, she realised, he reminded her more of Papa than of Henry.

Until he had kissed her and changed everything.

Not like the intrusive, disgusting embrace she might have expected from Henry or his remorseless friends. No, Ash's kiss had been compelling, passionate and intense. It had felt *real*, and Marianne relived it in her memory every night on retiring, and every morning when she woke up. It had been, quite simply, one of the most wonderful experiences of her life.

But what did it *mean*? Ash was a London buck and, for all Marianne knew, kissing governesses might be acceptable within their set. She must not read anything into it. Even though her instincts were telling her to submit to allowing herself deeper feelings for him, imploring her to tell him the truth.

For a moment she considered it. She pictured herself trying to tell him about the true nature of his acquaintance Henry.

She would not be believed. Why, no one could believe it—it seemed impossible even to her!

Then, imagining his reaction when he found out she had been lying to him, she shook her head. No, she could not risk trusting him. Too much was at stake. She must be on her guard.

Ash jumped down from the carriage, his valet following. Pausing to scan the outside of the house, he was pleased to see a new neatness to the place. If he had thought about it he would have remarked upon the gleaming windows, new roof tiles and the paring back of the previously overgrown bushes that lined the beds below the ground-floor windows. Not being used to noticing such details, he was nevertheless impressed by the sense of care that the house now gave.

The impression was reinforced when he stepped into the hall. Two lines of servants waited to greet him—Mr Cronin on one side, with the new footman, and the female servants on the other, headed by Mrs Bailey. He went through the ritual of greetings and introductions, nodding his head genially to each of them. Once done, he made for the library, calling on Cronin to accompany him and requesting tea.

Inside him, impatience was building. Where was Miss Bolton? Why had she not been there to greet him? And where were Fanny and Cecily?

'Where are the ladies, Cronin?' he asked bluntly.

'Lady Kingswood and Lady Cecily are resting, my lord, as they usually do at this time. We had not expected you so soon today. Miss Bolton, if I am not mistaken, is in the side garden, negotiating with some particularly stubborn rose bushes.' He paused. 'It is good to have her back—Miss Bolton, I mean. She brings a vivacity that affects the whole household.'

Ash's eyebrows rose. It was unusual for Cronin to make such personal remarks. 'Why is she working in the garden?' He had visions of Lady Kingswood forcing Miss Bolton into manual labour on a whim.

'She chooses to do it, my lord. She says she finds it invigorating.'

Ash rose. 'The side garden, you say?'

Cronin affirmed it, and Ash stalked out.

This, he had to see.

'Oh, you horrible, loathsome, odious creature!' Marianne addressed the recalcitrant rose bush, which was resisting all attempts to tie it up. The blustery weather was not helping, as each time she tried to stake a few branches the wind would whisk them away again.

'And I was hoping for a welcome!' said a deep voice behind her.

Marianne straightened and whipped round, to see Ash standing there, his eyes twinkling with mischief. He looked so tall, and so handsome and so *real* that her foolish heart immediately began beating a loud tattoo.

'Well, you *are* odious, my lord!' she replied tartly, enjoying the brief flash of surprise in his eyes. 'Creeping up on me like that! Why, you should not be here for another two hours yet.'

'I apologise if my early arrival has inconvenienced you,' he returned, and the twinkle was back.

'Hrmmph!' she replied. 'I should have preferred the opportunity to finish my gardening and then wash my face and hands before you arrived.'

'But you look charming!' he offered. 'Fighting with rose bushes has brought colour to your cheeks and a sparkle to your eyes.'

Marianne ignored this—though her heart, she knew, was storing every word.

'If you mean that I am weather-beaten and wind-torn, then I fear you are right!'

She tucked a stray strand of hair behind one ear, noticing how intently he was watching her. The colour in her cheeks deepened.

His eyes crinkled at the sides. 'Weather-beaten? Never! Why, you are so formidable I suspect the winds themselves would obey you!'

'Not *this* wind,' she retorted. 'It is much too lazy.'

'Lazy? Why, it is anything *but* lazy! It is becoming as strong as a storm. In fact, we should go indoors before branches start snapping from the trees.'

'My mother always called breezes like this "lazy." The wind is too indolent to go around us, so it simply goes straight through us.'

He laughed, then sobered. 'She had wit, your mother.'

'She did.'

Marianne swallowed hard. *Do not think of Mama!*

'I shall be happy to go inside, for I am almost done with my gardening for today. But I need to tie up this bush first.' She eyed him speculatively. 'Could you perhaps assist me?'

He paused, and she flushed.

'I apologise—I should not have asked you, my lord.'

For answer, he reached for one of the flailing branches of the rose bush, bringing it into an upright position beside one of the stakes.

'Well, come on then! Before these thorns prick me, or the wind blows me away or—worst of all—my valet sees me. I honestly do not think my reputation with him would ever recover!'

She giggled, enjoying Ash in this unexpectedly playful mood. 'Mr Loveday is extremely intimidating—I confess I am quite in awe of him.'

'I have a similar confession to make,' he replied in a theatrical whisper. 'He quite terrifies me!'

They tied up the rose bush together, then walked in companionable conversation towards the rear of the house. Marianne tried to hide her hands, which were grimy with soil, and explained that she always went in through the kitchens when she'd been gardening, so as to wash her hands before going to her room.

'That makes perfect sense,' he told her. 'But then, you are an eminently sensible woman!'

'Not always,' she returned dryly, sighing inside at his prosaic compliment. 'You would not believe how naive and innocent I am! Why, when I went to London—to Mrs Gray's register office—it was my first time doing anything for myself. I had no clue about finding places, or paying for things, or using the stage. I—'

She broke off, conscious that she had said too much. She was supposed to be playing the part of a woman who had been the daughter of a lawyer. Such a young woman would not have had maids, footmen or chaperons at all times, and she would have had to develop a certain knowledge of the world.

'Yes? Go on—I should love to hear more of your escapades.'

She shook her head. 'My parents were very protective, so I did not experience the—the freedoms that some of my friends enjoyed.'

Hopefully that was a reasonable explanation. *Lord,* she thought, *how I hate having to lie all the time!*

'But I assure you I am quite well able to educate Lady Cecily!' She looked up at him in entreaty.

He stopped walking and looked directly into her eyes, frowning. She faltered, pinned by that intense blue gaze. She waited for him to say something, but after a moment he blinked, made an innocuous comment about the wind, and walked on.

What should I make of this? she wondered. *He affects me so deeply. He is only just home and already my thoughts are disordered, my heart and stomach are in turmoil, and my senses are alive to his nearness. I cannot risk trusting him, and I am forced to keep lying to him. Oh, how I wish that things could be different!*

She sighed and fell into step beside him.

Chapter Fifteen

Ash could not recall ever feeling so confused in all his adult life. He was normally a person of habit, of ease, of fixed routine. His London lodgings were to his liking, he had jovial and benign friends, and he enjoyed predictable equanimity in all his relationships.

Yet ever since John's funeral he had felt as though he were clinging on to the back of a runaway horse. He was throwing his own money at a house and estate he had barely remembered a few months ago, he was obsessed with a governess, and—shockingly—his London life was beginning to pall.

He had enjoyed a long and fruitful conversation with Mr Moreton, and had come away with ideas about turnips, fodder, and a four-year rotation cycle rather than three. Moreton had been surprised that Ledbury's farms were not already using the system for, he'd stated, its use was now widespread, with better-fed animals and more crops from the same land.

Ash was excited—genuinely excited—to share this new knowledge with Cronin and with Miss Bolton. He vaguely remembered Cronin mentioning it before, but their first priority had been to repair the buildings and provide funds for the farmers to start hiring new labourers.

Conscious that Cronin was awaiting them in the library, he nevertheless took his time walking with Miss Bolton.

He sighed inwardly, admitting to himself that he had missed her company. Just walking beside her was creating a swirl of emotions and desires—physical need, overwhelming tenderness and something akin to bliss. It was beautifully terrifying, and he felt like a boat adrift in a storm. He had missed the opportunity to ask her about her friend—Henry Grant's sister—simply because she had looked at him in such a way that all thoughts had left his brain.

They entered the kitchen through the back door, and Miss Bolton paused to wash her hands at the large sink that stood in the outermost scullery. She was unaware of his gaze, so he took the opportunity to run his eyes over her—her hair, soft and dark, her face in profile…the smooth line of her forehead, straight little nose, lips and chin.

Her form, in the same black dress that she always wore—or were there two of them?

He resolved to try to notice the details—though women's clothing was normally of little interest to him. But everything about Miss Bolton fascinated him. Why did she sometimes tap her fingers on the table when lost in thought? How long had she been in mourning? Where was she from?

These things were of great interest to him. He could not recall ever being so interested in another human being.

The sound of Miss Bolton's handwashing water sloshing in the sink had attracted attention. The door was ajar, and suddenly an unknown serving woman, wearing the uniform of a housemaid, bounced into the room.

'Oh, Miss Marianne!' she declared. 'There you are! I'm to tell you that the master is returned early! He—'

Catching sight of Ash, she clapped a hand to her mouth, blushed profusely, and began stammering apologies.

'Think nothing of it!' he responded genially, half amused. 'For how could you have expected to discover me in this—' he indicated the room '—this fine scullery?'

As he spoke her words sank in and his brow creased. *Marianne?* Had the maid said *Mari-*

anne? But Miss Bolton's name, he knew, was Anne. He knew it because he had studied the letter from the register office to Lady Kingswood in quite obsessive detail. The name Anne had become etched in his brain ever since.

He glanced at Miss Bolton and his senses sharpened. She was pale and trembling, and looking at the maid with an expression akin to horror. Her eyes flicked to him and then, with a visible effort, she addressed the maid.

'I have told you before, Jane, to address me as Miss Bolton. Only close family and friends use my given name—which is Anne, *not* Marianne.' Her demeanour was stern—most unlike her. 'As you see, I am already aware that Lord Kingswood is home. Now, go and be about your duties!'

'Yes, Miss Bolton.' The maid bobbed a curtsey, sent one final frightened glance towards Ash, then left.

Something was not right here. With a strong feeling of dread Ash knew he had to pursue it.

He glanced around. There were a couple of crude wooden chairs in the corner. Pulling them to the centre of the room, he placed them facing each other.

'Sit down, please,' he said.

She complied. He studied her face closely. Her

gaze dropped to her hands. She was the picture of guilt.

His jaw clenched. 'What is your name?'

She lifted her head and looked at him. 'A-Anne Bolton.'

She was lying. 'Why did she call you Marianne?'

She shook her head. 'I—I know not. Perhaps she has confused me with someone else.'

He raised a sceptical eyebrow and she flinched.

'You called her Jane. Is she Mrs Bailey's daughter?'

'Yes.'

Her hands were now holding on to a fold in her dress, twisting the fabric unconsciously. He was reminded of her behaviour at the register office, when Mrs Bailey had first walked in.

'And how long have you known her?'

'I met Jane in—in the register office.' She frowned. 'No, that is to say I met her *mother* in the register office. Jane I met when they both came to Grillon's in order to travel here a few days ago.'

She cannot keep the lies straight in her mind, he thought, somewhat incredulously. *But why on earth is she lying to me?*

'She seems remarkably easy in your company.'

She opened her mouth to reply, but no words came out. She eyed him helplessly.

Confound it! he thought angrily. *She is persisting with the lies. To me!*

Rage built within him. He had trusted her, and she had been lying all this time. Dimly, he was aware that beneath his rage there was hurt. He pushed it away.

'Perhaps,' she offered diffidently, 'that is her manner. Her mother may still be educating her regarding proper behaviour.'

'Perhaps,' he agreed shortly. 'And perhaps I am the King of China!'

She flushed and bowed her head. She closed her eyes briefly, and when she opened them again it was as if she had shuttered herself away.

There was no expression in her voice as she said 'I shall pack my things immediately.'

No! His instincts cried out against this.

'You shall do no such thing! You are my employee, and I do not choose to release you. However, I demand that you tell me the truth.'

This fired a response. Her eyes flashed and she sat up straighter.

'With respect, my lord, you may be my employer, but you are not my jailer. You cannot wish to continue to employ me now, and my troubles—my tales—are my own.'

Her defiance provoked him further. *Why can she not simply tell me the truth?*

'Respect? Respect would be shown by your being truthful with me!'

'You can have nothing further to say to me, my lord.'

She rose, and automatically he stood too.

She took a breath. 'Goodbye.'

And before he could formulate anything in response she had whirled and gone.

Ash stood there, his breathing ragged and his mind disordered, for quite a number of minutes. His mind was awhirl. He had suspected before that something did not ring true about her, but he had hoped—foolishly hoped—that his mind was being overactive and imagining things that were not real.

Anger was overwhelming all other emotions. He was vaguely aware of a sense of loss—of doom, almost—but he would not look at it. How *dared* she defy him? Did she think herself his equal? She, a servant? Or almost a servant... Never had he heard or seen such bold disregard for authority!

Fuelling his own self-righteous outrage, he stalked outside and made for the stables.

'Tully!' he shouted. 'Saddle my horse!'

A gallop through the fields was in order. Either that or he risked putting his fist into a wall.

Marianne reached the refuge of her room and closed the door. Immediately she pulled down her bandboxes from the closet and began throwing her possessions into them haphazardly. There wasn't much.

To think that she had believed she had found a home here! All was lost! She had been found out and he was angry with her. She could not bear it.

Just for a second she had contemplated trying to tell him the truth. But there would have been no point. He would never have believed her. A gentleman—one of his own acquaintances, at that—importuning an innocent woman who was his stepsister? He could not—*would* not—think his friend capable of such depravity! Better that she just go. But, oh, how her heart was breaking!

Unreleased tears gathered in her eyes, hurting her throat and creating an enormous weight somewhere in her chest. She must not let them flow. Not yet. She must go. *Now!*

Her second dress was not there—of course, Jane had it. *Jane!* The poor girl would be distraught that she had caused Marianne to lose her position.

Sure enough, a few moments later Jane appeared at her door. When she saw that Marianne was packing she dissolved into floods of tears, apologising incoherently through her sobs.

Strangely, her distress helped Marianne settle some of the disorder in her own mind. She put her arms around the girl.

'Jane, Jane—listen to me! This is not your fault. He would have found out in some way anyway.'

She meant it. Ash noticed things. Perhaps it was better this way rather than living on her nerves for weeks or months. Next time she would hope for an employer with less perspicacity. If there *was* a next time.

Once Jane had gone to fetch her dress, and to ask Thomas to prepare the gig, Marianne steeled herself and went in search of Lady Kingswood and Cecily. It was safe for now, as—according to Jane—the master had galloped off on his horse with a face like thunder.

Marianne aimed to be gone before his return. The thought of seeing him again—*ever*—was terrifying. His anger had wounded her deeply, especially since she knew that underneath it there would be disdain. Once his anger cooled he would probably show her contempt, and she would not be able to bear it. His good opinion of her had been one of her most treasured possessions, and now it was lost for ever.

She found the ladies in the drawing room, just awake from their nap, and initially a little bemused at Marianne's news.

'Leaving? What do you mean, *leaving*? Have you been sent on some errand, perhaps?' Lady Kingswood's brow creased. 'I must say it is dreadfully inconvenient! When do you return?'

Marianne repeated her news, and this time it sank in.

Lady Cecily promptly burst into tears and fell upon Marianne's neck. 'Oh, Miss Bolton, please don't go! For you are quite my favourite of all my governesses!'

Gratifying as this was for Marianne, Lady Kingswood seemed unimpressed by this evidence of her daughter's affection for the governess.

'That is quite enough, Cecily! I shall remind you that it is unseemly to display such emotion—particularly towards someone who is to all intents and purposes a servant. I remember a similar carry-on when your wet nurse went away.' She turned to Marianne. 'If you write to me with your new direction I shall ask Cronin to pay you whatever wages you are due.'

This was a blow. Marianne had been hoping to be paid before she left. Tearing herself away from Cecily—and she felt as if *that* separation would tear her heart in two—she murmured a polite thank you and left.

Conscious that she must—simply *must*—get away before Ash's return, Marianne did not dare take the time to seek out Mr Cronin herself. Besides, taking her leave of the steward, for whom she had developed a sincere fondness, would cause her more sadness, and she needed to be resolute.

So she hurried back to her room and finished her packing.

Mrs Bailey arrived, but her protestations fell on deaf ears. The housekeeper believed Marianne should tell the truth, and that her employer would forgive her! Marianne knew better. Despite Ash's kindness to her, she could not expect him to judge his own friend and believe her story— which would sound wildly impossible to his ears. In addition, Mrs Bailey had not seen nor felt the force of Ash's anger.

Mrs Bailey sighed. 'But will you write to me? I will worry about you. I need to know that you are safe!'

Marianne hugged her then, saying gruffly, 'I know not where I will be next. I hope that Mrs Gray can find me another governess position. If not I shall offer to be a scullery maid, or work in a tavern.' She lifted her chin. 'Whatever it takes, I will contrive. Somehow.'

They clung to each other for a long moment. Marianne reflected that this might be the last time she would feel warmth, affection or love from anyone. Then she stepped back, donned her cloak and bonnet and picked up her bandboxes.

Both of them recognised the similarity with her previous flight, though neither commented on it.

And so it was that Marianne Grant left Ledbury House in the late afternoon, her gardening work unfinished and her heart full of pain.

Lady Cecily, Jane and Mrs Bailey waved to her as Thomas drove the gig out of the yard. Marianne lifted her hand in farewell, her eyes taking in as much detail as possible of them and of Ledbury House. Her home.

Chapter Sixteen

'Hup!' Ash urged his stallion on and they cleared the ditch with a graceful leap. The horse was clearly enjoying their dash through the country-side, revelling in the jumps and the speed.

Eventually, conscious that he did not want to harm the animal, Ash finally turned back. As Ledbury House came into view he realised he was no nearer to deciding what to do about Miss Bolton—or whatever her real name was.

Marianne.

That was clearly her true first name.

Marianne.

His lips and tongue silently formed the word, enjoying an agonised pleasure in feeling her name in his mouth. It suited her. Oh, she had tried to hide underneath the cloak of a plain Anne, but Marianne did justice to her inner beauty, her complexity and her intelligence.

His rage had subsided somewhat, enabling him

to think a little more clearly. She must have a reason. He had to trust his instincts that she was deeply uncomfortable about the deceit. Or had she simply been uncomfortable at getting caught?

He slowed his mount to a walk and directed him towards the stable yard. He would question her again, as soon as he went inside.

A sudden memory came to him—of the moment when he had spontaneously and without any clear reason told her that she could confide in him if she was troubled. That had been just after they had left the register office. She had been upset, and he had wanted to comfort her.

Of course she had been upset. With hindsight, he realised that she had been distressed not so much from hearing Mrs Bailey's tale but from seeing Mrs Bailey herself! It was obvious now.

Lord, how foolish he had been! Embarrassment and a feeling of not being in control stung him again. Confound it, his emotions were in disorder! It would not do.

He stomped his way to the front of the house and into the hall. Cronin was there to meet him, his face a mask of inscrutability. Deuce take it, he had completely forgotten about his appointment with the steward. Although the man was an employee, he deserved more courtesy than that.

'Afternoon, Cronin. I apologise for keeping you

waiting, but I decided to ride first. I hope you were informed?'

'Indeed I was.'

There was a rigidity about Cronin's demeanour that let Ash know he was unhappy.

'I am at your disposal, my lord.' He bowed stiffly.

Ignoring the implied criticism—which was, he realised, entirely justified—he continued breezily along the corridor, the steward beside him.

'Just let me change out of these clothes—and I need to speak to Miss Bolton about something. Then I will be right with you.'

Silence.

He glanced at Cronin. 'What?'

Cronin's face twisted. He seemed to be considering what to say.

Ash stopped, awareness prickling at the back of his neck. 'Tell me!'

'She's gone, my lord!' The words erupted from Cronin. 'Thomas drove her away in the gig about a half-hour ago.'

'Damn it all!' Ash felt the blood draining from his face. Her words about packing came back to him. But he had not thought she would actually go—and certainly not this quickly. 'Where has she gone?'

'We believe to Netherton. The stage comes

through in the early hours of tomorrow morning. She intends to wait at the inn until then.'

The inn at Netherton. The place where he had first seen her.

He wheeled around. 'Tell them to prepare my phaeton. I am going to get her.'

The tap room at the inn was unchanged. There was the hearth. There were the tables. There, at the bottom of the room, was the landlady. Yet so much had happened in Marianne's life since she had last been there.

Maintaining what she hoped was an air of confidence, Marianne walked to the landlady, ignoring the two farmers at a table to her right. Using some of her precious cash, she bought a ticket for the stage.

'And would you like to hire a chamber, miss? Or a private parlour, perhaps?'

This was tempting, as the alternative was to sit in the taproom for the next six hours, until the stage arrived. But her money was so scarce she could not justify it.

'No, thank you,' she said calmly. 'I shall be fine here.'

The landlady shrugged and returned to her task of cleaning the table underneath the taps.

Marianne looked around, then selected a table

against the wall. Somehow she felt a little safer with solid stone at her back. She stowed her band-boxes under the table, clasped her hands together and tried not to think. About anything.

She watched the inn's patrons come and go—mostly locals, calling in for some cool ale after their day's work. Occasionally a carriage pulled into the yard, its occupants entering the coolness of the inn looking for food, or drinks or the use of the comfort chamber.

After a while Marianne ordered a glass of milk and drank it as slowly as she could manage. Eventually though, it was empty. When she came to take it away the landlady brought two books for Marianne to read, to while away the time.

Grateful for this small act of kindness, Marianne opened the first book, pleasantly surprised to find that it was the first volume of a novel written by 'A Lady.' Perhaps it would be entertaining enough to divert her mind from her situation.

She squinted at it in the dim tavern light but could not make out the words. April sunshine was streaming in from the door to the yard, so she stepped outside to the yard and sat on the low windowsill, allowing the mild spring warmth to soothe her a little. She lowered her head and gave the book her full attention.

It worked. The first few chapters were well-written, and contained such interesting characters that she became quite engrossed. Which was why she did not notice the man standing beside her until it was too late to evade him.

Sensing him there, standing unmoving, she looked up. Shiny black boots, fashionable breeches of the finest quality, a rust-coloured waistcoat beneath a tightly fitting coat by Stultz. Her gaze continued upwards as her heart contracted with fear. He was smiling—a smile that filled her with dread.

'Well, well, well,' he said. 'Finally I have found you, sister dear.'

Chapter Seventeen

Ash drove the phaeton himself. When he brought her back—as he fully intended to do—he did not want Tully or anyone else to witness the conversation he wished to have with his runaway governess. The words were burning in his mind, ready to be unleashed.

What a trimming he was going to give her!

How could she just disappear like that—without his leave, and without even saying goodbye to him?

Already he was thinking of the questions he would ask her, just as soon as he had unburdened himself of his frustration at her foolish flight. He was determined to get the truth from her—and to discover if there was, in fact, a valid reason behind her deception.

He checked his timepiece, then encouraged his horses to go a little faster. The stage was not due for another four or five hours, and an inn was not an appropriate place for an unaccompanied lady—particularly in the evening time.

Ten minutes later he pulled into the inn yard, which was empty. He jumped down and stalked directly into the taproom. A quick glance around showed no sign of her. Thankfully it seemed she had had the sense to reserve a private parlour—or a bedchamber.

He frowned. If she had already retired he would have trouble getting to her. Hopefully she was in a parlour.

'Good evening, my lord. How may I serve you?' The landlord, wiping his hands on a towel, was approaching him.

'I am seeking a young lady who came here earlier. My servant, Thomas, brought her from Ledbury House.' Ash spoke brusquely, not wishing to reveal anything that was not strictly necessary.

The landlord looked puzzled. 'There are no young ladies here, my lord.'

'What? *What?*' Ash realised he looked and sounded foolish, but this was so unexpected that he was struggling to take it in.

The landlord looked uncomfortable. 'Leastways I am not aware of any. I was gone all afternoon—at the market, you understand—so my wife was here by herself for a time.' He gestured towards a nearby table. 'I shall go and ask her, if it pleases you. Please, be seated.'

Ash sat, still reluctant to believe the landlord. Of *course* she was here! She had to be. She knew no one in the area—as far as he knew—and Cronin had been certain that her plan was to take the stage to London. This information had been relayed to him, apparently, by Mrs Bailey. And besides, where else would she go? There was nothing for miles except a couple of hamlets and Netherton itself.

The landlord returned, looking a little sheepish. 'Apologies, my lord. My wife informs me that there was a young lady here earlier. Dressed in black and with two bandboxes.'

'That would be her, yes.'

'She left 'bout a half-hour ago, the wife says.'

'Going where?'

'I asked my wife that—for I reckoned you would want to know, my lord—but she did not know. The lady drank some milk, read a book and then left in a carriage, she thinks.'

'Did she—? Was she happy to go?' This made no sense. Why would she go with someone?

The landlord frowned. 'My wife did not see her leave, but she did not notice anything untoward, my lord—for if she had I am certain she would have told me of it.' He drew himself up, puffing out his chest a little. 'I do hope there is nothing *villainous* or *notorious* going on, for my inn is a respectable establishment, my lord, and I don't hold with no misconduct!'

Ash made haste to reassure him, suggesting that there had been a simple misunderstanding about the young lady's travel arrangements, and left the inn shortly afterwards. Driving to the edge of the village, he pulled up at the crossroads. Straight ahead was the road to London—her most likely destination.

Who was she with? She had gone willingly— that much seemed clear. Yet he had only discovered her deception a few hours before. How could she possibly have had time to contact someone? And why had she deceived him in the first place? What had her plan been? Extortion? Theft? There was nothing to suggest either option.

Reluctantly he concluded that he had no right to go after her. She was free to leave his employment if she wished, and there was absolutely nothing he could do about it. Refusing to listen to a small inner voice that encouraged him to continue his reckless pursuit, he turned the horses towards home.

What on earth was going on? He pondered this the whole way back to Ledbury House, racking his brain to try and figure out just how complex her deception had been. He came up with exactly nothing, save that he had clearly been duped by a seemingly innocent woman. Luckily he had stumbled upon her deception, and now she was gone.

Except he didn't *feel* lucky. Not in the slightest.

Henry spent the first hour of their journey congratulating himself on discovering Marianne's whereabouts and pointing out to her how clever, resourceful and determined he had been.

'I saw you, you see—that day when I had my accident. You were with Ashington.' He sneered. 'What an arrogant booby he is! Thinks himself a man of the town, but I outfoxed him!' He leaned forward. 'It's common knowledge that he paid off his last mistress in January—just around the time you left—and that he has been spending an inordinate amount of time at this country house he's just inherited. Of course, once I'd seen you and him together I knew *exactly* why he was spending so much time at his little nest in the country!'

'But, no!' Marianne protested. 'How could you even *think* such a thing?'

She was horrified at Henry's assumption—not just for her own sake but, more importantly, for Ash's.

Henry laughed. 'His friends actually believe he

has developed a passion for farming!' He shook his head. 'Completely ridiculous. His passions are much more carnal than they realise.'

Unaccountably, Marianne was reminded of that kiss in Ash's carriage—a kiss characterised by carnal passion. She flushed.

Seeing her reaction, Henry made a disgusted sound. 'You rejected *my* advances but you must have gone to *his* bed within a week of leaving home. What did he offer you, eh? I see no fancy gowns or jewellery. You have devalued yourself, my dear sister.'

He flicked a casual finger down her cheek, and she flinched.

'Oh, fear not,' he muttered testily, 'I will no longer be pursuing you. I would not take *his* leavings—not for all the gold in England. Your only attraction was your innocence, and now that is gone. Besides, I have other plans for you.'

Marianne could hardly breathe. If she protested that she was still innocent—that his assumptions about her connection to Ash were wrong—would he attack her again? Though it did not sit well with her, she realised that for now it was safer to allow him to keep believing that she had been Ash's mistress.

'It was an easy matter,' Henry continued, 'for me to discover the name and general direction of his country house. When I got as far as Netherton I went into the inn to ask for further directions—and there you were!' His eyes narrowed. 'But tell me, sister, why were you at the inn? And with your bandboxes? Has he tired of you so soon?'

He looked at her expectantly.

Marianne swallowed. 'He—we had a disagreement and I left. I was planning to take the stage to London.'

She was so tired of lying. At least this was—more or less—the truth. Her voice had caught a little as she'd remembered the 'disagreement'—the look of baffled disappointment on Ash's face as he'd realised she had been lying to him.

Henry sniggered. 'I see that you are wounded by him. Poor Marianne! Did you think yourself in love with him?'

In love? With *Ash*?

Henry's words reverberated inside Marianne's head.

In love with Ash.

Her breath stopped in her throat.

In love with Ash.

Of course she wasn't! That was quite impossible. Why, she had never been in love with anyone!

In truth, he was the best person she had ever met—apart from Mama and Papa. The kindest, smartest, most attractive… Sometimes grumpy, sometimes completely infuriating, but always dear to her. She valued his friendship. She saw his good qualities. But she couldn't possibly be *in love* with him!

Henry, with the benefit of their long acquaintance, read her expression precisely. He threw back his head and laughed, his hilarity ringing cruelly in her ears.

Her hands balled into fists. *Oh, if I were a man,* she thought, *I would box your nose, right now!*

'Oh, Marianne—you always were a soft fool. He has seduced you and tired of you and you have given him your heart. What a sad, sad tale.' He leaned forward, speaking in a theatrically lowered tone. 'You have a lot to learn, my dear. Keeping the attention of a man like Ashington, renowned as a connoisseur of women—' his tone was scathing '—requires a great deal of skill in the bedchamber. If you truly aspire to be a courtesan I can send you to people who can train you better.'

Before she had even thought about how to respond to this she found that she had already done so.

The slap of her hand on his face shocked them both. Her fingers, palm and wrist throbbed and stung—she had hit him with her open hand.

For a second there was silence, as they both

realised what she had done. Then his expression turned ugly and he hit her back. Hard.

Her head was knocked backwards and sideways by the force of the blow, and blackness briefly threatened to overcome her. She slumped into the corner of the coach and tried to focus on his face, which was strangely blurred.

He was leaning forward over her, his fist raised as if he was preparing to hit her again. 'There! How do *you* like it? Have you not realised yet that you are entirely in my power? That as your guardian I can have you sent to Bedlam or locked in the attic and no one can stop me?'

His tone was menacing, his face purple with rage, and Marianne knew real fear. Her body was shaking uncontrollably, her ears were ringing and the entire left side of her head was a blur of pain. She could taste blood in her mouth, too.

Lord! she thought. *Is he going to murder me?*

To her intense relief he seemed to check himself, lowered his fist and sat back in his seat. His face was set in the sulky expression that she knew well. He would refuse to speak to her now for a time.

Her fear was not limited to the chance of more physical harm at his hands. It was also because, legally, what he had said was right. She was entirely in his power. Oh, *why* had Papa appointed him her guardian? Such foolish faith in his son! But then, none of them had understood Henry's true nature. And now, because of Papa's will, she had no choice but to obey Henry.

Fear, combined with her existing upset at leaving Ledbury House, had left her temporarily vulnerable at the inn. Oh, she had tried to resist him, had called out for help, but no one had heard her and no one had come. Besides, by law he had dominion over her. Even if someone from the tavern *had* tried to intervene he would have simply told them that she was his runaway sister and she would not have had the strength to deny it.

Within less than a minute he had wrestled her into his closed coach, her bandboxes flung casually into the back, and she had been trapped. The coachman and groom were unknown to her, and they had carefully averted their eyes as Henry had put her inside, then climbed in behind her.

And so here she was, travelling to an unknown destination, all that glorious freedom removed from her. As a child she had accepted her parents' authority—of course she had—but having had a taste of independence as Miss Bolton she had found that she quite liked it.

The insecurity had been frightening, and worries about being found out had haunted her, but she had loved the feeling of *purpose* she had known as Miss Bolton. She had felt useful, and had known that she was valued by Lady Cecily, by Mr Cronin, perhaps even by Ash.

Now it was all gone. She was back to where she'd started, desperately needing to protect herself from Henry. Only this time he was angry with her. *So* angry.

Her left ear was still burning and her head was throbbing, but the dizziness had passed. She blinked hard to prevent her tears from flowing. She refused to show Henry weakness! The independent, confident Miss Bolton might have disappeared today, but part of her lived on in Marianne.

Looking out of the window, as the sky began to don its sunset cloak of glorious red and orange and deep pink, she tried to make a plan—any plan. But her thoughts were all disordered and her mind in turmoil. In her mind's eye she pictured Ash, walking beside her from the garden to the back door. That was the last moment when all had been well—before he had found her out, before she had run away. Before Henry had found her.

Leaving Ledbury House had been difficult enough. But it was the severing of her connection to Ash that hurt most deeply. She had lost her home, her friends, all sense of belonging. She was truly alone.

* * *

'Ash? Is that you?'

Fanny's voice was querulous, high-pitched, demanding. The door to the drawing room was ajar, and Fanny now appeared in the doorway, peering out at him.

Ash sighed, but kept walking down the hallway. 'Not now, Fanny.' The last thing he needed was Fanny in a fit of temper or histrionics.

'But I have questions and I demand answers! Why is Miss Bolton gone? And where have you been?'

Ahead, Cronin and Mrs Bailey appeared at the end of the hallway. They had clearly been awaiting his return. Ash nodded to them to indicate he wished to speak to them.

'Miss Bolton has left—as she is free to do.'

His tone was flat and emotionless. *Good.* The last thing he needed was for his own emotions to break through his mask of unconcern.

'And I have been out on my own business.'

He opened the door to the library and stepped inside. 'Cronin, Mrs Bailey—I wish to speak to you about some matters of business, if you can spare some time.'

'Of course, Lord Kingswood.'

'Yes, Lord Kingswood.'

They both spoke at the same time, exchanged

a glance, then followed him into the library and closed the door.

Ash sat in the winged leather armchair beside the fireplace and casually examined the cuffs of his jacket. 'Cronin,' he said nonchalantly, 'tell me what you know of Miss Bolton.'

The steward nodded grimly. 'I know little of her background, or what she did before she came here. But I know a lot about *her*.'

'Go on.' Ash steepled his fingers together and adopted an air of mild interest.

Inside, he remained all disorder. Why had she gone? What was her real name? Why had she lied to him? Who was she with now? Was she a practised deceiver, manipulating him for some nefarious purpose? Or a wronged and vulnerable young woman? *Was she safe?*

This last thought threatened to overpower him as the very thought of Miss Bolton in danger played havoc with his stomach and his gut. Perhaps hearing Mrs Bailey's and Cronin's perspective would assist him in deciphering the puzzle that was Miss Bolton. Certainly he had come to trust Cronin's judgement during his time at Ledbury House.

Cronin took a breath. 'I know her to be kind and clever and accomplished. I know her wit and her serious nature. I know how she became an important part of this household, how interested she was in the improvements you were making. I believe her to be honest and upright and—and a *good* person.'

Ash simply stared at him blankly. This, he had not expected. Hearing her virtues listed filled him with a sense of loss and confusion, and of abject woe—all at the same time. Never could he remember being so close to losing command of himself.

Carefully, deliberately, he pressed his fingertips together, watching them turn white until he had himself under control again.

Then he looked back at Cronin. 'And if you discovered that Miss Bolton was not who she said she was? What then?'

Cronin did not flinch. 'Then I would imagine there to be very good reasons for it. Whatever those reasons are, I believe at heart she did not practise her deceit in order to harm us in any way.'

Ash nodded to indicate that he had heard Cronin. The steward's acceptance of Miss Bolton's innocence was understandable, since he wished to believe the same himself. But she had not been close to Cronin in the same way she had been to him. While Cronin and the governess had enjoyed a cordial friendship, Ash's own relationship with Anne—with *Marianne*—was much more complicated.

He turned his attention to the housekeeper. 'Mrs Bailey?

'Yes, my lord?'

Her face was white and he noticed her hands were trembling. He decided to go straight for the knockout blow.

'Is Bailey your real name?'

This appeared to surprise her. 'Oh, yes! My name was Mary Higgins until I married Ned Bailey, nigh on twenty-six years ago, and we had our Jane a year after the wedding. Ned died when she was nine and I have never remarried.'

'And what is Miss Bolton's real name?'

He barked the words out and Mrs Bailey's face crumpled.

'Oh, my lord, I can't tell you,' she said, 'not even if you see fit to dismiss me! I can't! I simply can't!'

Cronin shifted slightly and Ash saw that he was looking at Mrs Bailey with compassion.

Ash was torn. He was desperate to find out more about the elusive Marianne. Bolton was clearly not her surname, so in his mind he refused to use it further. Yet he could see that Mrs Bailey was genuinely distressed.

'Is there *anything* you can tell me?' he asked, admitting defeat.

'Yes. I can tell you that all the things Mr Cronin said about her are true. She is a good girl, Lord Kingswood, and I'm sure she felt bad not being able to be truthful with you.' Mrs Bailey's expression was filled with entreaty. 'She did have good reason. I can tell you that.'

Not being able to be truthful with you.

Mrs Bailey's words stayed with him long after she and Cronin had left. That was the nub of it. No one disagreed with the fact that she had lied. What he wanted to know was *why* she had lied.

Then there was this notion that she had good reason. As far as he knew people generally changed their names to hide from criminal behaviour in their past. Had she committed a crime? A crime so serious that she felt she'd needed a new start?

No references from the registry, and yet Marianne was a good teacher, highly proficient. Her manners and accomplishments proclaimed her a lady—or gentry, at least. He frowned, remembering her tale. She had said her father was a lawyer. Could it be true…? Was it, perhaps, her *father* who had committed some crime, staining his daughter's reputation? Embezzlement, perhaps?

Lord! His imagination was running riot. He was, he realised, creating reasons in his mind—reasons that would allow him to forgive her. Yet the anger remained, and with it a strong sense of betrayal. If she had needed assistance why had she not simply told him the truth? If she'd had good reason he would have accepted it.

Yet he acknowledged that she might not have known that. Anger had been his foremost reaction on discovering her lies—and he had dealt with it by galloping over ditches and through fields and returned with a thousand questions. If only she had not left so quickly! He was sure he would have had the forbearance to listen to the truth from her, and to decide for himself whether her reasons were good.

The fact that he had been denied the opportunity was frustrating. She had not trusted him enough. The realisation pierced him.

Stop this! he told himself. *She is a governess who was working in your household. She has resigned. Now she is gone. That is all.*

If only that were true.

Marianne awoke with a start. The carriage had stopped its slow swaying and there were noises outside. She opened her eyes and gently touched the side of her head. There was a lump there from

Henry's blow, and she still felt a little sick and dizzy. She could see that it was almost fully dark, and they seemed to have arrived at their destination.

The coachman opened the door and let down the step, and Henry exited the carriage.

'Welcome to my London townhouse, sister,' he said. When she did not move, he added, 'Well, come on then!'

Marianne stood stiffly and followed him out. They were in a well-to-do street, with elegant houses of various sizes and designs on both sides of the road. They had stopped outside a narrow, newish-looking three-storey house, and as Marianne looked at it, the front door opened. Two servants came out and wordlessly took Marianne's luggage and a trunk that presumably belonged to Henry.

Although unsure exactly where in London she was, or what was happening, Marianne wondered if this might be a chance to escape. She glanced furtively around. Perhaps now, while Henry was distracted—

'Do not even *attempt* to leave again, Marianne.'

He was right next to her, speaking quietly in her ear.

'Next time I will not be so kind.'

Kind? *Kind?* Her head was still throbbing with

pain—she had been half aware of it even as she had dozed in the carriage. If this was Henry being kind, then she dreaded to think what he intended when he wished to be *unkind*.

Slowly, she went up the steps and into the house.

The door closed behind her.

The bedchamber was perfectly comfortable, Marianne had to admit. The furniture was of good quality, the hangings were fresh and the whole was pleasing on the eye. But, *oh!* She would have given anything to be back in her sparse, plain governess's room in Ledbury House. There she had a place, and friendships, and the chance of seeing Ash, of speaking to him, of experiencing the thrill of being in his company. Here she was incarcerated in a well-decorated prison.

And a prison it was.

Standing in the hallway, Henry had given her clear instructions in front of the servants—a deliberate humiliation. She was to remain in the house at all times, though she could take the air in the garden to the rear of the house if she wished.

He had hired this house and all the staff in it. None were known to her, and all, he'd said, had been instructed to carry out his wishes. The servants all knew that he was her legal guardian, and that she had run away before. They had been instructed to ensure that she did not do so again.

A housemaid had brought her to this room, helped her undress, and tended to her head with soothing cold cloths, ointment—and silence. She was an older lady, with a grim face and stiff demeanour, and Marianne had found her quite alarming. Finally, she'd left, and Marianne had mechanically prepared for bed.

Now, lying in bed in the darkness, Marianne considered how her world had changed in a day. So suddenly and so completely. Last night she had lain in her narrow bed at home, anticipating Ash's return. Tonight she was under Henry's control, and would likely never see Ash again.

It was too much.

Finally, hopelessly, she let the tears fall.

Chapter Eighteen

'You are quiet tonight, Ash.'

Fanny's words penetrated Ash's reverie. She had been speaking incessantly this evening. A stream of noisy nothingness had accompanied dinner, and now that Ash had joined Fanny and Cecily in the drawing room the torture had been renewed.

Why can she not just be silent for once?

He shook his head at his own lack of charity. Fanny was John's widow and should be respected. Yet he needed time, and solitude, for thoughts of Marianne were plaguing him.

What if she was in trouble? Mrs Bailey's words had impressed him, and he needed to believe that she had had good reason for not confiding in him. Now, though, his mind was filled with conjecture about Marianne's abrupt departure from the inn. He had not mentioned to anyone that Marianne had gone away with a man. For a start, he did not wish to make it any more obvious that he was taking a particular interest in the governess, and also he was not clear himself what to think or feel.

Confiding in Fanny was out of the question, and to share his worries with the servants would be inappropriate. For the first time he bemoaned the lack of true friendship in his life. Oh, he had dozens of friends, to be sure, but none close enough to confide in. Since John's marriage to Fanny had created awkwardness and coolness between them he had never again allowed any friend close enough to betray him.

How strange it was that now, with the benefit of nearly fourteen years' experience, and the trial of having to endure Fanny's company on a regular basis, he realised that his youthful infatuation—though strongly felt at the time—had in reality been a narrow escape. He and Fanny would have irritated each other no end, and the thought of being leg-shackled to her for life made him shudder. John had been much more phlegmatic and placid in character, and had probably made a better job of tolerating Fanny's annoying habits.

'Ash?' Fanny was persistent.

'Apologies. I was a hundred miles away. What did you say?'

She looked a little miffed, but straightened, giving him a winsome smile.

'Just that I love our cosy evenings together—just you, me and Cecily.' She leaned forward to pat his arm, and her hand lingered for a moment. 'I know I was not particularly welcoming at first, but I did not then know how amiable you are.'

'Amiable? Me? You have mistaken me for someone else, I fear.'

She laughed as if he had made a great joke. 'Oh, Ash, your sense of humour is as dear to me as ever it was.'

He raised a cynical eyebrow. 'Is there something in particular that you wish to say to me, Fanny?'

She frowned crossly. 'Oh, you are the most provoking creature! Cannot I speak my heart to you without there being something particular behind it?'

He let this pass, although he was itching to point out that he had apparently gone from 'amiable' to 'provoking' in less than half a minute.

'However, now you come to mention it, I do intend to take dear Cecily back to London again next week, once our half-mourning begins. Our new dresses will be ready by then, and I confess I am looking forward to being out a little. No public events or balls, of course, but I wish to widen Cecily's acquaintance in readiness for her Season in a few years. And I suppose I shall have to hire yet another governess. Why do the wretched women never stay? Why, this last one was only with us for two months! Another ungrateful wretch!'

'Mama!' gasped Cecily, greatly daring. 'We do not know why Miss Bolton had to leave so suddenly, but I am certain it was important. She was quite my favourite.'

Fanny sniffed. 'That's as may be, but it is not *she* who will have all the bother of securing yet another governess. Did Miss Bolton even *think* about the impact on me? Did she? No, she did not! Such selfishness!'

Cecily subsided, clearly deciding not to argue the point further.

And why should she? thought Ash. *Miss Bolton will still be gone, no matter what we all have to say about it.*

Fanny smiled at him again. 'I should hope to borrow your carriage again, Ash, if you will permit?'

So that is it! he thought.

Fanny frowned in concentration. 'And I must speak to the lawyer about getting more money from my funds.'

Ash's forehead creased. 'Go easy on the spending, Fanny. John left you a tidy amount, but you will need to practise economies.'

'Now you sound just like John. He was forever telling me what I could not have.' She pursed her lips. 'I admit it has been surprising to learn just how much it costs to have the little luxuries of life. Why, did you know that one of the milliners charged me half a guinea for that straw bonnet—the one with the ostrich feathers? I was never so shocked when I received the bill. I did not even *like* it!'

'Well, if you did not like it, why on earth did you buy it?' Ash was rapidly losing patience.

She pouted. 'Perhaps I need to find another husband—one with fortune enough to allow me to live as I ought.' She eyed him speculatively.

'I think that a very good idea, Fanny—though if you expect *me* to introduce you to eligible gentlemen you quite mistake the matter.'

The last thing he needed was to take on the role of matchmaker for Fanny—although without someone to make her practise economies she would likely find herself in dun territory in two years.

Someone as pretty as Fanny would, of course, never end in debtor's prison. She would marry some unsuspecting fool long before. Ash pitied her as yet unknown future husband. She would remain demanding, verbose, and entirely oblivious to her own selfish nature. But if a man were looking for an expensive, empty-headed, beautiful companion, she would serve perfectly well.

His tastes were otherwise.

She sniffed. 'That is not what I meant at all!'

Tired of the subject, Ash turned to Cecily, who had also been unusually quiet this evening. 'How do you, Cecily?'

'I am well, thank you,' she responded dutifully, but he saw how her shoulders drooped, and how she struggled to summon a smile.

He felt a pang of sympathy. She, too, was missing Marianne. 'I am sure your mama will find another governess whom you will admire just as much as your previous one.'

She looked up at him and he saw tears welling in her eyes. 'I do hope so.'

She did not believe it. Nor did he.

Abruptly he rose, and bowed to them both. 'If you will excuse me, I shall retire early tonight. I have a slight headache, and I have much to do in the morning.'

They replied with polite 'Goodnights,' but the last thing he saw as he turned to leave was Cecily's sympathetic expression. They both knew what ailed him, and it was not a headache.

* * *

Marianne had not slept well. She had tossed and turned for an age, desperately trying to quiet her mind, which persisted in showing her images of the day's events: Ash's angry, disappointed face; Henry standing in front of her in the inn yard at Netherton; Henry again, with his fist raised.

And, as if that was not sufficient to prevent her from having any rest, her mind also created a series of plays and stories which were *not* true and had *not* happened, yet which seemed as real as if they were happening in that instant. Chief among these was one in which she tried to escape this house and was inevitably caught, and another in which Ash berated her remorselessly for being false to him.

The dawn had already broken by the time Marianne at last fell into an exhausted doze, and soon she woke suddenly as the same housemaid from last night entered her room, opened the curtains wide, and informed her that breakfast would be served in twenty minutes.

Marianne's body went instantly from exhausted sleep to full, fearful alertness.

'Where is my brother?' she asked, unable to prevent a slight tremor in her voice.

'The master does not rise before noon,' was the

response. 'However, he has instructed that you are to follow a set pattern while you are here.'

While you are here. What did that mean? She remembered that yesterday Henry had said he had plans for her. She shuddered to think of what wicked scheme he had in mind.

She rose, and washed, and allowed the disagreeable housemaid to help her into her second-best black dress. She descended to the middle floor and endured a solitary breakfast in a room that would otherwise have been quite pleasant. The food tasted like sawdust to her, but she knew she must eat, so forced herself to have tea and porridge.

Afterwards, knowing that Henry was still asleep on the top floor somewhere, she decided to explore the middle and ground-floor rooms—it was a small act of rebellion, but she was determined to find small ways in which she could exercise a measure of control over her world.

The house contained a pleasant collection of drawing rooms, parlours, a dining room, a library and even a modest ballroom. If she had been here as a house guest she would have found it delightful. It was surely the most comfortable jail in England.

All the while she was conscious of the staff. There was a footman on duty by the front door at all times, it seemed. This was not particularly un-usual, but when she tested the situation by walk-ing dangerously close to the door the footman rose and blocked her way.

'Sorry, miss,' he said grimly, and it was clear that he was determined to follow his master's orders.

A little shaken, Marianne retreated, but it did not deter her. Somehow she would find a way to get out!

The garden was surprisingly large, with a pleasant walkway bordered by shrubs and a few young trees here and there. There was no gate, and it was surrounded by high walls. No escape this way.

As she neared the bottom of the garden she sur-prised an elderly gardener, who was diligently digging out a bed for planting.

'Oh, sorry, miss, I did not see you there!'

He eyed her warily. She saw his jaw drop as he took in the bruising on her face. His gaze slid away.

She lifted her chin. 'I am Miss Grant.' How strange it was to be able to say her real name again. *But, oh, how I loved being Miss Bolton!* 'What is your name?'

He scrambled to his feet and removed his cap. 'Ben Forshaw, miss. At your service.'

Marianne indicated the bedding plants, sitting in a neat row of pots. 'What are these? I have never seen them before.'

'Them's called lobelia, miss. They'll add some nice colour here and here.' He indicated the places where he intended to plant them.

'May I help?'

Suddenly Marianne knew that to do some gardening would help her cope with her imprisonment.

Ben assented—well, what else could he do?—and soon Marianne was kneeling at the edge of the path, her hands gloriously soiled. The sun gently warmed her back, the smell of rich earth filled her nostrils, and briefly she almost forgot her troubles. Had it been only yesterday that she had been tending to her garden at Ledbury House and waiting for Ash's return?

All too soon the task was done, and Marianne had to go back inside. She looked at the stairs down to the servants' quarters, wishing she had the confidence to go to the kitchens to wash her grimy hands, but she dared not. The house servants seemed universally hostile. At least the gardener, Ben, had been civil to her—a small kindness that had made her day more bearable.

Giving up on the idea of going to the servants' quarters, she climbed all the way up to her room on the top floor and washed her hands and face carefully there. She then moved the chair to the window and sat, hands folded in her lap, watching all of London, it seemed, go by.

She saw servants going about their business, families pass by, perhaps on their way to the park, and a young couple laughing together in the sunshine. Silent tears streamed down her face. Her heart was breaking, she was a prisoner in a gilded cage, and she had absolutely no idea what was to become of her.

She waited.

An hour passed, then another. She half dozed in the chair, her head nodding, then jerking upright. Finally, soon after the small clock on her mantel had struck two, she was summoned.

'Miss Grant.' It was the disagreeable housemaid. 'The master would like to see you in the library.'

The maid waited, clearly expecting Marianne to accompany her immediately.

'I shall be downstairs directly.'

The maid's lips tightened, but she did not argue.

When she had gone Marianne took a few deep breaths and checked her appearance in the mirror. Her hair was neatly contained in its pins, her dress was reasonably clean and tidy—and the lump on the side of her head made her look as though she had been involved in a prize fight.

She peered at her reflection, gingerly touching the soft swelling above her left ear. It distorted her face, somehow, made her look strange. It hurt still—*really* hurt—and she was glad that her parents were not here to see what Henry truly was... what he had done to her. Ironic, since he was only able to have such power over her because they were gone.

Actually, that was not quite right. It was *Papa's* death that was key. If Mama had not also died in the same carriage accident Henry might have allowed her to live with Mama and not bothered her. Papa's will—from what Marianne understood—gave Marianne no choice whatsoever. Papa had made Henry her guardian in all circumstances.

Marianne did not know the detail of Papa's will, as she had collapsed before the lawyer had read to the end. Not for the first time Marianne wished she had been more alert in those early days after her parents' death.

She descended the staircase slowly, her heart pounding and her palms damp. *'Ash...'* she murmured to herself, and immediately felt a little better. Even the thought of him, the shape of his name in her mouth, gave her strength.

She entered the room without knocking.

Henry was seated behind the writing desk, a cluster of papers in front of him. When she entered he shoved them all into the desk drawer on the right-hand side and closed it firmly. He then took a small silver key out of his pocket and locked the desk drawer. Looking up at her finally, he visibly recoiled at her appearance.

'For goodness' sake, Marianne, you look a mess! Did that maid not treat your head last night? That lump is disgusting!'

She would not accept this. 'If I look a mess, it is because you hit me! Or have you forgotten so soon?'

'I only retaliated after *you* hit *me*!'

There it was, the sulky tone. She remembered it of old.

'You must learn not to provoke me,' he said.

The injustice of this was immediately apparent to her, but before she could respond, he spoke again.

'You have caused no end of trouble by running away as you did.'

'And what would you have had me do? Stay at home for you to—to—' She would not complete the sentence.

He laughed. 'Your months as Lord Kingswood's trollop have made you no less a prude, I see! Yes, you *should* have stayed at home and allowed me into your bed. You achieved nothing by running away, apart from making life difficult for me.'

Oh, but I did, she thought. *I learned that I am strong, and capable, and resourceful. I travelled on the stage by myself and conquered my fear of London. I won a position in a genteel household. I was a good governess, and I learned about farming and estate management. I looked after myself without a maid, and I met some wonderful people.*

Aloud, she said, 'How did it make your life difficult? I thought you would not care that I was gone.'

'In truth,' he said, 'I did not, at first. But then ill-natured people began to spread foul stories about me. They questioned my character and my good name.'

Marianne was confused. 'Why? How did our—our quarrel affect your reputation?'

'Some of my—I hesitate to call them *friends*… Two or three of the men I had invited that weekend turned out to be false friends. Naturally I have cut them off—I am no longer willing to give them the benefit of my company. They actually accused me of cheating at cards, and of not paying debts they said I owed them! Absolute nonsense, of course.'

Biting back a sceptical retort which might, if uttered, earn her a second blow to the head, Marianne decided to keep him on track. 'But what has that got to do with me?'

'As part of the lies they are circulating about me, they suggested that I was ill-treating you by keeping you in the country. Which, of course, is a total falsehood!'

Marianne was conscious of a feeling of bewilderment. Had he no self-awareness? No sense of irony? Here she was, standing in his presence with a swelling to her head and a broken lip which he had inflicted, and he was maintaining that he did not ill-treat her!

This time, she could not help but emit a small bark of cynical laughter.

He had the grace to flush. 'Yes, well, you know that I have never raised a hand to you before— not since we were children, I mean. And we both know that what happened yesterday was *your* fault.'

Marianne was barely listening. She now understood why he had needed her to return—and that she had more power here than she had realised. 'So what is it that you require from me?' She wanted him to admit it.

'Not much,' he said, though he was avoiding her gaze. 'I will take you about a little...introduce you to people. Perhaps hold a dinner party here. That will silence the naysayers.' He glanced at her head. 'Not yet, though.'

'I should think not!' she retorted. 'There is something else, though. Something you are not telling me. What is it?'

'Nothing—nothing at all,' he responded as his gaze slid away.

He was clearly lying, but at this moment she had no way of getting the rest of the truth from him. Still, at least she knew what he wanted. And could use it to negotiate with him.

'I shall need new clothes,' she said. 'We are out of mourning and it would not be appropriate to have your stepsister going about in two well-worn black dresses.'

He eyed her dress with disfavour. 'Agreed,' he said. 'You do me no credit, looking like that. But if you think that visiting dressmakers will give you the chance to run away again you can forget the notion. You will be accompanied everywhere by your personal maid and by my most loyal foot-man. They will be acting on my direct orders to watch you at all times.'

Dash it! That had been exactly what she was planning.

He smiled cruelly. 'Your thoughts are so evident, Marianne! Now, go and *do* something. I have things to attend to.' He put the silver key back in the drawer. 'Go!'

She went.

Chapter Nineteen

One week later

'Such a pleasure to meet you, Miss Grant.'

As he spoke, the man's gaze swept over Marianne insolently, lingering on her bosom. She withdrew her hand from his and nodded coolly. She would not lie by pretending the pleasure was in any way mutual.

'Grant!' he bellowed, without removing his gaze from Marianne. 'I take it back. You *do* have a sister, and a comely one at that.'

It was Henry's dinner party, and Marianne was acting as hostess. She had put it off as long as she could but had finally run out of excuses. Her new wardrobe had arrived—Henry had been surprisingly generous, and she had been able to order a range of beautiful dresses, petticoats, shoes and hats, as well as spencers, pelisses and a new cloak.

Bluntly, he had reminded her that the only reason he was spending money on what he called 'fripperies' was because he wanted society to understand that he was looking after her well.

As per his orders, the servants had ensured that she was closely watched each time she left the house for a dress-fitting, and she had had no opportunity to slip away into the bustling London crowds. Her head had now healed completely—she had tested earlier for any trace of the painful swelling, but it was gone. Inside, though, the scars would take much longer to heal.

While she no longer believed herself to be in immediate physical danger from Henry, she despaired at times, wondering what his plan was for her after she had sufficiently repaired his reputation. At best, she would be banished to their old home in the country. At worst, he would retain her as his hostess, and her own reputation—and her innocence—would gradually be lost through exposure to Henry's rakehell friends.

Like this one.

The man raised his quizzing glass to one eye which, as Marianne looked at it, became magnified to a monstrous degree. 'A fine-looking girl, indeed, Grant. Doesn't look much like you, though!'

He guffawed at his own joke, while Henry looked put out.

'Henry is my stepbrother,' Marianne said firmly. 'My own father died, and my mother's second marriage was to Henry's father.'

It was strange to remember that dear Papa had not actually been her natural father, so caring had he been towards her—his wife's child from her previous marriage.

'Oh, that explains it.' Henry's friend chuckled. 'Might have guessed you weren't related by blood. Fine-looking girl,' he repeated.

'Yes, well...' said Henry distractedly. 'Shall we go through for dinner?'

Thankfully, Henry's lecherous friend was seated midway down the table, so Marianne was not forced to engage with him during what felt like the longest dinner she had ever experienced. She was, naturally, at the foot of the table, and divided her conversation between the two young gentlemen on either side of her—one of whom was more interested in the food than in conversation, and the other whose focus, seemingly, was in seeing how much wine he could imbibe without seeming rude. He had two glasses in the time that others drank one, and kept nodding at the footman to refill his glass each time he drained it.

Marianne, needing her wits about her, was taking impossibly small sips from her own glass.

She glanced down the table. Beyond the young

men were two widowed ladies, neither of whom seemed to be as refined as Marianne would have liked. In addition there were a number of men and women whom she had never met before, but who did not look like the sort of people she would wish to become better acquainted with.

She ate her food and engaged in just enough conversation for politeness. And so it was that she was easily able to hear the conversation between one of the widows and the man beside her when, to her shock, the name Kingswood was mentioned.

'Yes, recently widowed and on the catch for the *new* Lord Kingswood, they say. She had the Fourth Earl, and now she will have the Fifth!'

The man murmured something in response, and the widow tittered in delight.

'Indeed! And just when we had all quite given up on the notion of the new Lord Kingswood ever marrying! The Earldom needs an heir, no doubt. They say she was his childhood sweetheart, you know… No—no date as yet, but Lady Kingswood has been dropping the broadest hints. She is still in mourning for her husband, so they will likely wait a few months. Though why she would wish to give up her widow's weeds, I know not. I find it perfectly agreeable to be a widow!'

Marianne remained frozen, her fork gripped

tightly in her hand. Ash was to marry Lady Kingswood? *It could not be true!*

She could almost hear the crack as her heart split open. As if it was not enough that she had had to leave him. That he felt anger and disdain towards her. That she had never been able to tell him her true name.

Despair and impotent frustration washed over her. He would marry and she would never again enjoy his company, nor see his smile, nor feel that leap of her heart when she saw him.

It was not impossible that it was true, she realised. She had seen Ash fall in love—not particularly with Fanny, but with Ledbury House. He was truly engaged in the life there, as she had been, and she believed he had developed a lasting interest in the estate.

Fanny was mistress of Ledbury House, Ash was Cecily's guardian—and the deceased Lord Kingswood had been Ash's friend as well as his cousin. It made sense from a certain point of view. It might even, she speculated, have been John's intention when he'd written his will the way he had, giving Ash responsibility for Cecily. Perhaps Ash felt it was his duty to marry Cecily's mother. Perhaps he wished to be the girl's stepfather.

Like Marianne, Ash had come to enjoy life

there, she thought—or was her own anguish at leaving Ledbury House leading her to make assumptions?

The Earl had a perfectly cordial relationship with Lady Kingswood, but honestly Marianne could not say that she had seen any spark of passion between them. In fact she had often had to intervene to prevent them from irritating each other. The news that Fanny and Ash had been sweethearts before her marriage was surprising, but it meant that there was a long history and an understanding between them.

The thought of Lady Kingswood and Ash married was hugely disturbing. It could not be good for the happiness of either party.

His relationship with Cecily was more affectionate—more like his warm interactions with Marianne herself had been. Her heart squeezed in pain. Her deceit had destroyed that warmth. It was painful to think he was out there somewhere, angry with her and planning to marry Fanny.

There was a lump at the back of her throat, begging to be released as sobs, but Marianne held firm. She ate and drank nothing more, barely spoke, and spent the next hour in a daze.

Somehow she survived the dinner, and the increasingly raucous antics in the drawing room afterwards. The guests had begun to pair up, and she firmly discouraged both the lecher and the drunken sot before quietly announcing—though no one was listening—that she was retiring.

She fled upstairs to the sanctuary of her chamber, placed a chair against the door handle to dissuade any night-time invaders, and cried herself to sleep.

'A great success!' Despite the heavy eyes and pained expression that told of the after-effects of too much wine, Henry was pleased with himself. 'They thought you cold and standoffish, but none of them could say that you were being ill-treated.'

Cold and standoffish? To be fair, that was not an unreasonable reflection of her manner towards Henry's friends. She held them in disdain, and had not been afraid to show it a little.

Henry rubbed his hands together. 'Now for the next part. I shall accompany you to Lady Annesley's ball on Friday night. You will smile. I shall bring you ratafia and help you find dance partners. It is expected to be a crush—all of the *ton* is clamouring for an invitation. That should put paid to any remaining rumours.' His expression grew sly, and then he added with a casual air, 'Oh! The lawyer has some papers he wishes you to sign. Nothing important—just matters related to the estate.'

Marianne was conscious that the hairs on the back of her neck were suddenly standing to attention. What was he up to?

With an equally casual air, she replied, 'Of course! But what shall I wear to the ball?'

Her diversion worked in the way she had intended. He laughed.

'I might have guessed that would be your first thought! You ladies have little in your heads beyond fashion.'

Resisting the urge to challenge him on this—for Marianne's mind was working furiously, trying to consider what these 'unimportant' papers might be—she said, 'Well, you can hardly hope to present me in a half-dress and have people believe that I am not ill-treated! And, it being only five days until the ball, it may be difficult to get a gown made in time.'

He chuckled. 'I see your game! You hope to squeeze more money out of me for an expensive gown! Very well—but know that this will be your last evening out for quite some time.'

She frowned. 'What do you mean?'

'I *mean*, sister dear, that you will be living in the country until I can arrange a marriage for you. I have been considering which of my friends should have the burden of your care. I invited all the likely ones last night, but only two are showing an interest in pursuing you. I am quite torn between Eldon and Hawkins. Both are well-juiced, but I may be able to squeeze Eldon a little easier than Hawkins.'

Marianne felt sudden rage boiling within her. 'Do I not choose my own husband? And Hawkins? The drunken sot from last night? Why, I would not marry him for all the gold in England!'

'Ah, but his family *own* much of that gold. And, no, you will not choose your own husband. My father's will gives me that right. *My* father,' he repeated, 'not yours. He was never yours.'

'So this is about money? You will sell me to the highest bidder?' Marianne could barely contain herself. 'What happened to all the money you inherited?'

He smiled again—he was clearly enjoying her outrage. 'Ah, well, I found it was not quite enough to keep me in the lifestyle which I prefer to have.'

'You mean, I suppose, that you have squandered it at the card tables and the horse racing?'

He was unperturbed. 'Not only there, my dear. There is also the cock-pit and the bawdy house.'

She gasped. 'How dare you speak of such things to me? Papa would be ashamed of you!'

Without warning, he hit her in the stomach. She doubled over in pain and discovered that she could not take a breath. Her chest muscles seemed frozen, and she struggled in agonised panic as her lungs screamed for air. She sank to her knees.

He stepped closer and leaned over her in an intimidating fashion. '*Never* speak of him to me again!'

He pointed his finger at her to emphasise his point. She cowered, sure he was about to hit her again.

'Do you understand me?'

Terrified, and still winded, she nodded.

Thankfully he stepped back. 'You may have bruising, but it will not show. If you defy me you will be punished—but in such a way that it cannot be seen by anyone else. Now, get up! You offend me.'

Oh, how she wanted to defy him! She wanted to hit him back. She wanted to spit in his face and tell him what she thought of him. But she had also to survive. So she scrambled to her feet, her breath coming in long, strained, noisy inhalations—as if her throat were almost closed. She stood there, conscious that her whole body was trembling and wishing he could not see her fear.

'Now, understand this,' he snarled. 'You will do what I say without question. You will retire to

Papa's house immediately after the ball. While you are there you will speak to no one and see no one, apart from the new servants I have hired. You will marry whomever I choose. And, most importantly of all, you will tell no one false stories about my treatment of you. Oh, I see that you believe yourself to be ill-used... Believe me, you are very well-treated in comparison to many women. So I expect you to be grateful.'

Grateful? She could scarcely believe what she was hearing. But she knew that to oppose him directly would bring her more pain. *Just get through this,* she told herself. *Get out of the room and you will not be hit again.*

She had to think. Surely there was something she could do to escape this nightmare? She tried, but her mind simply would not function. Stupidly, sluggishly, it refused to provide any answers. It was as though all rationality had left her. All that was left was terror.

'Now, go to your room and stay there for the rest of today. It makes me sick to look at the ugliness of your person.'

The contempt in his voice and in his facial expression almost proved her undoing, but she refused to submit completely. She straightened her spine and looked into his eyes. His gaze dropped.

Wordlessly, she turned and left the room, still

shaking, her eyes blinded by the tears that were ready to flow. But as she slowly climbed the stairs, and the horror began to subside a little, she made a vow to herself.

I promise, she said in her head, *that I shall escape from you, Henry. Somehow I will. And I shall always remember that I was loved. Mama and Papa loved me. I promise never to let you take that away from me. I was loved. I am Marianne. I shall survive this.*

Chapter Twenty

'Are you going to Lady Annesley's ball tomorrow night, Ash?'

Barny is a good soul, thought Ash, *but his eternal cheerfulness can be wearing.*

'I have not yet decided, Barny. I told her that I would try to attend, but matters of business might take me away from London tomorrow.'

'Oh, but surely there is nothing so pressing that it cannot wait for one more day?'

Ash sighed. 'I suppose not.'

In truth, he had no energy or joy for anything these days. Since Marianne's departure he had been wavering between worrying about her, desperately trying to think of ways to find her, and absolute rage at her for deceiving him, then running away. He still did not know whether to think of her as the victim of some unknown misfortune or a practised deceiver.

Ledbury House without her was unbearable,

and yet he had to persist with the work there. Cronin, Mrs Bailey and Cecily never mentioned Marianne, yet her absence was an unspoken bond between them. Fanny, of course, did not mention her either, but only because she did not give a fig for Marianne or anyone else.

Thankfully Fanny was spending more time in London, and Ash rarely saw her. Although mourning limited her from attending large or public events, she was still busy visiting drawing rooms and tea rooms, and from what he could make out she was still spending much more money than she could afford.

She insisted on dining with him every few days, and he did so for Cecily's sake. The girl was more subdued than ever, and clearly missing Marianne. As was he. She had, it seemed, quite without him noticing it, become a part of him. Now that she was gone he felt as an amputee must—ever-conscious of the absence, of someone or something that should be there but was gone.

'Here we are!'

Barny's words brought him back to the present. He had somewhat reluctantly agreed to accompany his friend to a coffee house in New Bridge Street in Blackfriars which was, Barny assured him, all the rage. As they stepped down from the carriage he caught a fleeting glimpse of a lady climbing into another carriage nearby, followed by a footman and a maid. He glimpsed a flash of dark curls peeping out from beneath a fetching straw bonnet, and there was something about the way the lady moved—simply the *shape* of her— that made him stop dead in his tracks.

Marianne!

Without thought, he ran towards the carriage just as it pulled away. There was a crest on the door, he noted. To his great frustration, the street being fairly clear, the carriage moved ahead, and before long he had to give up his pursuit.

He stood at the side of the road, pondering what he had seen, until Barny huffed up to him.

'What on earth are you at, Ash? Running up the middle of a London street—have you taken leave of your senses?'

'Do you know, Barny, I believe I have. But tell me—who owns that coach? Did you see the crest? It was not one I recognise.'

'Of course I saw it—and I know *exactly* whose coach it is. It belongs to Henry Grant.'

Marianne put her cloak and bonnet in her chamber and left the room, intending to go to the library and read. During these past two weeks it had become quite a habit with her to read there in the middle of the day.

Thankfully Henry had gone off with his friends for the day. He was promised to a cock-fight in Richmond and a card party tonight. He would not return until the early hours of tomorrow—the day of the ball.

It was such a relief to know he would be gone all day and all night. Her steps felt a little lighter, and even the continuing presence of her jailers did not daunt her.

Henry had overslept this morning, and his valet had been helping him into his jacket even as they had descended the stairs. Yet still he had taken the time to remind her that the servants would remain vigilant.

'They have been told,' he'd said, 'that you are only to leave to see the dressmaker, and you are to be accompanied at all times when you are out of this house.'

She had already taken the measure of the servants. Apart from the disagreeable housemaid, her other chief jailer was a sullen footman named Trout. It suited him. Both Trout and the housemaid were to accompany her on all the trips to the dressmakers and milliners. The rest of the servants kept out of the way, and while they were no longer actively hostile, they made no attempt to help her either.

As she descended towards the middle floor her

eye was caught by a metallic glint on one of the stairs. She bent down and picked up a small silver key. It looked familiar.

A moment later her heart began pounding furiously as the realisation came to her. Henry's desk key! She had once tried the drawer where he kept his papers, but it had of course been locked. As far as she knew he kept the key with him at all times. And now it was resting in her hand.

She closed her fingers over it and continued downstairs. Such a tiny object, and yet it might give her access to some clue about the mystery of Henry's furtive behaviour. What *were* the papers stuffed into the locked drawer?

He had never been interested in business while growing up. Papa had continually tried to get him involved in meetings with the steward, or the lawyer, or the banker, but Henry had had no time for it. Of course Henry was now responsible for his own business affairs, so the drawer might simply contain legitimate dull papers.

They might, but Marianne's instincts told her otherwise.

'Miss Grant!'

A deep voice sounded sharply behind her, making her jump in fright. She turned and schooled her features into calmness as Trout approached.

'I am to inform you that the master has invited two guests for dinner tomorrow evening before the ball—Mr Hawkins and Mr Eldon. He left instructions that you are to confer with Cook about the menus, and to ensure that all is made ready for his friends.' His eyes narrowed. 'Is something amiss?'

Lord! Her fear of getting caught with Henry's key must be showing on her face. Not for the first time she wished her thoughts were a little less transparent.

'Nothing save the fact that you frightened me half out of my wits, addressing me like that!'

His jaw hardened, but he did not argue. He, too, maintained the pretence that he was a footman, not a prison guard, so his insolence was somewhat contained. Under normal circumstances he would have been given his marching orders for speaking so to his master's stepsister.

She pursed her lips, every inch the serene lady of quality. 'Please tell Cook to meet me in the green parlour at four o'clock with a suggested menu.'

She inclined her head graciously, indicating that the conversation was at an end, then turned and walked smoothly to the library.

Eldon and Hawkins—the two suitors Henry

had identified as wealthy targets he could squeeze for cash if one of them became Marianne's husband!

She half expected Trout to challenge her again, but he let her walk on. She felt his gaze boring into her back and it took every ounce of her strength to keep walking, head held high, until she was safely inside the library.

Closing the door, she leaned against it, her body sagging in relief.

Chapter Twenty-One

So it is true! thought Ash. He and Barny had enjoyed an almost silent dish of coffee, and they were now back in Ash's carriage. After leaving Barny at his lodgings Ash intended to go for a long walk in the Green Park, to try and return his mind to sanity.

She had deceived them all and was obviously a high-class courtesan. After a short time pretending to be an innocent—a *governess*, for goodness' sake!—Marianne had shown her true colours.

Henry Grant had seen instantly what she was. Ash's own instincts had been dulled, he now realised, by his immediate and compelling attraction towards 'Miss Bolton.' Besides, she had introduced herself as a governess and, while he had realised there was something not quite right about her, he had had no idea of the scale of her deceit.

Grant had seen her in his company and made

an incorrect assumption about their relationship, but he had been entirely accurate in realising that Marianne was a lightskirt.

Either that or he had known her already, and had been seeking an opportunity to continue a previous liaison or pursuit. It was also still entirely possible that Marianne, as Grant had said, did know Grant's sister. Barny had told him that Grant's sister never came to London. With Grant having installed a mistress in the capital, Ash now knew exactly why the sister would never be allowed to venture into Grant's world.

Grant had been open in his pursuit of Marianne—going so far as to blatantly try to steal her from Ash, whom Grant had assumed was her current protector.

And in a sense I was, Ash mused. *As Cecily's guardian, I paid her wage. I paid for her keep in return for her services. Just not in the usual way.*

Whatever quirk of fancy had inspired her to try her hand at being a governess, it had not lasted long. The minute she had been unmasked she had vanished, gone on to find a new victim. Henry Grant.

The fact that he already intensely disliked Henry Grant should have made it easier to take. Instead it was harder. The thought of Grant bedding his Marianne had fired a rage inside him that was begging for release. Seeing her willingly climb into Grant's carriage—arrayed in fine new clothes, if he was not mistaken—had put to rest any lingering doubts he had had about her true vocation.

He was not ashamed to admit that along with the sense of betrayal and hurt there was a sense of relief. Stupidly, he had actually thought himself to be in love with her! He had even, he admitted to himself, considered making her his wife! He, who had vowed long ago never to let any woman into his heart after the disaster of his mooning calf love for Fanny all those years ago, had actually thought that he quite adored Miss Bolton.

But Miss Bolton did not exist.

Or did she?

His tortured mind wavered between condemning her and wanting nothing more than to be with her again. It was easier to find refuge in anger than to handle the vulnerability of love.

Thankfully, he told himself, the notion that he loved her was now passing. The revelation that she was not the innocent miss he had thought her, that she had knowingly and deliberately deceived him about everything—not just her name and her past, but her very nature—had put an end to any deeper feelings.

Though his determination to bed her remained,

the warmer feelings had vanished under a hail of anger—mainly anger at himself, for his own stupidity. She had made a fool of him, and he did not like it.

And yet part of him desperately wanted a different truth. He wanted to find that she was true, and innocent, and that there was some reasonable explanation for her departure with Henry Grant. How could he uncover the truth? For he *must* know.

'Barny,' he said casually, 'where does Henry Grant play cards?'

Marianne fitted the small silver key into the lock. Her hand was trembling, and it took two or three tries before it went in properly. Her breath sounded loud in her ears as she strained to listen for the sound of footsteps in the hallway. She was terrified that someone would enter the library and catch her prying.

She turned the key and it gave with an audible click.

Now to see what Henry was hiding!

She slid the drawer open. It was stuffed full of papers—some heavy parchments, some small scraps with scribbled words on them. Cautiously, she began sifting through them. There were so many!

Stopping to think for a moment, she rose and swiftly walked to one of the bookshelves. Selecting a book at random—Ovid's *Metamorphoses*—she set it on the desk, open as if she were reading. There! That might help if someone was to walk in.

The small bracket clock on the oak side table struck two, making her heart jump.

Keep a cool head! she told herself. *This is your chance to learn something that might help you escape!*

The first paper she picked up seemed insignificant—a bill from Henry's tailor for a new coat. The next two were also bills—these from a dressmaker, Mrs James, and she recognised the description of some of the clothes she had ordered.

Her heart sank. These were ordinary, everyday documents. There was nothing special or secret or controversial about them. Was there to be nothing of significance among them? But then why would he lock the drawer?

Staying with her task, she persisted. The next two were vowels—IOUs to other young men. Gambling debts, she assumed. After that a bill for the rent on the townhouse, dating back four months.

Before long, a pattern emerged. Every document related to money owed. There were scores of unpaid bills and IOUs, some going back many months. There was no way that he could afford to pay all of them. Papa and Mama had lived comfortably, but never with this sort of extravagance.

Henry was in serious, pressing debt.

The extent of his debts—that was what he was trying to conceal from her. And that was clearly why he wanted to marry her off—so that he could lean on his future brother-in-law for funds. He had talked of trying to work out which of his friends he would find easier to squeeze—this was what he had been thinking of. She was to be sold to fund his future. And tomorrow night's dinner with Hawkins and Eldon was part of his plan.

'We shall see about that!' she muttered to herself.

She rummaged through the rest of the drawer, checking that the remaining papers all looked similar to those she had already studied. At the bottom of the drawer was something different— a flat vellum wrapper, tied with leather cords. Carefully, holding her tongue between her teeth, she slid it out. Resting it on her lap, behind the cover of the desk, she opened it.

It contained three documents. The first was the Last Will and Testament of George Grant. *Papa's will!*

She gasped. Although tempted to read it in detail immediately, she first looked at the other two documents. One was a letter, asking about the whereabouts of the daughter of Charles Bolton.

This was entirely unexpected. Charles Bolton was a part of who she was, yet someone she had never known. He had died of scarlet fever when she was a baby, and Mama had married George Grant two years later. Although she had been raised as Marianne Grant, she was also, in truth, Marianne Bolton. That was why she had chosen the name. It had made her lies a little easier to bear.

She frowned. Before succumbing to the temptation of reading Papa's will, there was one final document.

Her heart froze as she glanced through the parchment. It was a legal draft, beginning, *I, Marianne Agatha Bolton Grant, being of sound mind...* It went on to award Henry George Grant all her goods and possessions as 'a gift'. There was space at the bottom of the second page for Marianne to sign.

She almost laughed. The only items of value that she owned were Mama's jewels. Henry had clearly discovered that she had taken them with her the night she had run away. Of course he would wish to have them. He would no doubt sell them instantly and waste the proceeds on his debts and his hedonistic lifestyle.

Suddenly everything was clear. Henry's scheme was to coerce her into signing Mama's jewels over to him before he married her off to a soft-willed husband who could be 'squeezed' in future. Her own opinions and wishes, and any sense of morality, were as nothing compared to his need to see himself on a better financial footing.

Strangely, having seen the mountain of debt contained within this one drawer, Marianne could almost feel sorry for him. *Almost.* But not enough to be a willing victim in his schemes.

Setting aside the unsigned parchment, she began to read the will.

Ash was filled with a new sense of purpose. Gone was the sadness, loss and lethargy of the past week. Everything had been transformed, and at last there was something for him to do. He knew where she was and he would see her again!

Having got Grant's direction from Barny, he was now on his way to the man's townhouse. He desperately hoped that Miss Bolton was not living there—that Grant had simply offered to take her to London via a chivalrous impulse.

He snorted. From what he had heard of Grant that was highly unlikely.

More plans were being formed in his head as his carriage moved swiftly through the streets. Oh, but it was good to be doing something! He could not shake the notion that she was in need of rescue, yet part of him was terrified that she was Grant's willing paramour, and would laugh at him for his foolishness.

Tully pulled the horses up and jumped down. 'This is the address, my lord.'

'Thank you, Tully. Now, tell that urchin that I have a task for him.' He indicated a young errand boy who was just then crossing the street.

'Yes, my lord!'

A few moments later the boy, following Ash's orders exactly, mounted the steps to Grant's house and banged the knocker. The door opened, there was a pause, and then the boy turned on his heel and returned to the carriage.

'My lord,' he said breathlessly, 'I did just as you said. I told the footman that the flowers were for Miss Bolton, from an admirer. The footman said there was no one there by that name, so I said the flowers were for the young lady as lived there. And he took them.'

Ash tossed him a coin. 'Thank you. I do like a person smart enough to follow precise instructions.'

The boy grinned, bit the coin to check its authenticity, then sauntered off, whistling.

Ash stayed a moment longer, looking at the house. He frowned. He still did not know for sure if she was there. There could be another young lady— But, no. If there *was* a young lady living there it had to be Marianne.

She was there—inside that house. He just knew it.

Of course he was no nearer to knowing if she was Grant's willing mistress or his captive. Even so, she would have retrieved the flowers and would be wondering who her admirer was.

He smiled to himself at the thought, conscious of a strange joy that she was not lost to him for ever. How he hoped she was well!

He tapped the roof of the carriage with his cane. 'Let's go, Tully!'

Now for the card party.

Engrossed as she was in the documents, Marianne was nevertheless still keeping her ears open for any sound from the hallway. And so it was that when the young footman who was on duty that afternoon knocked on the library door she was able to offer a near instant invitation for him to enter.

When he came in, he would see Miss Grant

seated comfortably behind the desk, reading a book. Nothing untoward at all.

'Miss—Cook says to let you know it's after four and do you still want to meet her?'

He looked a little awkward, as he always did when he spoke to her. She often wondered if he was a little uncomfortable about Henry's treatment of her.

'Lord, is it that time already?' Marianne glanced at the clock. 'Please tell Cook I shall come directly.'

'Yes, miss.'

He withdrew, and Marianne quickly opened the drawer again, checking that the folder of documents was in the right place, and that everything looked more or less the way it had when Henry had last locked it. She locked the drawer, returned the book to its shelf, and stepped out into the hallway.

As she did so the footman was just opening the front door. Marianne heard a child's voice. She could not quite make out the words, but as she got closer she saw that a young boy was standing outside, a posy of flowers in his hand.

'There's no Miss Bolton living here,' the footman replied, sounding genuinely confused.

Marianne froze.

'Then I'm told to give them to the young lady as lives here,' said the boy confidently.

'I see,' said the footman, and accepted the flowers.

The boy turned and left, and the footman closed the door.

Marianne started walking again. 'Who was that?'

The footman turned towards her, a frown creasing his brow. 'An errand boy,' he said, holding out the flowers. 'He says these are from an admirer.'

An admirer? Someone who knew the name Miss Bolton. Her heart leapt. Could it possibly be *Ash*? Immediately she discounted the idea. Why should Ash send her flowers? For a start, he had no idea where she was. Secondly, and more importantly, he despised her. And thirdly he was going to marry Lady Kingswood.

Could they be from Mrs Bailey? With a hidden message, perhaps?

Automatically she took the flowers, then ran lightly upstairs. There was a small ornamental vase in her room, so she filled it with water from her washing jug and arranged the flowers.

Though she searched carefully, there was no message. The flowers were beautiful, though. Whoever her 'admirer' was, and whether there had been some mistake or not, at least she now had some beautiful flowers to brighten up her well-decorated prison chamber.

And someone out there was trying to make contact with her. A feeling of warmth spread through her ches and tears pricked her eyes. Perhaps she was not quite as alone as she had feared.

On the way back downstairs, she carefully placed the silver key on one of the stairs—over to one side so that it would not be noticed, but obvious enough that when Henry realised it was gone and sent his valet to look for it the man would find it with no difficulty.

Breathing a sigh of relief, she continued down to the parlour and her meeting with Cook.

The hour was late. Ash dimly recalled hearing a clock strike three, but that had been some time ago, and there were now telltale shards of light knifing through at the edges of the heavy velvet curtains. One by one, the other players had given up, collecting their winnings or accepting their losses, until now, at dawn, only two remained.

Ash did not so much as glance at the pile of coins and vowels in front of him. Nor did he allude to the fact that Henry Grant, having won and lost substantial amounts during the course of the night, had now surrendered all his winnings and was on a persistent losing streak.

Their play was being observed by a small but dedicated group of onlookers, including the club's host—there to record the debts and ensure fair play.

'Damn it to hell!' Grant threw down his cards as another round went in favour of Ash. 'What devilment are you using against me?'

There were gasps among the onlookers. Was Grant accusing Ash of cheating?

'Steady on, Grant!' muttered one of his friends. 'He's winning fair and square and we all know it!'

Grant flushed and ran a finger under his neckcloth, as if finding it too tight. 'I'm only saying my damned luck has to change some time!'

His friend disagreed. 'Maybe call it a night, Grant, old chap. When the luck isn't with you, it isn't with you.'

'When I wish for your opinion, Hyle, I shall ask for it!' he snapped. 'Play on!'

Ash remained unperturbed. 'If you insist.'

It had little to do with luck, he knew. Grant had lost his ability to play cleverly, and desperation was causing him to make reckless choices in his play.

On they played. Occasionally Grant would win a hand, but over time the pile of scrawled IOUs he passed across to Ash increased. In the end Ash, calculating that he had done enough, gave a theatrical yawn and announced that he was done.

Grant paled. 'Might I speak with you privately...?'

Immediately the onlookers began shuffling away, or pointedly began conversations. As everyone was aware, Grant's request was code for a discussion about his gambling debts and when they might be paid.

'Of course—but not now.' Ash stood and stretched out his back. 'If you will furnish me with your direction I shall call on you later today, if that is convenient?'

Grant wrote down the address of the townhouse—the house where at this very moment Marianne slept. Ash pocketed it with satisfaction. Tomorrow—later today—he would see her again. And he meant to find out once and for all what was going on.

Was she the innocent victim of a lecherous young man, forced to accept her lot? Or had she all along been deceiving Ash as to her true nature?

Chapter Twenty-Two

April the twentieth, the day of the ball, began with rain. No doubt Lady Annesley was cursing the bad fortune that had seen almost two weeks of dry weather lost to persistent drizzle interspersed with more determined showers. Nevertheless, most of the *ton*—England's high society—looked forward to what would surely be the most glittering event of the season.

Marianne had spent the day in relative calm, intending to begin her preparations in the afternoon. She had tried very hard not to think too much about her situation, and avoided thoughts of Ash completely, since even the thought of him sent pangs of anguish through her.

Marianne's sense of loss—akin to the grief she had experienced when Mama and Papa had died—was at the absence of his regard for her. His friendship.

Just a short time ago she had had everything—

her home in Ledbury House, her friendships with the staff, her time with Cecily. And Ash.

Should she have told him the truth? She had continued to agonise over that question and had come to the conclusion that she had made a huge mistake in not being honest with him. Even if he had reacted badly her situation could not possibly be any worse than it was currently. And perhaps—maybe—he might even have believed her.

She set down the book that had been lying idle in her lap and pulled the bell in the library. 'Please ask Cook to attend me here,' she directed the footman who responded. 'And send a maid to my room afterwards. I shall begin to dress for the evening shortly.'

'Very good, miss.'

As he exited the library Marianne distinctly heard the front doorbell. Since deliveries, of course, all went to the servants' entrance, this could only mean that one of Henry's friends was calling.

Marianne's heart sank. The last thing she needed was to encounter one of Henry's lecherous friends—especially with the ordeal of the ball ahead. She opened the library door to listen, and sure enough she heard male voices. Too late to dash upstairs!

'If you would be so good as to wait in this parlour, I shall inform the master of your arrival.'

Hopefully she would not be asked to entertain Henry's guest until he came downstairs. Henry had not yet arisen, and the servants had informed her that it had been after dawn when he had arrived home. If he was the worse for having been drunk the night before he would not appreciate being awoken from his stupor earlier than he'd intended. He would probably take some time to appear.

Marianne hoped his friend did not mind kicking his heels in the parlour for a half-hour while Henry rose, shaved and dressed.

In fact it was a little over twenty minutes later when Henry descended the staircase and entered the parlour. Marianne knew this because the housekeeper arrived to join her and Cook in the library at much the same time. They had been discussing the dishes for tonight's dinner, and now the housekeeper begged to know how many bedrooms to make up.

'None, I should think,' Marianne responded. 'We are attending Lady Annesley's ball afterwards, so I do not expect any overnight guests.'

The two servants had a fairly lengthy debate about the deployment of housemaids—apparently not one but two scullery maids were ill—and

Cook did a masterful job of negotiating for one of them to assist her in the kitchen for the day.

Finally, to Marianne's relief, they finished their discussion and left. Keen to avoid seeing Henry before she had to—particularly if he was the worse for wear—Marianne moved quickly through the hall towards the main staircase.

Her timing, naturally, could not have been worse. The parlour door was just opening and Henry's guest was emerging.

'I shall see you tonight, at Lady Annesley's ball,' the man was saying in farewell.

He closed the door behind him as he stepped into the hall. Marianne stood frozen, unable to move or think. *She knew that voice!*

Ash haunted her. Not just in her dreams, but in any idle waking moment. Thoughts of him were by turns distressing, then comforting. She had thought never to hear his voice again, never see his face. Now he was here—not more than three yards away.

Her eyes devoured the shape of him—his tall, strong figure, the familiar dark hair curling over his collar…

He must not see her!

She stayed there, stock-still. Perhaps he would not look this way. Hopefully he would continue to the entrance hall. He had no reason to look back.

Somehow she could not think what to do. She watched, transfixed, with a sense of hopeless inevitability as he stopped abruptly, then slowly turned to face her.

'Well, well,' he said, stony-faced. 'Miss Anne Bolton. The quiet, sensible governess.'

She could not breathe. 'Ash! My lord!'

'Good day, Miss Bolton. What a surprise to see you here!' His tone was mild, uninterested, and yet his eyes burned with unexpressed emotion. 'Or, should I say Marianne?'

His use of her first name was shocking. Insulting. Yet hearing it on his lips made Marianne's heart cry. How she had longed to hear him say her true name! But not like this. Not when she could see anger in his expression.

His eyes narrowed. 'I have been discussing you with Grant.'

What? What was this?

'I am pleased to say our discussions went well. I have an engagement tonight, but tomorrow I shall come here to talk to you.'

'Dicussions about me? What do you mean?' Her voice was little more than a croak. Then it dawned on her. Her heart leaped in hope. 'Do you mean that you wish to—to marry me?'

'Lord, no!' he said harshly. He stepped towards her. 'After what Grant has just told me that is now impossible. Though if you had kept up your pretence a little longer you might have won that particular prize.' His arm snaked around her waist. 'Kiss me!' he ordered.

It was wrong. It was all wrong. Though she had dreamed of seeing him again, dreamed of kissing him, she had never imagined anything like this.

It was Ash—and her heart and her body were responding to his mesmerising presence—and yet, her mind insisted, it was *not* Ash. She loved him for his integrity as much as his other attributes, and she could not cope with him like this. And what was he saying? Did he believe her to be a *lightskirt*?

He leaned in and claimed his kiss. Despite this being exactly what she had wanted, Marianne froze. *Not like this!* She stood firm, keeping her eyes open and her lips pressed tight shut. In a blur, she could see his face, topped with his dark hair. She could feel his arms around her, her body pressed tightly to his chest. His scent—delicious, masculine and seductive—drew her in.

Oh, how she wanted to submit! The feeling of being wrapped in his warm embrace was so tempting—and not just to her body. It offered warmth, contact, a connection in her cold, loveless world. And the sensation of his lips on hers was stirring her body, urging her to respond.

He moved his mouth to her cheek, trailing featherlight kisses along her cheekbone. Her eyelashes fluttered down, her eyes almost closing. She could feel herself softening. She needed him so much!

But not like this.

Summoning all her strength, she raised her arms and pushed against his chest. She twisted her head to one side. 'I do not wish for you to kiss me! Is this who you really are, then—a man who importunes unwilling maidens?'

It worked. His head jerked up. He stared at her angrily for a moment, and then his face twisted with what looked strangely like anguish.

'You are no maiden, madam. Henry Grant has confirmed it. You are living in his house as his mistress. That in itself gives the lie to your protestations.'

She gasped, but he ignored it.

'As I said, I shall return tomorrow to speak to you,' he said grimly. 'Be ready.'

Turning on his heel, he strode towards the entrance hallway.

He was gone before Marianne had even the time to protest.

Oh, why did I not speak? she thought. *I should have shouted out. No! Henry lied!*

But it had happened too quickly. There had only been a few heartbeats between Ash telling her of Henry's lies and his departure.

She sagged, putting one hand on the wall to steady herself. Was this an actual nightmare? Her senses were almost overwhelmed. Desire, anxiety, hopelessness… Her breathing came in short gasps as she placed her other hand on the wall. Her knees felt soft, as if they would not support her weight. Her mouth was dry, her heart was pounding, and she felt as though she could not think, or act, or even *be*.

How long she stood there she did not know. Thankfully no servant came by to witness her distressed state. Her happiness had vanished the day her parents had died, but she had worked hard and been brave in order to create a new life for herself—a life that had included friendship and regard and support.

Now she had nothing. Only a prison created by her guardian. Threats of beating. No control over important decisions.

And now this. Ash had believed Henry's lies. Why? Why had he not questioned Henry's assertions?

It is my own fault, she realised. *He knows me for a liar.*

Ash's insulting behaviour was the final indignity. She craved his kisses, but needed his regard. Kisses were not enough. Because she loved him. She loved him and he did not—*could* not—ever love her back. He had made no attempt to veil his outrage at her deceit. It slayed her.

It is not fair!

She had refrained from wallowing in self-pity as best she could, but her sense of injustice at this moment was overwhelming. She had only ever tried to be good, to do the right thing, to obey the rules she had been taught as a child. She had never knowingly harmed anyone, never cynically manipulated anyone. She had only resorted to deception in dire need.

And doing so had led to this—a broken heart, humiliation and powerlessness. In truth, she had never before experienced a feeling like this. She felt worthless, empty, as if she did not even exist. *Should* not exist.

To love and be loved. Was there anything more important? If there was, she did not know of it. In all this world there was no one who loved her. And in all this world those she had loved were gone.

Mama—gone. Papa—gone.

Friends from home—long gone in her mind.

Mrs Bailey. Jane. Mr Cronin. Cecily. All lost to her.

Ash—lost.

To see him again so unexpectedly, and to have him treat her with such disdain, was almost too much to bear.

Almost.

Somehow she found a reservoir of strength inside her. She closed her eyes, summoning it, uncaring if there were any servants watching, and took a few deep breaths. Then, straightening her spine, she walked slowly but steadily towards the parlour. She would survive this. She had to.

And one thing was certain—she needed to know more about what had just passed between Ash and Henry. Ash would return tomorrow, giving her a chance to tell him the truth. If there was to be any hope of regaining his regard, she had to continue.

'I am brave, Mama,' she whispered. 'See?'

Henry was pouring himself a drink when she entered the room. He glanced at her, groaned and threw the whole measure of brandy into his throat.

'What do *you* want?' He poured himself another.

'I want to know why Lord Kingswood was here and what you have discussed with him.' Her voice was quiet, calm. She heard it with a curious sense of detachment.

'It is none of your business, sister dear.'

'It is my business if it affects me,' she persisted.

'Lord, what did he say to you?' He frowned.

Her heart skipped a beat at the memory. 'He—he insulted me!'

A cruel smile flashed briefly on Henry's face. 'If you mean that he kissed you, then I know not why you are complaining. It is not, after all, the first time he has done so.'

She flushed, unable to deny it. 'That is not the point. I did not wish to be kissed!'

Henry shrugged. This clearly meant nothing to him. *What a guardian I have!*

She drew a breath. 'He said that he had been discussing me with you and that he would return tomorrow.'

This hit a mark. Henry's gaze slid away, and his response confirmed Marianne's worst fears.

'What did you say to him?'

'My father placed you under my guardianship,' he returned sullenly. 'It is for me to decide what is best for you. The law allows and society supports.'

'What is *best* for me? Do I not have a part to play in deciding what is best for me?'

'No!' he bit out. 'Only *I* have oversight of the

entire situation—the fact that you ran away, that you were his mistress, our financial circumstances—'

'*Your* financial circumstances, you mean!'

His eyes narrowed and he marched towards her. 'What are you suggesting?'

She flinched—she could not help it. Her palms were suddenly sticky, and fear pooled coldly in her belly. *If he discovers I have been prying—*

'I know what you yourself have told me, and I have the evidence of my own eyes,' she replied shakily. 'You have admitted that you are living beyond your means.'

'And where do you think that dress came from?' he snarled, pointing to it. '*My* money has paid for it, and you are *my* property just as much as that dress or this brandy!' His voice dipped menacingly. 'And, as my property, I shall dispose of you in whatever way I see fit!'

The sudden rage was upon him again, terrifying her. She had to think!

His money worries might be behind the temper. Change the focus—move away from the money! she told herself. She needed information, and ideally she wished to get it without physical injury.

'What have you told Lord Kingswood?'

He smiled. 'Actually, all I did was confirm his assumptions about you.'

She frowned in confusion. 'What assumptions?'

Henry moved back to the window and poured himself another drink. 'Oh, he believes I will succumb to his demands—all over a few gaming debts. But I am playing a deeper game than he knows.'

His gaze became unfocused as he thought through his plan.

'I need either Hawkins or Eldon to come up to scratch, and then one of my new brothers-in-law will, of course, be forced to settle my debts in order to avoid shaming themselves. They both favour you, and I would rather deal with *them* than with the arrogant Lord Kingswood.'

Focused once again, he added, 'I admit that is the part I find strange, for I cannot see the attraction, myself. Kingswood, too? What magic are you working on these men?'

She snorted. 'Nonsense! Hawkins thinks more of his wine than he does of me, and Eldon is nothing but a lecherous rake!'

'And Lord Kingswood?'

Her lips tightened in sudden pain. 'He is motivated by anger, nothing more.'

'He is certainly angry with *you*, that is for sure. He has no idea that you are my sister—'

'Stepsister!'

'That you are my *stepsister*, and he asked if you are my mistress.'

'And did you not tell him the truth?'

'Of course not! I told him that we are lovers—that we had been together before and that you had left his bed to return to mine.'

Marianne gasped. 'Henry—how could you?'

He shrugged. 'I may tell him the truth eventually. Perhaps I shall do so tonight, in public, or tomorrow if he dares call. That way I can earn a measure of revenge against him.' He grimaced. 'However, if you do not become betrothed tonight, then I might in truth have to accept his demands.'

She held her breath. 'Which are…?'

'You as his mistress in return for cancelling all my debts to him.'

She gasped. 'How much?'

'Ten thousand pounds.'

So much money!

She grasped the back of a nearby chair. 'How did you come to owe him such a sum?'

'The devil's own bloody luck was with him all night. Either that or he cheated me!'

'But *ten thousand pounds*? In *one night*? What on earth were you *thinking*, Henry?'

She had spoken without thought, but even as she did so she knew she had gone too far. His rage, barely contained, was unleashed. From across the room, he threw his empty glass at her with full force. It hit her right shoulder painfully and bounced off, to shatter against the hearth in a thousand glittering shards.

He thundered across the room and she retreated in fear behind the nearest chair.

'Listen to me, Marianne.' His voice was harsh. 'By the end of tonight's ball you will have accepted an offer of marriage from either Eldon or Hawkins or it will be the worse for you. Do you understand me?'

She could not do it. Even under the threat of violence. 'No! You cannot just sell me to the highest bidder!'

He raised his fist. 'I said, *Do you understand me?*'

'No! I cannot—'

He stepped closer. 'Do you *understand* me, Marianne?'

Desperately she brought her hands to her face, to protect herself from the blow she knew was coming. She would not submit to his tyranny.

She waited.

The blow did not come.

Opening her eyes, she looked directly at him, and what she saw terrified her. He was smiling.

'Oh, Marianne, you think yourself so clever, don't you? You *wanted* me to hit you in the face so as to ensure you do not go to the ball tonight!' He chuckled. 'But I am up to all your games. Save them for your husband—or for your Lord Kingswood. But only after I have secured my future!'

He flung her to one side, then spun away from her.

'Now, get out.'

Something is wrong. Something does not add up.

Ash sat in the line of carriages, awaiting his turn to alight outside Lady Annesley's well-appointed townhouse, worrying over the same inconsistencies that had bothered him since leaving Grant's house earlier.

Oh, Grant himself had been just as Ash had expected—embarrassed by the extent of his debts, completely without the means to pay them, and directing his resentment towards Ash, Lady Luck and the world in general.

Their conversation had been in line with Ash's expectations, with Grant's hope that Ash might somehow forgive the debts turning to sullen anger as he'd realised Ash had no such intention. Gradually Ash had brought the conversation round to Marianne, whom he had described as 'the woman living in this house'.

Grant's eyes had widened, then narrowed as he'd considered the possibilities. 'Are you asking about my—about Marianne?' he had queried.

Ash had leaned forward. 'Tell me why she is here.'

Grant had smiled slightly at this, and preened a little. 'She is here because she is my doxy, of course. She left me in January—a trifling quarrel—and I am relieved to have her back. I am pleased that I was successful in discovering where you had put her.'

Ash had formed his hand into a fist, conscious that all his hopes were being dashed by Grant's words. Miss Bolton, innocent governess, was in truth Marianne, a courtesan. His chest had tightened in pain.

'Am I to understand,' Grant had continued, 'that you are interested in—in renewing your own liaison with Marianne?'

It had taken every ounce of restraint for Ash to respond calmly to that. He had casually flicked though the pile of IOUs in front of him, resisting the impulse to plant a firm blow into Grant's smug face.

'I believe we might be able to come to a mutually satisfying agreement,' he had said.

He would seek to persuade Marianne to leave Grant and come to him. At least *he* cared about her!

Five minutes later he had left Grant's parlour, with a promise from the younger man that he would consider Ash's offer.

Reflecting on it now, Ash was confident about the outcome. He had seen desperation in Grant's eyes and knew that the man had few options. Best to let him stew—perhaps take the opportunity to reinforce the current balance of power between them at tonight's ball—and then return to speak to Marianne on the morrow.

His heart had been badly wounded by Grant's confirmation that Marianne was his mistress. Somehow Ash had been hoping for—*something else*. He knew not what. Something that allowed Miss Bolton to be real.

But there was no Miss Bolton. There was only Marianne.

Marianne!

His heart leapt as he recalled seeing her today. She had looked so beautiful, so alluring, in her gown of green silk. Through a haze of hurt, anger and lust he had treated her unkindly today. Had treated her badly. He knew it.

Her resistance to his kiss had been unexpected, and at the time he had sought only to push through it. And he had almost succeeded! He had sensed her beginning to soften, to respond to him. But her challenge had doused his ardour as effectively as a dip in a freezing cold bath. As she had intended, no doubt.

He had never in his life forced himself upon an unwilling woman, and he regretted that he had not handled the situation with Marianne well today. She expected—and deserved—respect. That he could certainly give her.

He frowned. So what was this constant nagging feeling at the back of his mind? This notion of wrongness, of something that didn't quite fit? He recalled her as he had last seen her, looking pale and distressed because of his treatment of her.

Well, she should not have lied to me! he thought. *It is perfectly understandable for me to be cross with her.*

The difficulty he had was that some part of him persisted in seeing her as Miss Anne Bolton, innocent governess, even now. And there was still the possibility that Grant had taken her by force.

The sick feeling in his stomach returned immediately. It simply did not bear thinking about—Marianne, frightened and hurt, being overpowered by an evil man.

Even if she was a courtesan, he wanted to know how she had come to be so. Recalling Cronin's defence of her, he could not help but agree with the steward that Marianne was good-hearted.

The carriage lurched forward another few yards and Ash glanced outside. Finally he was nearly at Lady Annesley's house, and finally the rain had ceased.

He rapped on the roof of the carriage with his cane. 'I shall walk from here, Tully!'

'But, my lord! The mud!'

Ash sighed and relented. 'Very well.'

Tully had the right of it. The road was a veritable mire. Best to be patient a little longer and use the wooden slats laid down by Lady Annesley's servants.

He just wanted this ball out of the way, so that he could speak to Marianne on the morrow. Tonight patience was not his strong suit, it seemed.

The disagreeable housemaid, despite her hostile demeanour, had done an excellent job of preparing Marianne for the ball. She had spent an age bathing her, soothing her bruises and dressing her—and all with barely a word.

It had suited Marianne perfectly, giving her time to think about what she had learned today, what she had discovered in Henry's locked drawer and what she might do about it all. As a woman, she had limited choices. All around her were men believing they knew her, making decisions for her and controlling her. Tonight it would all come to a head, and she had absolutely no clue as to her best course of action.

Finally the housemaid was dressing Marianne's hair. She created two small plaits and integrated them into Marianne's curls, sweeping her hair up into an elegant topknot. She then softened the style by ensuring that Marianne's glossy brown side curls perfectly framed her face.

Marianne's ball gown had arrived today, just after nuncheon, and in other circumstances Marianne would have been delighted with it. The gown was blue silk over a pale blue satin underdress, and flowed like a wave over Marianne's form, clinging in all the right places and covering her bruises. The bodice, hem and sleeves were trimmed with pale blue embroidery, and there were three lines of pin tucks along the flounce.

It was beautiful.

Marianne had looked in the mirror and saw that *she* looked beautiful, but the thought made her slightly sick. It suited Henry for her to be attractive. Tonight she wished to be the most unattractive, unmarriageable hag possible. She was to be paraded before her suitors like a prize heifer, her future up for the highest bidder.

Henry had forced her to preside over the dinner earlier, with both Marianne's suitors in attendance, along with Henry's favourite widows to make up the numbers. Whatever Henry had said to the men had worked. They were falling over each other to pay her extravagant compliments, beg for her hand at tonight's dancing and generally compete with each other to bid for the prize.

Henry had sat back, an amused half-smile on his lips, and contented himself with listening to the widows' prattle, while Marianne had winced and tried to pretend she was elsewhere. Promoting competitiveness between Eldon and Hawkins was an inspired tactic on Henry's part. If either man had reservations about his choice of bride they had been lost in the desire to best his rival.

As the ladies had left the room Henry had reminded Marianne of his expectations, and of the fact that marriage—*any* marriage—should be preferable to being any man's mistress, and that their family name would be exposed to shame if he were to be declared a bankrupt.

He had done all this in a hurried, low-voiced rant, his grip painfully tight on Marianne's glove-covered left arm, before straightening, smiling and declaring that he and the other gentlemen would join them very shortly, for Lady Annesley's ball promised to be the event of the season.

And so it proved.

They'd spent quite half an hour in the line of carriages before finally descending, and were now taking their place in the queue of people waiting to mount the stairs to greet their hostess.

Marianne was reflecting on Henry's hissed words to her earlier. Was it really true that marriage would be preferable to being Ash's mistress? Oh, she knew that as an unmarried lady to be known as the *chère-amie* of a gentleman would be her ruination. But the thought of marriage to Hawkins or Eldon filled her with horror.

She shuddered. To have Hawkins's wet lips on hers—or, worse still, Eldon's clammy hands—was repugnant. Ash—handsome, lean, and muscular as he was—was infinitely preferable.

Despite this, when Ash had kissed her in the hallway—kissed her as a man who intended to make her his mistress might—she had not responded. And she knew exactly why. Ash was handsome, and no doubt skilled in these matters, and his nearness did strange things to her senses. Yet even as her body had been responding to him her heart had cried out in pain.

For she wanted more than kisses. She needed his regard, his good opinion. *His love.* To become his mistress would be a delight—but in the end it would destroy her. Of that she had no doubt.

Yet the thought of simply staying with Henry was horrific in a different way. No matter which way she stepped, no matter which choice she made, she would be the loser.

'Lady Annesley! So delighted!'

Marianne came back to the present with a start. Henry was playing his part to perfection.

'May I present my sister, Miss Grant?'

Marianne curtseyed to the older lady.

'Why, Mr Grant, I had only recently become aware that your sister was finally visiting town. But you are delightful!' This she directed at Marianne, with a kind smile. 'A beauty! You shall have all the young gentlemen falling over themselves to dance with you tonight!'

'I have already secured the first two dances, Lady Annesley,' Mr Eldon interjected smoothly from over Marianne's shoulder.

Marianne's smile—which had been a genuine response to Lady Annesley's warmth—became a fixed grin.

'And I the following two,' added Mr Hawkins, not to be outdone.

'I see,' said Lady Annesley, her gaze flicking briefly to Marianne.

She greeted Eldon and Hawkins, and the two

widows—both of whom, surprisingly, were clearly welcome in polite society—before turning back to Marianne.

'Well, as hostess, I shall come and find you after that, Miss Grant, as is my duty.'

'I shall look forward to it,' said Marianne, with rather more enthusiasm than was appropriate. 'I mean—I am *so* looking forward to the ball!'

It sounded forced, even to her own ears.

'Lady Annesley, if you do not mind my asking...' It was Henry, his cultured, easy, 'public' mask firmly in place. 'How did you hear of my sister being in town? For apart from my closest friends—' he indicated the two gentlemen behind him '—I have not talked of Marianne to many people, and this is her first time attending a London ball.'

He smiled. Marianne saw his charm. It sickened her.

'I had hoped to cause something of a stir by bringing her here tonight.'

'Oh, I cannot recall, exactly,' replied Lady Annesley airily, 'though I believe you are right and her presence is not widely known. My dear—' this was directed at Marianne '—I do hope you enjoy the ball.'

'Thank you.'

Marianne could not help smiling warmly at

Lady Annesley. The older woman's kindness, charm and warmth reminded her of Mama. A sudden lump came into her throat, and her eyes shone with unshed tears.

A slight frown appeared on Lady Annesley's brow.

'I hope that my sister makes the most of the occasion,' added Henry quickly, diverting his hostess's attention to himself, 'for she is likely to be returning to our family home in the country tomorrow.'

'Oh, what a shame!' Lady Annesley seemed genuinely put out. 'I had hoped to get to know you a little, Miss Grant.'

'Perhaps next time,' murmured Marianne, knowing that unless she agreed to marry one of the two ghastly gentlemen behind her on the stairs Henry would indeed banish her.

In truth, she would welcome it. He was becoming more volatile by the day, and she lived in constant fear of triggering his temper. If she could be sure he would leave her alone at their family home she would be perfectly content. It might even be worth signing that document and letting him have Mama's jewels, if he would then leave her in peace. But, given that he saw her as a means to access funds from her future husband, she knew that he would not rest until he had achieved it.

As she moved with the rest of the party towards the ballroom, where a country dance was already in full swing, she noticed a grand clock standing there, its perfectly balanced swinging weights and polished wood case testament to the care and attention involved in its creation.

It was just after nine o'clock.

Lady Annesley excused herself from a conversation among a group of chattering matrons on the shocking cost of furniture. Having a beautifully furnished, comfortable home, and no intention of purchasing new furniture any time soon, she had no interest in such matters.

She made her way out to the hallway where, after a very few moments, she found Forbes, her butler.

'Forbes! There you are!'

'My lady.' Ever conscious of his duties, he bowed graciously. 'I can report that all is well from my perspective. There is plenty of wine and ratafia, and although the gentlemen in the card room are consuming rather more port and brandy then I had anticipated, I have had two footmen fetch more supplies and place them upstairs.'

'Very good, Forbes. Now, I have an unusual request.'

'My lady?'

'Do you remember the person who called yesterday, seeking me out? You placed him in the small parlour.'

'Indeed, my lady. I do hope,' he added with a touch of anxiety, 'that I did right? He seemed to be a respectable person—I thought him to be perhaps a banker or a lawyer. Not a tradesperson who should be directed to your secretary or to Cook.'

'You did right, Forbes, never fear. At the time I had no idea that there *was* even a sister, so of course I could not help. But now...' She paused. 'Yes, I shall have to meddle. That poor girl!'

'My lady?' Forbes, who knew his mistress of old, prompted her gently to come to the point.

'He left me his card. Name is Mason, I think. I put it on the mantel in the small parlour.' She paused for further reflection.

If Forbes wondered why Lady Annesley was focusing on this in the middle of her grand ball—an event which she had been planning with an obsessive attention to detail for at least two months—he gave no sign.

After a long moment, she seemed to come to a decision. 'Forbes!'

'Yes, my lady.'

'There is nothing else for it! She might be whisked away tomorrow to goodness knows where. It will have to be tonight.'

'Tonight?'

'Yes. Direct someone to find Mr Mason and bring him here. Put him somewhere private and send for me once he is here. Tell him it relates to the…to the business we talked of when he called.'

'Yes, my lady.' Forbes bowed and left.

If his mind was filled with speculation regarding his mistress's sudden request he gave no sign of it.

Eleven o'clock. Hearing the distant chimes, Ash yawned, stretched, and rose from the card table. 'I shall return shortly,' he told his friends. 'If I stay here much longer I shall fall asleep at the table, so I shall take a look in on the dancing.'

It was true. Having reached his bed well after dawn, he had spent the morning in fitful sleep, anticipating seeing Marianne again. The lack of rest was now catching up with him, and the brandy at his elbow was having a soporific effect.

'I shall come with you,' said Barny, heaving himself out of his chair.

Together they walked along Lady Annesley's sumptuous hallway to the ballroom.

'Lord, what a crush!'

'Lady Annesley will be delighted,' Ash replied. The dance floor was filled with couples moving through the intricacies of a waltz, while all around the edges of the room dowagers, wallflowers and young men watched proceedings.

Ash spied Henry Grant at a table along the left side of the room, deep in conversation with some of his cronies—the entire group looked decidedly foxed. He grimaced. Unsurprisingly, Grant had stayed away from the card room tonight.

His gaze travelled on. The dancers were taking turns to move up the set in pairs, and he espied Mr Hawkins cutting a comic figure as he moved his ample figure through the steps. His partner, who had her back to Ash, was gently trying to guide Mr Hawkins, with limited success. Then she half turned, and Ash went completely still with shock.

Marianne! If he had thought she looked beautiful earlier, nothing had prepared him for the vision of beauty that she presented tonight. Her gown was in various shades of blue, and it shimmered as she moved elegantly through the figures. The low-cut bodice—traditional for a ball gown—gave him ample opportunity to appreciate her white bosom, and pearls glowed around her neck. Her hair was dressed in an elaborate style, complete with a diamond pin, and a delicate painted fan dangled from her wrist.

He could not have named the elements of her dress, nor said exactly *why* she looked so well. He only felt the force of it.

But why was she here? Had Grant the audacity to bring a courtesan to a *ton* party, expecting to get away with it? He reflected for a moment. No, even he would not be so bold. She must, then, be eligible to be here through family connections or status. Not a courtesan—or at least not *only* a courtesan. Yet she was not a governess either.

Although she was dressed in the pale colours of an unmarried woman, she might possibly be a widow. Was that it? Had she been married, lost her husband, and been forced to take work as a governess? But no—for that would have been perfectly respectable. No need to lie to him.

What, then?

His mind was working furiously, trying to find the answer to the riddle, when the music ceased and Mr Hawkins began leading Marianne off the dance floor.

Swiftly, and without a word to the disconcerted Barny, Ash moved to intercept them. They were ahead, and Hawkins was lightly stroking Marianne's arm as he whispered something in her ear. She visibly shuddered and shook his hand away.

Ash smiled grimly. So Mr Hawkins was not to be favoured, then?

Just how many men does Marianne have dangling after her?

An instant before Ash reached them Lady Annesley stepped in front of them both, smiling broadly. Whatever she said elicited a protest from Hawkins, and Ash caught the word 'terrace'. So he'd hoped to take Marianne outside, had he? Away from the people and the lights.

'And here he is!'

Lady Annesley had noticed Ash, and now reached for his arm, propelling him with force into the conversation.

'I am afraid, Mr Hawkins, that your delightful partner is promised to Lord Kingswood for the next dance!'

Hawkins, his face set, could not openly challenge his hostess, so he bowed, muttered something about finding his acquaintances, and left.

Marianne, stony-faced, did not even look Ash's way.

'Ash,' continued Lady Annesley, unperturbed, 'might I present—?'

'We've met,' interrupted Marianne shortly, adding a belated half-smile to make her utterance more acceptable.

'Oh, you have? How wonderful!' Lady Annesley smiled broadly. 'I shall leave you in Ash's capable hands, then. But...' She lowered her head to speak to Marianne directly. 'I wish to speak to you in private later. There is something I must discuss with you.'

Marianne nodded, looking somewhat bemused. She had gone rather pale, Ash noted.

Ha! She might well do so!

He had question after question tumbling over each other, and he intended to get some answers.

Lady Annesley was not yet done. Standing on her tiptoes, she whispered in Ash's ear, 'I saw you looking at her during the dancing. A diamond, is she not?'

She patted Ash's arm, winked at him, and turned away just as the musicians struck up a chord to call the couples to the floor for the next dance—a cotillion.

'Shall we?' he said urbanely, offering Marianne his arm.

She hesitated, then her shoulders slumped in what looked like defeat.

'Very well.'

Chapter Twenty-Three

This is all it needed, thought Marianne as she walked towards the dance floor, her gloved hand tucked into Ash's strong arm.

At a glance, she had taken in his effortless elegance. He was attired in the traditional evening dress of knee breeches and an evening coat of dark blue superfine. Yet somehow he outshone every gentleman there. His snowy cravat seemed whiter, his coat a more perfect fit, his easy gait the epitome of unforced masculinity. Not that she was prejudiced in any way.

Appreciating his physical and sartorial splendour did not, however, reduce her anxiety about having to interact with him. They were in a public place. She had deceived him. He was angry with her. Oh, and he intended to make her his mistress and would 'collect' her in a few hours. So, yes, she was angry with him too.

Still, after enduring dances with her two suitors dancing with Ash could hardly be worse.

Mr Eldon, predictably, had used the dance to leer at her, throwing lingering glances towards her bosom, while Mr Hawkins had clearly been uncomfortable, capering through the dance with a look of pained endurance on his round red face. Both had tried to persuade her to accompany them out onto the terrace for fresh air—though their real intent might have been to propose marriage.

Despite her fear of Henry, Marianne had not been able to bring herself to co-operate with either suitor. She had been rescued from Mr Eldon by Mr Hawkins, coming to claim her for 'his' dances, and now Lady Annesley had rescued her in turn from Mr Hawkins. But at what cost?

Heaven knows what Ash will say to me now! she thought abstractedly.

She stole a glance at him. His expression was inscrutable.

The musicians played the first few bars—it was the cotillion known as La Vandreuil—and they moved into position without speaking, one of a quartet of couples forming the four sides of a square. The silence grew thick between them as the pressure of expectation built and grew.

The music began properly and they completed

the introduction and honours with a bow and a curtsey. Marianne's heart was pounding with a strange mix of excitement and fear, but some part of her mind was urging her to enjoy every moment of this brief time with Ash.

They moved into the first figure, all eight dancers joining hands in a great round. They circled with the other couples, looking only into the circle, though Marianne was supremely conscious of his hand in hers.

The next step was for her and Ash and the other top couple to move towards each other. Marianne took the hand of the gentleman opposite while Ash did the same with the gentleman's partner. After skipping with the gentleman towards the side couple, and looping around the side gentleman, Marianne re-joined Ash and they whirled round in a right-hand star, *en moulinet*, finally going back into place.

She stole a glance at him. He looked preoccupied, but not angry. Not the way he had looked earlier. Her heart ran faster. Should she say something? Tell him the truth? She might not ever have another opportunity.

'Can I tell you something?'

Suddenly she had his full attention. His gaze bored into hers like shards of midsummer sunlight penetrating a dark forest.

'Will it be the truth this time?'

Almost she reacted angrily, but she held herself back. This was important. 'Yes.'

'I am listening.'

He was. She could see it.

They moved into the next pattern, separating to *vis-à-vis* at the corner with the side couples, then came back to their places to stand while the side couples led in, performing the same pattern from the beginning.

She took a breath. 'My name is Marianne Grant and I am no man's mistress.'

'Grant?' His eyes widened. 'You are *married* to that idiot?'

'No! But his father married my mother.'

He frowned, considering this as the dance briefly took them apart. When they came back together, he nodded grimly. 'Go on.'

'My true father was Charles Bolton. He died when I was a baby. Papa—George Grant—was like a true father to me.'

'Then Henry Grant is your stepbrother?' His jaw set. 'I begin to understand.'

'After Mama and Papa died Henry was appointed my guardian.'

They clasped hands in the dance.

'I cannot imagine he took his duties very seriously. I am sorry to say that I find him one of the most feckless, dissolute men of my acquaintance.'

She spun away, curtseyed to another gentleman, clasped hands with him as they moved around each other, then came back to Ash. They joined hands again and moved around each other, first with their right hands joined, then with their left.

'On the contrary, he took a great deal of interest in me. Unwelcome interest.'

His grip on her hand tightened as her meaning became clear to him. 'He *what*?' He looked thunderous.

'Hush! People will stare!' She pasted a smile on her face, trying to present an impression that all was well and that she was not, in fact, sharing her deepest secrets with her partner on a dance floor.

'Is that, then, why you became a governess?'

She nodded. 'It was the only thing I could think of. I had to leave home with great urgency. I had no recommendation, but I had always worked hard at my studies and I had taught Jane—my personal maid.'

'Mrs Bailey's daughter. It all becomes clear now.'

Again the dance required them to part briefly. She smiled politely at her temporary partner, then glanced at Ash. His brow was creased in thought as his mind worked furiously to put it all together.

Next time they came together he had his questions ready. 'Why did Grant not tell me your true identity?' he asked. 'Why did Mrs Bailey and Jane leave? And *why*—' he gazed at her intently '—did you not trust *me* with the truth?'

Her heart sank. She might have known he would get to the heart of things quickly.

She answered the easiest question first. 'Henry tried to interfere with Jane, too. Mrs Bailey believed that if she stayed Jane would be in danger.'

'Was she correct to hold that belief?'

'Without doubt. My stepbrother has no sense of morality. He lives only to please himself and has no concept of other people having feelings of their own.'

Ash's grip tightened on her hand. 'Once we are somewhere less public I wish to know how much you have suffered at his hands.'

She looked up at him, hardly daring to hope. 'Then—you believe me?'

'Of course I believe you, you foolish woman! You should have told me this long ago!'

He looked as forbidding as ever, but this time it did not frighten her. This time she knew he was not angry *with* her. Instead he was angry on her behalf. It scarcely seemed possible!

Although she was dancing around Lady Annesley's ballroom, it suddenly seemed to Marianne that she was, in fact, floating on some sort of cloud.

He believes me!

Ash had been on board a ship fewer than ten times in his life, yet each time he had found the movement of the deck beneath his feet most disconcerting. Everything had *looked* the same, yet his feet would not move properly, his balance was lost, and he found himself gripping nearby objects in a most undignified way.

At this moment he was conscious of a similar loss of equilibrium as his assumptions vanished like mist, to be replaced by blinding new truths.

He moved through the remaining figures of the dance without consciousness, his entire mind focused on Marianne's revelations.

That was why she had gone away with Henry Grant! A wave of guilt washed over him as he recognised his own part in her departure from Ledbury House that day. And *that* was why she had lied about her identity. He frowned as he thought about what it must be like for Marianne, to be under the control of a man like Henry Grant. His stomach clenched as he considered the attack or attacks upon her person that had caused her to run from her childhood home.

He had to know the whole truth.

'Marianne—' His voice cracked.

She looked up at him, and her face creased at what she read in his eyes. 'He did not...succeed... in violating me.'

Her voice was low, but he heard her words. Relief coursed through him.

Confound it! When would this dance end? He had a hundred more questions, but felt too overcome with emotion to make sense of his own thoughts. He was simply overwhelmed by notions of what Marianne must have endured.

If Henry Grant was in front of me right now, he thought, *I cannot say what I might do.*

Fast on the heels of anger came pride. He watched her move serenely around the dance floor, her head held high. What a woman! She was simply magnificent!

Finally the music ended. He claimed her hand and led her off the floor, searching for somewhere they might speak with a modicum of privacy.

'Shall we go to the terrace?'

She raised an ironic eyebrow. 'You are the third gentleman to invite me to the terrace tonight. Mr Eldon and Mr Hawkins both made it clear that they had the intention of taking me there and making me an offer of marriage.'

Marriage? He was momentarily stunned. 'So you'd have the means to escape permanently from your brother?' Fear coursed through him at the thought that he might lose her again.

'My *step*brother,' she corrected. 'And, no, I do not favour either gentleman—not even to escape.'

On reflection, he saw the wisdom of this. Neither Eldon nor Hawkins would make a good husband for Marianne.

And then he was suddenly certain that she must marry no one but him.

'Does your stepbrother encourage you to marry?'

'Yes. He has told me that I must accept one of them tonight as his debts are most pressing. If I do not he will punish me.'

They had reached the terrace doors, and he stood back to allow her to precede him.

'Punish you how?'

'Either by giving me to you, and ruining me—'

'Oh, Marianne! I apologise for my foolishness— my flawed assumptions. I should have questioned the lies he told me.'

He took her hand and she felt his warmth through her thin evening glove.

'I should have known that my hot-headed notions were wrong. I who had the chance to know who you truly are. Our time together at Ledbury House was truly the happiest I have ever known. I—'

'*There* you are!'

It was Lady Annesley, bustling and fluttering up to them.

'Ash, I must steal her from you. Please come with me, Miss Grant. There is someone I should like you to meet.'

Ash, on the verge of declaring himself, could not have been less pleased to see his hostess. Why must Lady Annesley appear at such an inopportune moment?

Marianne squeezed his hand in a clear signal. She, too, wished to continue their conversation.

'I am afraid that I was about to speak to Miss Grant on a most pressing manner. Can you give us a few moments?' he asked.

Lady Annesley's eyes widened, and then she smiled broadly. 'Sits the wind in *that* quarter?' She peered at Marianne, and nodded, as if satisfied. 'Well, you two shall make a fine match!' She tilted her head to one side and thought for a moment. 'No! It is better to— Yes, I believe it can only help.'

She took Marianne by the elbow.

'I regret it cannot wait. There is someone here to see you. But Ash can accompany us, if that is your wish?'

Marianne nodded, clearly as mystified as Ash himself.

'I have put him in the small parlour downstairs,' Lady Annesley continued cryptically. 'Follow me!'

As she led them through the ballroom Ash automatically turned his head towards the table where he had earlier seen Henry Grant. Through a brief gap in the crowd he spotted him, still with the same group of inebriated young men. As if sensing his gaze, Grant looked up. He took in the strange procession—Lady Annesley, Marianne and Ash—and frowned.

The seething host of revellers swarmed again, and Ash could no longer see him.

Rage boiled within him at Grant's treatment of his stepsister. How dared he treat any woman with such callousness? The fact that he had also importuned Jane added to the sense that this was a pattern with Grant. Ash recalled Barny's words—it seemed to be a habit with that entire group of dissolute young men.

His hand closed into a fist. *Oh, but there will be a reckoning between us!*

Marianne followed Lady Annesley in something of a daze. She had no idea whom she was about to meet, and frankly she cared little. Her heart was singing at her reconciliation with Ash.

He believed her!

But it was more than that. Her senses were tingling and her insides were churning delightfully at his manner towards her. The warmth in his tone, the heat in his eyes… Could she possibly hope that he felt something for her?

Lady Annesley had assumed that Ash was about to make her an offer of marriage. But Lady Annesley knew nothing of what had actually passed between them. Ash had genuinely wished to speak to her on a pressing matter, but naturally Lady Annesley would come to the most logical conclusion—in this case inaccurate.

Marianne's rational mind came back with a warning. *Do not assume anything!* Of course Ash would be feeling mortified, and regretful and possibly even a little guilty on discovering the truth. It did not necessarily follow that he would wish to pursue her in any way.

In fact, receiving kisses from him would be *less* likely now that he knew the truth. As a gentleman, he could not and would not renew his efforts to take her as his mistress.

She was not surprised to feel a pang of regret at the realisation. No lady could *wish* to be ruined, but if it were to happen then she would certainly choose for Ash to do the ruining.

She stifled a giggle. What on earth was wrong with her? She was living with an unpredictable, selfish guardian, and her options were still limited. Despite all that, she was enjoying a sense of elation.

Lady Annesley led them downstairs to the entrance floor, and into a pretty parlour with an elegant ormolu clock on the mantel. The time, Marianne noted, was ten minutes to midnight. Might that matter?

There was only one person in the room—a quite elderly gentleman, in neat, dark clothing that proclaimed him a man of business. He looked vaguely familiar.

Where have I seen him before? thought Marianne.

The man evidently recognised her. He rose, relief written clear on his face, and approached her.

'Miss Grant—I am so glad to see you! You can have no notion of how long I have spent searching for you! Indeed, I had almost given up hope when I received word that a young lady had left Mr Grant's townhouse to visit a certain dressmaker—a Mrs James of New Bridge Street. My sources confirmed the dressmaker was making a ball gown that was to be delivered to your guardian's home by today.'

He joined his hands together with an air of satisfaction.

'I knew I would not be permitted to speak to

you there, so I took it upon myself to discover where tonight's ball would take place and I boldly approached your gracious hostess.' He bowed to Lady Annesley. 'Thank you again, my lady.'

Lady Annesley dismissed his gratitude with a wave of her white hand. 'Think nothing of it. I am happy to help.'

The man looked across to Ash. 'Er... I do not believe we have met. I am Mr Mason.'

'Kingswood.' Ash's tone was carefully neutral.

The lawyer's eyes widened. 'Lord Kingswood—forgive me—your acquaintance with Miss Grant is of recent duration?'

'I stand as her friend,' said Ash.

Marianne's heart turned over in a rush of love and tears pricked her eyes. He had said it—he was once again her friend.

Mr Mason nodded, seemingly content. He turned to Marianne. 'Miss Grant, I—'

'What the deuce is going on here?'

It was Henry, erupting into the room with all the elegance of a bull.

Mr Mason jumped, clearly startled, and looked put out.

No one spoke. Marianne felt fear pool coldly in the pit of her stomach. Henry was enraged. This would not end well for her.

'Marianne, we are leaving!' Henry glared at her. *'Now!'*

Lord, he would probably begin berating her as soon as they got into the carriage, away from witnesses. He might even offer her violence once again.

Marianne was torn. She absolutely did not wish to go with him, but to disobey him would enrage him further. She looked at the clock. It lacked only five minutes to the hour.

'Just a moment.' Ash's tone was one that commanded respect. Everyone looked at him. 'I wish to hear what Mr Mason has to say—if Miss Grant permits?'

Marianne nodded. It took every ounce of courage she had to defy Henry so openly. She knew she would pay for it later. But at least if she stayed here there was a chance—albeit a small one—that the situation might improve. And she too was curious about Mr Mason, and why he had sought her so persistently.

'Very well.'

Mr Mason remained standing, as they all did. To sit might trigger Henry's insistence on leaving with Marianne. The tension in the air was palpable.

'You may remember me, Miss Grant, from the

day of your parents' funeral. I was your father's lawyer, and I am your trustee.'

So that was why he looked familiar! 'I am sorry, Mr Mason,' she said, her voice a little hoarse as she tried to force words through her tight throat. 'That day is somewhat blurred in my memory.'

'Perfectly understandable,' he responded kindly. 'I have tried to visit you on a number of occasions during the past year, but I have been prevented from doing so by your guardian—Mr Grant.'

Henry scowled but did not deny it.

'In February I was informed that you no longer resided at your family home, yet no one could say where you were. I admit I feared the worst.'

'But why did you wish to speak to me?' Marianne asked, confused. 'Papa's will left everything to Henry, bar my mother's jewels, and made him my guardian.'

'Ah...' said Mr Mason. 'Perhaps I should have been clearer. I was not only your *stepfather's* lawyer, but also your *father's*. I worked for Charles Bolton many years ago. He left a substantial amount in trust for you, to come to you when you were of age.'

Suddenly many things became clear.

'So, Henry, is that why you wanted me to sign a legal paper giving all my possessions to you? I thought you wished to take Mama's jewels. I did not know there was more.'

Rage blazed in his eyes. 'Have you been snooping among my personal papers?' he snarled. 'I did not ask you to sign *any* paper.'

'But you had the document there, ready to use at the right moment, didn't you? Once you had broken me. But I am not broken.'

Henry did not reply.

Marianne turned to Mr Mason. 'What of Henry's guardianship of me?'

Mr Mason's brow creased. 'That, too, ends on the day you come of age.'

Marianne nodded, relief flooding through her. She turned to her stepbrother, furious. Now she could say what she truly wished to say. 'You only needed me to *believe* that document was valid. I would not have had the knowledge or the resources to fight you in court. I did not even know about my father's legacy to me.'

Henry's gaze shifted away. 'Be quiet, Marianne!' he spluttered. 'I have heard enough!' He stepped towards her. 'I am leaving, and I am taking my ward with me!'

He reached out and gripped Marianne's left arm. Instinctively, knowing that she had friends in the room, Marianne struggled. Henry grabbed

372 The Earl's Runaway Governess

the sleeve of her ball gown with his other hand and pulled her towards him. Marianne resisted and the dress tore at the shoulder.

It all happened in a flash. One moment Marianne was struggling with Henry, the next her stepbrother was lying on his back, having been floored by a superb punch from Ash. Marianne looked from one to the other blankly. Had that really just happened? Had someone hit Henry for her sake? Had *Ash* hit Henry for her sake?

Ash, his face pale with anger, leaned over Henry. 'Get up, you piece of filth! And if you ever lay a hand on her again you will answer to me!'

Henry scuttled backwards on the floor. 'I believe you have broken my nose!' he exclaimed petulantly, pulling a large handkerchief from his pocket. Sure enough, blood was beginning to flow. He scrambled to his feet, being careful to stay out of range of another blow. 'And you have no legal rights over my sister! It is I who is her guardian!'

Marianne looked around the room at the others. No one could deny this. Not yet.

Ash turned towards her. His eyes swept over her, coming to rest on her exposed shoulder. 'What is this?'

His hand gently touched the uncovered skin, creating a wondrous tingle that spread throughout Marianne's body. Dimly she knew that this was an inappropriate reaction, given the situation, but her senses were heedless to common sense.

'Oh, my dear!' Lady Annesley bustled forward. 'It is a recent bruise. Has he been abusing you?'

For answer, Marianne removed her left glove. Clearly outlined on her arm were a series of fingertip-shaped bruises, where Henry had grasped her earlier.

'The one on my shoulder is from the glass that he threw at me yesterday.' She looked at Ash. 'He was careful to hurt me only in places where the bruises could be hidden.'

Ash's face turned grim and he strode across to Henry. 'Mr Grant', he said, his tone deceptively cordial, 'I declare you a coward, an extortionist, an abuser of women, and a man who writes IOUs that he has no way of honouring.'

Henry blanched.

Ash slapped his face—hard. 'You may name your seconds!'

'A duel!' breathed Lady Annesley. 'I do not normally approve of such things, but occasionally nothing else will do.' She turned to Henry. 'Mr Grant, you are no longer welcome in this house. And I mean to ensure that your true character, your wickedness, is widely known.'

With this pronouncement, given Lady Annesley's position in society, Henry's reputation was lost.

In the background, the ormolu clock began to strike midnight.

Henry's face twisted in a sneer. 'You may do what you will, for I care not! London holds nothing for me any more! Come, Marianne!'

Ash took a step forward.

'Do not seek to interfere between a guardian and his legal ward,' Henry snarled.

Ash, frustration etched into his face, paused.

'Wait!' Marianne found her voice. 'Mr Mason, you say that when I come of age Henry will no longer be my guardian?'

'That is correct.' His eyes narrowed.

'And does there need to be any legal process in order for me to be free of his guardianship?'

Mr Mason shook his head. 'It is automatic, as soon as you turn twenty-one.'

Marianne's heart was thumping loudly. 'I did wonder about that... I hoped that tonight... Then—I am free!'

They all regarded her quizzically.

She indicated the clock. 'As of this moment, it is my twenty-first birthday!'

'But how wonderful!' declared Lady Annesley, clapping her hands.

Mr Mason's lined face broke out in a smile. 'I

knew the date could not be far off, but I confess I had not recently checked. I was just relieved to have found you—'

He broke off, his eyebrows lifting, as Marianne was bundled into a rough hug by Ash.

'Dash it all, Marianne!' Ash muttered incoherently.

His arms swept around her, giving her the benefit of his warmth, his delicious scent and his nearness, yet he was careful not to hold her too tightly.

After a moment he pulled back to look into her eyes. He did not speak, but Marianne saw with wonder that a tear was making its way down his cheek. She reached up with her gloveless hand to catch it, and he turned his head slightly to kiss her fingers.

'Ahem!'

A polite cough brought them back to the room. Lady Annesley was gazing at them fondly. Mr Mason looked disconcerted. Of Henry there was no sign, but the door was ajar.

'Apologies!' said Ash huskily. 'Mr Mason, I thank you for your diligence in searching for Miss Grant. But now I need to speak with her alone.'

'Of course you do!' said Lady Annesley. 'For I interrupted you earlier. Mind, you can only take a few moments—I must return with you to the ballroom shortly or there will be talk.'

She smiled.

'Miss Grant, I see that you are a well-bred young woman, and that you have been much put-upon. I do not know if my offer will be welcome, but I shall make it, regardless. You are welcome to live here with me for as long as you wish.' She sent a sly glance towards Ash. 'Or, more accurately, for as long as you and Ash need to organise your wedding!'

'Oh, thank you so much, Lady Annesley! But—'

Wedding? Marianne's mind was awhirl—so much so that she could barely think straight.

Her hostess bundled Mr Mason out of the room, extracting a promise from him in the process that he should return on the morrow. They shut the door behind them.

Instantly Ash and Marianne turned to each other, their lips meeting in a kiss of such passion, such love, such tenderness, that Marianne found her head spinning and her knees going soft. Her soul was soaring, her heart swelling so much that she believed it might burst, and her fevered mind was lost somewhere in a fog of happiness and physical desire.

'Marry me?' Ash seemed similarly afflicted,

his voice husky as the words seemed to erupt from him.

'Yes!' she replied. 'Yes, and yes, and yes!'

'Oh, Marianne! How I love you! When you disappeared from Ledbury House I was bereft. I was so hurt that you seemed to be a fake and a deceiver, for truly I have not loved before!'

She smoothed his hair back from his brow, marvelling that she was now permitted to do so, that he was now—miraculously—hers. 'What of Lady Kingswood? I have heard that you loved her before her marriage.'

She knew before he spoke what his answer would be. 'The calf love of an eighteen-year-old moonling—no more!'

Since this was exactly the conclusion she herself had reached about his relationship with Fanny, she did not pursue it. She was sure he had no notion of the rumours Fanny was circulating about his future intentions. No doubt Lady Kingswood would be most displeased when Ash married Cecily's governess, but at this moment Marianne cared not.

He went on. 'Truly, I had no notion of what love was until you arrived and bewitched me with your warm heart, your lively mind and your beautiful soul. I am yours, Marianne, whether you will have me or not. And Ledbury House is empty without you.'

'I have already said I will have you. I wish nothing more than to be your wife.' She smiled at him through her tears. 'I love you, Ash.'

He groaned and kissed her again.

After a few moments, he raised his head to say, 'First you were Miss Bolton, and I loved you. Then you were Marianne, and I was angry with you. Tonight you became Miss Grant, and I found you once more. But soon you will be Lady Kingswood, and we will never be apart again.'

'Never!' she affirmed, and it felt like a vow.

She reached up with both hands and pulled him close for another kiss.

'Never.'

Epilogue

The new Lord and Lady Kingswood had decided not to have a honeymoon, but instead to travel directly from the simple wedding breakfast to their country home—Ledbury House. The bride wore an elegant wedding gown in dove-grey silk, topped with a stylish ribboned bonnet, and the groom—whom many had said would never marry—a coat of blue superfine which showed his athletic figure to advantage.

Their witnesses, Lady Annesley and Lord Kingswood's astonished friend Barny, congratulated them warmly as they entered their carriage to depart from London. The bride had been a guest of Lady Annesley for nigh on six months, and the wedding had been a quiet one, given the tragic circumstances.

Everyone knew that the bride's stepbrother, Mr Henry Grant, had died in a dreadful carriage accident on his way home from Lady Annesley's ball in April—more or less at the same time as his stepsister and Lord Kingswood had been causing speculation by sharing adoring glances while dancing together.

It was said that Mr Grant had been driving his carriage at breakneck speed, and with a good deal of drink taken, when he had rounded the corner at Piccadilly much too quickly, overturned the carriage and broken his neck. It had not been his first accident, and those who had known him had shaken their heads at the news, commenting sagely that they had known all along that it would be the death of him. No one had expressed surprise.

Of course no wedding could take place while Miss Grant was in mourning, so today—the six-month anniversary of Mr Grant's death, and the first date on which it became acceptable—the quietest of weddings had been contracted in St George's Church in Hanover Square.

'Finally!' Ash said fervently as the carriage began to move through the streets of the capital.

He reached for his bride and they enjoyed a long, enthusiastic kiss.

Marianne sighed in happiness. 'Finally!' she echoed.

Their love for each other, so long denied, had strengthened during their long betrothal. They had spoken at length, and on many occasions, about the misunderstandings that had separated them prior to Lady Annesley's ball, and of the depth of feeling that each held for the other.

Ash smiled. 'Do you mean *finally* we are married?'

Marianne kissed him softly. 'I do.'

'And do you mean *finally* you will return to Ledbury House?'

He trailed a line of light kisses along her jaw. She tilted her head and he accepted the invitation to kiss her neck. She quivered.

'Mmm, yes…that as well. It was good to see Mrs Bailey and Jane and Mr Cronin when they came to London, and it is always good to see Cecily, but Ledbury House is my home and I cannot wait to live there again. But…' Her voice tailed off as he reached her earlobe.

A long moment later, he prompted her again. 'But…?' His lips traced a path along her cheek.

'But that is not what I meant.' Marianne's voice cracked a little.

'Tell me what you meant.' There was a smile in his voice.

'I meant—' she took a breath '—that *finally* I will share your bed.'

'*Marianne!*'

His mouth swooped on hers and they kissed ferociously, all the pent-up longing of six months finally being given freedom.

When they eventually separated both were breathless and flushed with desire. By mutual agreement Marianne shifted from Ash's knee onto the seat beside him. He groaned as she did so, but contented himself with taking her hand and kissing it.

'I wish we could have had this night many months ago, but we both know why it was better to wait.'

She nodded. 'The last thing we wanted was for me to end up with child a full six months before our wedding. Still, I have learned much about you—and about a man's desire—these past months.'

He chuckled. 'The Marianne of old would not have dared talk of such matters without blushing. And, yes, we have done almost everything save the deed itself. But never in a bed...and never with the luxury of sleeping in each other's arms afterwards.'

They grinned at each other at the thought of the night to come.

Yet as the carriage continued on towards Ledbury House—the home they would make together—Marianne's thoughts shifted beyond the night ahead to the months and years they would enjoy together. She could never have hoped for such happiness.

I was strong, Mama, she thought, *and love came to me. I am loved again, Mama. I am loved.*

* * * * *